Shades of Gray

KIM SANDERS

Shades of Gray is a work of fiction. Names, characters, places, and incidents are a product of the author's imagination or used fictitiously. Any similarity to actual persons, places, or events is unintentional.

Copyright © 2011 Kim Sanders

ISBN-10: 1463731272
ISBN-13: 978-1463731274

Cover Design © Rachel Browne Photography

DEDICATION

To Paul,
the reason I believe in happily ever after.

ACKNOWLEDGMENTS

Thanks to Rachel Browne Photography
for the cover artwork and inspiration
and
to my editor, Fletcher Ryan,
for the fabulous support.

CHAPTER ONE

Sam ran. For the first time in her life, the isolation of her island scared her. Zigzagging along the edge of the surf, she slipped away into the deep morning fog, shivering as sweat beads tracked down the back of her neck like fine hairs.

Sanctuary loomed ahead. She pictured the weathered gray steps to her home and turned in their direction. Sanctuary, she thought again and froze in her tracks. Running had always been her refuge, not a house or a place. She closed her eyes, trying to push away the image of Ben and the unthinkable. She needed to forget, if only for a moment. She felt the rumble of the thunder and listened to the waves crash against the shoreline. She let the storm push away the fear and stoke her anger. Lifting her head, she pushed a loose blonde curl away from her pale blue eyes and ran across the battered dunes.

Flying up the steps, two at a time, Sam finally stopped and settled into an oversized rocking chair on the back deck. She pulled her knees up to her chin, wrapped her arms around long bare legs, and stared out across the empty beach. A beautiful rising sun danced across the sea, but Sam didn't see diamonds on the water. She saw only darkness as the storm clouds reflected on its surface and reclaimed the light. A piercing scream splintered the air, and Sam jumped, sending the rocker into motion. She gripped her knees tighter and reminded herself to breathe. Not Ben, her mind chanted, a seagull, not Ben.

She pictured Ben as she had seen him last—asleep, peaceful, and tangled in a sheet. She had shut the door behind her without saying goodbye. If only she could just go back and ask him what was wrong. He'd wanted to tell her something. He'd been excited, but nervous. She knew he needed her to ask, but it'd been easier to pretend she hadn't noticed. She liked the distance, the separation. She hadn't wanted the secrets of his personal life—until now.

Sam closed her eyes and turned her face up to welcome the barrage of god-sized teardrops that now mingled with hers. She cried silently until there was nothing left and blessed the return of the emptiness.

When she opened her eyes again, the rain had stopped. She wiped her wet face with wet hands and felt a chill as the cool air brushed over her skin. A deep whimper sounded from the other side of the screen door, and a small smile tugged at her lips as her thoughts turned to Wallie.

The swinging door squeaked on its rusty hinges, and Wallie bounded out. A black head the size of a bowling ball rested on the arm of her rocker as he made grumbling noises in the back of his throat.

"I'm okay, Wallie." She reached over to rub between his two tan eyebrows that were arched in concern.

Thunder rocked the porch again, and Wallie barked, bumping his head against Sam, practically knocking her out of the chair. Dimples peaked out at the corners of her cheeks and the crease between her eyebrows disappeared.

"I know. You hate storms."

Wallie barked again, adding a growl for good measure. Then his ears perked up, and he dashed back inside. Sam heard the front door open and bang shut.

A voice from inside called, "Samantha, where are you?"

"I'm out on the porch, Maggie."

Maggie pushed the screen open just enough to poke her head out. "Sam, dammit, get your ass in this house before lightning fries your curls. You're giving credence to the phrase *dumb blonde.*"

Sam grinned and grabbed her wet ponytail, shaking the frizzing curls at the end. "Oops. Too late!" she said, hoping she sounded nonchalant. "Don't worry. I'm coming in. I was just unwinding after my run."

"That's my Sam, always running from something. Run, run, run," Maggie mumbled as she turned back into the house.

"You say something, Maggie?" Sam inhaled and wiped once more at the dampness on her cheeks as she uncurled her body and stepped into the house.

"Me? God forbid," said Maggie, noting her friend's strained red eyes without comment.

Maggie was what most men would call a real woman. Tall and athletic with flawless mocha skin and a body that would make Aphrodite jealous. Standing next to Maggie always gave Sam flashbacks to her awkward tween years when she was the skinny geek with wild fuzzy hair. By all rights, she should resent the hell out of her flawless friend. But it was impossible. Every pore of Maggie's body oozed love alongside that beauty—even when she scolded. And when she was done scolding, she wrapped her victims up in those long arms and crushed them to life with her surprising softness, leaving her loved ones hard-pressed to find an air pocket. But that act was for her empathetic moods—she was definitely in scolding mode this morning.

"I can't believe you're just going to turn yourself in. You know you can't trust a suit, Sam. Stay here until it all blows over. They'll find Jimmy Hoffa before they find you."

"I can't, Maggie, you know that. I have to face this. I didn't do anything wrong, and I'm not hiding from anyone."

"That's debatable," commented Maggie dryly, but she held her hand up before Sam could argue. "Nevermind. Didn't mean to detour from the topic. But Sam, this is the time to hide. I can tell you from experience; in the South, the law is lazy and crooked. Once their first suspect shows up, they have no reason to keep looking."

"I'm going, Maggie."

"Dammit, girl, you're as naive as you are stubborn."

"Yeah? Well, the naivety is just a part of my Southern charm, but I learned the stubborn from you." Sam was trying to lighten the mood, but one look from Maggie told her it wasn't working.

"Look, I'll be okay, I promise," she continued. "And with you keeping Wallie happy, I'll be free to fix the whole mix-up. Trust me, I've got to work this out my way."

Maggie sighed and her hard gaze fell. "Do it however you want, but promise me you won't tell them about this house or this island. If you wise up and discover that you're the easy way out for those suits, just get back here as fast as those size nines will take you. You run and hide, and I'll lock and load."

Sam smiled naturally at the old joke. The first time they met, Sam had been running on a day she thought she was the only one on the island. She had run up on Maggie who was standing with her legs braced apart, gun drawn and pointed straight at an unfortunate ghost crab that had just kidnapped a baby loggerhead from its nest. Sam would have run the other way that day if Maggie hadn't been wearing her federal parks uniform and muttering about nobody messing with her babies. They had been best friends ever since.

"I promise, if things get too bad, you're the only place I'll run."

Maggie nodded in resignation, and before Sam could protest, Maggie squeezed her tight and whispered with veiled tears in her voice, "You're my best friend. Watch that tiny ass of yours."

Maggie released Sam and swiped at her watery eyes before throwing back her shoulders and grabbing Wallie's giant bag. "Well, come on, Wallie, I've got work to do. Say goodbye before those storm clouds open up again and mess up my gorgeous do." She patted her own short, weatherproof curls and opened the door.

"Bye, Maggie. I owe you."

"Just watch your back and call me. And remember if that giant dog of yours touches my babies, you're getting him back in pieces."

Sam laughed. They both knew Wallie would guard Maggie's babies like he was the mama loggerhead.

Sam stooped down and gave Wallie a bear hug. He placed a wet kiss on her left cheek and eyed her with a sad wariness before trotting off behind Maggie to the old truck in the driveway. He leapt through the open driver's door to the passenger's side, and Maggie slid in behind him. Sam smiled and waved as they reversed down the narrow dirt road.

She watched in silence as the truck disappeared from sight. She tilted her head to rest against the doorframe and continued to watch the empty road until fresh rain washed the tracks away. Sam closed the door and then did something she had never done before—she locked the door from the inside.

She had two hours until the ferry left. Shivering, she walked back to her bathroom to strip out of her wet clothes. She had created her dream bathroom just a year ago with money from a very successful photography assignment in London. In fact, she had found the old claw-foot tub while wandering around an English antique shop. The tub was huge, and she had envisioned this room the minute she saw it. The shop owner had arched his eyebrow and literally looked down his hooked nose at her when she had asked to have holes cut in the sides. Now the sizable claw-foot tub, equipped with modern Jacuzzi jets, sat under giant windows that opened like French doors toward the sea. The floor was covered in old world Tuscan blue tiles and the walls were rough-cut with exposed beams and a coat of white wash. Filling the tub with hot, steaming water, Sam flipped on the jets and opened the windows.

On a normal day, Sam would grab a book and hop in the tub after a long run. Her muscles would slowly turn to Jell-O as the salt air brushed across her face. But today her body refused to relax and the hot water seemed incapable of warming her. She felt old, well beyond her twenty-eight years.

Sam closed her eyes and pictured Ben. She let her head slide below the water line until the agitated water enveloped her. The muffled roar of the motor drummed in her ears as the popping bubbles pricked her skin. Cold raindrops blew through the open window and lanced the water like icy daggers. When her lungs screamed for air, Sam surfaced without opening her eyes and leaned back against the cool porcelain. Her crescent-moon lashes dripped with beads of water like crystal tears as the steam engulfed her face. She concentrated on the small white dot on the inside of her eyelids and willed her brain to stop thinking.

Sam dozed. When she opened her eyes and glanced at the clock, it was already nine a.m., and the water was lukewarm at best. She still felt exhausted but knew it was time to go. Self-pity wasn't helping Ben.

With a new determination, she quickly washed and rinsed her hair, stood, and grabbed a towel. She roughly dried a body any runway model would envy—endless legs, small breasts, small waist, small hips—a perfect physique of which Sam was eternally oblivious.

She dressed in a pair of faded cutoff jeans and a ragged pink t-shirt with a small Care Bear barely visible in the corner. An unskilled seamstress had hacked off the sleeves and cut a small v in the front neckline to assure the wearer unobstructed movement. The haphazard fashion statement should have looked like a Salvation Army castoff, but instead it was casual chic, accenting the lean muscular arms and legs. Sam topped off the outfit with hiking boots.

"What should I pack?" Her voice echoed back to her. She shook her head. "Right, Wallie, you're gone and I'm talking to myself."

Sam packed casual clothes. Jeans, t-shirts, running shorts. After all, she'd only be in one meeting with the *suits*. Opening the top drawer of her dresser, she grabbed underwear and tossed it in the bag on top of the other clothes. The bright fancy bits of lace looked as if they had jumped into the wrong suitcase. It never occurred to Sam that her choice of underwear did not fit her clothing style. She simply liked the whimsy and the feel of silk against her skin. Besides, it wasn't as if anyone would ever know what her underwear looked like. She'd only been with one man her entire life and that experience had proven once and for all that life with a canine was her best option. Before zipping the bag, she reached in her closet and added her only black suit. Grabbing the duffle bag, she headed outside to load her Jeep.

Sam's Jeep was yet another enigma. While Sam tried to hide in faded nondescript clothes, her Jeep shouted for attention. The Jeep was a rusty orange with off-roading wheels that would make any redneck proud. Even with legs like stilts, Sam had to use the attached black metal step to climb in her seat. Tossing camera bags in the back with her clothes, Sam slammed the door and walked back to the house.

Sam's home sat alone on the corner of a small island overlooking the Atlantic Ocean. Its cedar siding was aged; and the tin roof, a reflective pewter. The entire house would have been completely camouflaged on a day like today if not for the Caribbean blue storm shutters that framed every window.

Thunder rumbled deep and long as Sam walked out onto the back porch and began closing the shutters. She smiled faintly and touched the rough wood. She had bought the shutters on a whim—color to her otherwise gray life.

That same color had crept stealthily into the house over the years. A large, blue, over-stuffed couch and matching chair filled the living area. A plush blue and cream checkered rug covered the unfinished pine floors in the center of the room. The remaining furniture was secondhand but had been sanded and whitewashed. Bits of sea glass, driftwood, and other ocean treasures were scattered across the tops. The windows were large, and after the storm passed, sunlight would fill the room and rainbows from dangling prisms would dance across the walls breathing life into the framed gray works of art that covered the whitewashed walls.

The gray works were Sam, though she simply thought of them as assignments. When Sam looked through the lens of a camera, she saw souls. It didn't matter if she photographed the wet sands on the beach or the face of a smiling sick boy: she had a gift, and that gift made her walls speak. Sadness, fear, loneliness. The voices of the portraits cried out from their framed cells.

One black-and-white photograph, more than any other, reached out to haunt its viewers. A small, pale child swallowed by a leather office chair looked straight into the lens. His big eyes twinkled with a shy smile, belying the thin face, and luring the unsuspecting observer to lean into the photograph. But upon closer inspection, the twinkle revealed a shadow, a shadow of misery usually reserved for the wrinkled, faded blue eyes of war veterans, not the large teddy bear eyes of a three-year-old. At least, that was the opinion expressed by the editors of *Time* magazine.

Sam gently touched the boy's face with the tip of her fingers, turned, and walked out the front door, pulling it shut behind her.

CHAPTER TWO

Sam drove her Jeep down the narrow streets of Charleston looking for the two-story pink B&B. The Jeep bounced over cobblestone streets as she maneuvered through the historic district. Citadel boys strutting along the sidewalks stopped to grin and whistle whenever she slowed down. It was only May, but sweat dripped down her face even with the top down, and her hair felt like a tangled ball of yarn. But when a girl drives a jacked-up Jeep through the streets of Charleston, the Southern boys stand and salute. As she turned another corner, Sam shook her head. She was certain the honors were aimed at the Jeep, not the girl.

The street paralleled Charleston Harbor. Sunlight glinted off the water as sailboats, big and small, skated across the glassy surface. Without conscious thought, Sam scanned the water for dolphins. Her eyes rounded as she spotted a submarine surfacing between two unsuspecting boats. A helpless laugh escaped her lips. Not exactly what she was looking for, and probably not the best of signs.

The Palmer House Bed and Breakfast was just to her right. She had splurged and rented the B&B's small carriage house for the week. The carriage house had two small bedrooms so she could sleep in one and set up her equipment in the other. The master bedroom boasted privacy along with a view of the harbor. She drove down the narrow driveway along the side of the home and parked in the small gravel lot reserved for guests. Parking was a premium in Charleston, so it was almost worth the price of the room just to have a parking space. Almost. But it was within jogging distance of Ben's apartment. And that would be priceless.

Jerking up the parking brake, Sam reached across the seat and pulled out the small bag containing her camera and lenses. Next, she unloaded the two larger bags from the back. As she pulled the luggage around to the front stoop and lugged it up the first step, a man who could only be described as a business clad surfer dude, complete with Brad Pitt's face and the shoulders of a body builder, looked down at her.

"Hey, honey, need some help?"

Sam looked up into gorgeous blue eyes and bit back a retort. Why did men call everything with shaved legs "honey"? But she was tired, and bumping the bags up the steps was not the way she normally treated her equipment.

"Actually," she said, "I could use a little help. Do you work here?"

"Nah," said Surfer Dude, effortlessly picking up the two heavy cases, wheels and all. "I'm just here on business. Liked the hominess and the food better than the high-rise hotel down the street."

"Oh, well thanks." The man set the bags down at the top of the staircase. "Didn't mean to put you to work."

"No problem. My name's Dan Williams." He held out his hand. "Maybe you could thank me with a drink? Downtown later tonight, that is, if you're here alone." She could have sworn he wiggled his eyebrows.

"Samantha," she said, extending her hand and tensing as she waited for a sign of recognition. She was still front-page news in Charleston. Instead, he smoothly grasped her fingers and pulled her hand to his lips for a quick kiss before she could jerk it back. She released her breath, and the relief brought on a genuine smile. He was slick, but no reporter.

"Sorry, maybe after my murder trial," Sam quipped. She almost bit her tongue at her own comment and quickly turned to roll the suitcases across the verandah and through the open doorway.

"Your what?" he called to her back.

Sam decided she needed sleep. She was getting punchy. She was careful not to turn back to look at the stranger.

He stared at her back a moment before laughing. "Okay, Samantha-With-No-Last-Name. Anytime. I'll be here all week if you need a good attorney."

Sam stopped and looked back, but he was already down the steps. Hell, she thought, she did need a good attorney. She shook her head and went to the registration desk.

The receptionist sat behind a small antique desk doing paperwork. She peered up as the suitcases clattered across the heart of pine floors.

"Good afternoon, you must be Miss Jennings. Welcome to the Palmer House."

Sam glanced back over her shoulder to see if anyone had heard her name, but the room was empty.

"You are Miss Jennings?"

"Oh, yes. Thank you. Your inn is beautiful." Her eyes skimmed the room, taking in the 150-year-old furnishings and the breathtaking view out the floor-to-ceiling windows, which provided a wonderful breeze from the harbor.

"I'm glad you like it. I'm Suzanne. Should you need anything during your stay, just let me know, and I'll be happy to assist you." Reaching into her pile of papers, she pulled out a reservation form for Sam's review and signature. "Okay, all I need is a credit card."

Sam watched as the petite woman with a perfect cap of auburn hair swiped the card in a modern machine hidden inside a large, old wooden box. As soon as the card was verified, Suzanne rolled the desk lid down, effectively hiding the machine as well as a small laptop computer. With the exception of Suzanne in her modern dress, Sam imagined the room looked just as it had in the 1800's.

"You're all set." She smiled. "Here's your key to the carriage house. Karl will help you with your luggage."

A thin, lanky teenager appeared at her side and picked up the heavy cases as easily as Surfer Boy had. Sam reached across to test her own arm muscle and decided she needed to work out a little more. She followed Karl back out the way she had entered.

"Hey, Karl, I've got another bag in my Jeep."

"Okay. This it?"

"Yep."

"Cool wheels! I'm hoping to buy my own pickup one day, but I'd love to put some of these big wheels on it."

Sam smiled. Girls never appreciated her Jeep like the guys.

"You keep working this hard during high school and college and you'll get that truck." She slipped him a ten-dollar tip after he set her bags inside the front door of the carriage house.

He glanced down then looked up and grinned. "Thanks! Ask for me if you need anything, all right?"

"I'll do that. See you later."

Sam closed the door, dropping the heavy camera bag on the closest table. Air conditioning had been added and the cool air was a welcome change. It also would protect her equipment. She checked the extra bedroom and found it equipped with a long folding table as she had requested. She began unpacking her equipment, setting the computer, printer, and scanner on the long table. On the bed, she unpacked her cameras and extra lenses. Quickly, she examined the equipment to make sure the humidity had not harmed it. Satisfied, she went to the front hall and picked up her other bag and took it to her bedroom. She unpacked, placing most of her belongings in the antique dresser and hanging up the dull suit.

She walked out in the living area to discover a small plate of cheese, crackers, and petits fours. Chilling beside the plate was a bottle of white wine and a small note reading:

Welcome to the Palmer House. Brunch is served in the main house lobby every morning between 7 and 10 a.m. Mint juleps and hors d'oeuvres are served every evening between 4 and 6 p.m. Lunch and Dinner are available with reservations. Enjoy your stay.

Sam's empty stomach growled. She had forgotten to eat again. Opening the wine, she poured herself a glass, picked up the plate, and took her snack through her bedroom and out onto the porch. She placed the food and wine on a small table and sat down on the wicker settee. She leaned her head back and studied the harbor.

Exhaustion washed over her. It just didn't seem real. She'd always been a loner, and she liked it that way. She definitely had never been in trouble. The quiet, studious girl in the back of the classroom, who'd rather watch than join. Over her lifetime, she had learned to be wallpaper, sitting quietly and observing until people simply forgot she was in the room. Consequently, she'd listened and learned, mentally recording the world around her.

That gift was the reason she had chosen journalism as her major in college. She enjoyed writing about her surroundings. Then, she had taken a photography course. People looked different through a camera lens. For Sam, the camera was like her very own crystal ball. She saw emotions that were invisible to the naked eye. Her photographs quickly developed into unique creative expressions. She also discerned, to her great excitement, that with a camera in front of her face, she disappeared to a realm of freedom unsurpassed by anything in her past. By her third year in college, she found something she thought she had lost forever. Happiness.

Ironically, hiding behind her camera also brought her the attention she avoided. Unlike Sam, her photographs had a voice of their own, demanding to be seen and heard. After she graduated, Sam freelanced for various newspapers and magazines. Her photographs appeared in publications throughout the United States and, in time, the world. The works were often more art than journalism, creating a curiosity about the creator. Soon, much to Sam's annoyance, journalists sought to interview the journalist. Her agent demanded the interviews, and eventually Sam relented for what her agent called "business development." But she relented only to a point. Sam accepted the interviews and spoke in such abbreviated responses that the articles were filled with intense descriptions of the photographs and very little about the photographer. Much to Sam's amusement, she stayed the byline. At least she had until approximately two months ago.

Two months ago, it was Sam's face, not her photographs that appeared on the front page of *The Charleston Post and Courier*, *The New York Times*, and *The Washington Post*. In fact, a dated photograph of her face had hit the AP wire services and appeared in newspapers all over the country. "Famous Photographer Murders Lover." "Photographer Shoots to Kill." Sam sighed. It should have read "Photographer Framed." Fortunately for Sam, the wire photo had been taken during one of her interviews. She was wearing heavy television makeup and her hair had been ironed straight and pulled back in a severe French twist. She'd worn an elegant expensive black suit and pearls. It did not resemble the real Sam. And so far, no one had connected her with the woman in the newspaper.

Swirling the wine in her glass, Sam glanced out over the harbor. How had this happened? It just couldn't be real. Ben was dead, and these crazy people thought she had killed him. He was her only friend, other than Maggie. A tear slid down her cheek, but she brushed it away roughly. She didn't have time for tears. She stood up, deciding that she didn't have the patience to wait until tomorrow.

Grabbing her baseball cap, she jammed it on her head and pulled it low over her eyes. She exchanged her boots for running shoes, zipped a thin hoodie over her t-shirt, and walked out the front door. Slipping her keys into her pocket, Sam began a slow jog toward Ben's apartment.

Tomorrow, she was to report to Judge Seigler's courtroom to face charges of murder. She couldn't even afford a real attorney because she had invested all her earnings in buying her beach cottage and photography equipment. Money had never really mattered to her except when she was lusting after a new camera or lens, but she'd be damned if she'd take a second mortgage to make some sleazy criminal defense attorney rich. She hated to waste even five hundred dollars, but it would be worth it to end this insanity tomorrow. After tomorrow, she would sell her home if she needed the money to find Ben's killer. But tonight, she had to face his death.

Ben's apartment was only six blocks away. It was a small efficiency over a detached garage. The only entrance was at the top of an outdoor staircase that ran along the side of the garage. A dark alley running along the steps separated the building from the main house.

Sam hung back in the shadows of an untamed rhododendron and stared up the staircase. She wanted to go up but bright yellow crime tape barred her entrance. She glanced over at the main house and saw the silhouette of the landlady as she walked through her house.

Studying the street, she wondered if anyone else had been around that night. Most of the buildings looked empty. A slight movement in a dark doorway caught her eye, revealing a homeless man in a filthy orange t-shirt huddled in the corner. He met her eyes for a moment and frowned. He mumbled nonsensical words and took a swig from a tightly wrapped, brown paper bag.

Sam took a step toward him then stopped abruptly. He had pushed his body further in the corner as she'd approached, but he'd brought his hand to his chest. His eyes held hers as he grinned, revealing dark stained teeth as he fingered the open blade of a rusty pocketknife.

"I just want to talk to you," began Sam.

"Get yo'r own," he threatened.

He took another swig from the brown bag and raised the knife with his other hand. Sam backed up and glanced around the street again. She was alone with the man. Studying him, she memorized his face. She thought briefly of calling the police, but was afraid they would arrest her, not him. Tomorrow, Ben, she promised silently, and reluctantly left the man in his archway.

The man scratched his dirty scalp as he watched Sam walk away. He tucked the knife away and fingered the hundred dollar bill in his pocket. He grinned as he thought about the new one he would get tomorrow. Life was good. He stood up and pulled out the two shiny quarters and the tiny scrap of paper from the other pocket. He went only as far as the phone booth and punched in the numbers scribbled on the paper. After a brief conversation, he walked back to his doorway. He had a job.

He looked at the crumpled paper. He wasn't dumb. He pulled out the hundred dollar bill, folded the slip of paper into the middle of it, and stuffed it down the front of his pants. He was gonna keep that number 'til he got what he was promised. He patted his groin. Let's see that gloved hand find that. Smiling, he tucked his body tightly back in his corner to watch the little room over the garage.

CHAPTER THREE

The ringing jarred Sam awake, and she slapped at the bedside table trying to shut off her alarm. But the ringing continued. The phone. It was the phone. She opened her eyes, adjusting to the light filtering into to the room as she lifted up the receiver.

"What? What's happened?"

"Good morning, Miss Jennings. It's six a.m. and this is your wake up call. Breakfast is available in the lobby at seven."

"Oh, yes, thank you," stammered Sam before her mind noted it was a recording. The receiver clattered into place. Rolling over onto her back, she stared at the ceiling and groaned. Her shoes were still on, and the door to the small porch was open. But at least she had slept. And there had been no dreams for the first time in four days.

Pushing the tangled mass of hair out of her eyes, she crawled out of bed and walked out on the porch. She scanned the sunrise on the horizon. Just as she turned to walk back inside, she saw it. A dolphin surfaced just enough to take a deep breath before diving again only to reappear with its mate about thirty feet closer. Then they were gone. She felt a spark of hope that made her stomach flip. It was silly. She knew that. But dolphins had always been her good luck symbol. And today she needed all the luck God could spare.

With a lighter heart, Sam showered and dressed. She was to meet her lawyer at his office at eight a.m. and go with him to the courthouse for a nine a.m. appearance before the judge. At least part of this nightmare would end soon. She wondered if she should tell the judge about the homeless man or wait and talk to the police.

Pulling her damp hair into a tight bun, Sam gelled it in place until it looked stiff and dark. Next, she slid into her rumpled suit. She frowned at her reflection. Maggie would have had some choice words for this outfit and the hairdo. Librarian gone frumpy. And she had no hose, but who could wear hose in this heat? She slipped on her sandals and stepped out on the porch one last time. She noticed the untouched cheese and cracker tray from the night before and her stomach growled. She couldn't remember her last real meal, but the blobs of grease made her queasy. Breakfast could wait until after the courtroom drama.

The attorney's name was J.D. Snelling. His office was in the basement of a historic tabby building just a short walk from the inn. Sam entered a grand lobby, and followed the arrows down a back staircase to Mr. Snelling's windowless office. The top part of his door was frosted glass with his name painted in bold black letters across the middle. The colorless hallway was dimly lit and the white of the checkerboard tile floor was dingy. Sam felt the loss of Ben in those surreal surroundings. Taking a deep breath, she knocked.

At first, nothing. She knocked on the glass this time, rattling the door.

"Come in," called a male voice from the back.

Sam opened the door and walked inside a dark office with one flickering florescent light above the middle of the room. There was an empty receptionist's desk in the front with a phone attached to an answering machine. Directly behind the desk was an open door.

"Come on back."

Sam walked around the desk and into the office. Illuminated by yet another florescent light, this one with new bulbs, was the most cluttered office Sam had ever seen. White cardboard boxes with case names and numbers were stacked in every corner. Papers were spread on the floor in front of some of the open boxes. Messy stacks of paper adorned the desk and the two old wooden chairs facing the desk. The boy, because that was what he was, a boy, looked up from the clutter, blushed, and pushed the hair out of his eyes.

"Hi, you must be Samantha Jennings. You're just a little early. But that's fine. I'm J.D. Snelling. Just shove some of those papers on the floor, have a seat, and we'll get started."

Sam felt like she'd slid down a rabbit hole. Now, she knew those dolphins had just come up to laugh at her predicament. She looked down and occupied herself with pushing some of the papers to the back of the seat. She was perilously close to laugher—which she knew would soon turn into hysteria. She perched on the edge of the chair and looked up again. Okay, Sam, get a grip.

"Um, you're J.D. Snelling?"

"Yep. I know; I look young. But not to worry. I finished law school last year and passed the Bar the first time I took it." He sounded so proud of this accomplishment that Sam was struck speechless. "Now, let's see. Have you got my retainer fee?"

Looking around at the shabby office, Sam guessed he could use every penny he got. She would have simply told him to get real, but the hearing was in an hour and she had no time to find a more experienced attorney.

"Yes," said Sam. She opened her purse, pulled out the check she had written that morning and handed it to him. He took it, glanced down, grinned, and placed it in his top drawer.

"Okay. That's out of the way. We probably need to head on down to the courthouse."

"Wait. Don't we need to discuss my case first?"

"Oh, yeah. Sure. How do you plan to plead?"

"What?" Sam stared at him in disbelief.

"You know, guilty or not guilty. Or you can plead no contest, which means that you're not technically pleading guilty but that you are not contesting the charges. Then, you just go through the sentencing part of the case. Saves the court a lot of time and energy."

Sam's patience was gone and so was her sense of humor.

"I know what pleading means, you idiot. Of course I'm pleading not guilty. I'm being charged with murder for God's sake. I did not murder my best friend. This is just an outrageous mistake that has gotten completely out of hand. I need you to go in there with me and straighten this mess out or give me my money back."

Snelling's baby cheeks flushed with anger. "There is no need to be verbally abusive, Miss Jennings. If you don't want me to handle the hearing today, I'll be happy to return your check. Although it might be difficult to find another attorney to represent you at this late date, you are legally allowed to represent yourself, you know."

The last was said with a smirk as he opened the desk to retrieve the check. He was young, but at that moment she knew why lawyers were equated to sharks. He was simply bumping up against his prey before sinking in those carnivorous teeth. She had no choice. Even an inexperienced attorney was better than none. Judges were known to chew up and spit out unrepresented defendants who didn't know the proper procedures and magical legal terminology. They protected their profession from those who tried to avoid paying legal fees. As much as she disrespected this man, this boy, she did not want to spend a single night in jail for a misunderstanding.

"I apologize if I offended you," she mumbled. "I am just a little stressed, considering the circumstances."

He relaxed, returned the check to the drawer, and leaned back in his desk chair. Sam barely stifled a laugh when he leaned too far and almost tumbled backwards. Fortunately, her face was composed by the time he glared back up at her.

"Very well. Now, how will you plead?"

She wanted to scream at him but controlled her temper. "Not guilty, as I stated. But I would like a chance to explain everything to the judge so the charges can be dropped and I can concentrate on finding Ben's killer."

He had the nerve to smirk again. If she had her telephoto lens, she would seriously consider bashing his head in. One less shark.

"Miss Jennings, this is simply a preliminary hearing for you to answer to the outstanding warrant for your arrest and for bond to be set. You will not be allowed to plead your case today."

Sam could not believe it. She had just paid someone five hundred dollars to say "Not Guilty." She would demand her money back that minute, but she knew nothing about bond or courtroom procedure.

"Well, we best be on our way. The judge will throw you in jail for contempt if you are even five minutes late. He has a full docket today."

Without another word, Sam walked out the door a few steps behind her personal shark. She had no desire to walk beside him. She could only pray that things went smoother in the courtroom. But her mind was stuck on the fact that, apparently, her ordeal might not end today. She frowned and decided she wasn't willing to accept defeat that easily. She just needed a minute of the judge's time.

The courthouse was only two blocks away, but the heat and humidity were stifling. Sam could feel the sweat soaking her armpits and was thankful that the suit was black and the stains would not show. As she walked up the courthouse steps, she noticed a handful of photographers to her left. At the same moment, she saw the almost imperceptible nod of her attorney as the flashes began.

"Miss Jennings, Miss Jennings, how will you plead?"

"Do you regret killing your lover?"

"Was it a crime of passion or did you plan it?"

Sam ducked her head and put her hand in front of her face. The bastard had alerted the press. She pushed her way into the courthouse where a deputy came forward and lightly touched her arm.

"This way." The deputy spoke softly, leading her to the front of the line so that she could go quickly through the metal detector. He was a large black man with considerate brown eyes. She could have wept; she wished he were her attorney. Not daring to look back, it occurred to her that he had left her attorney to stand in the long line while she went ahead.

"You reporters back off, you're barred from beyond this line today. Judge's orders," barked the deputy before the protests were even voiced.

"Thank you," Sam whispered.

"No problem, miss," he said with a grin. "Vultures. All of 'em."

"The reporters or the attorneys?"

"Both."

Sam smiled absently at the guard. She knew his comment was meant as a distraction. And it worked, especially when she thought of the irony; after all, she was a reporter too. She went through the metal detector and walked around the corner out of sight while she waited for her vulture. Her nerves had returned, and she was thankful she hadn't eaten. She had composed herself by the time her flustered attorney came around the corner. She saw a flash of relief cross his face when he saw her. It was clear that the publicity would bring him more business.

"You alerted the press," she accused as he walked forward.

"Nonsense," he said, but the red blush creeping up his neck defied his words. "The judge's calendar is a matter of public record. Published and posted outside his door weekly."

Sam stared at him and said nothing then turned and walked into the courtroom. Mr. Snelling stumbled forward chasing her, then almost collided into her back before realizing she had stopped abruptly just inside the door.

Sam felt the blood seep from her face as she stepped into the courtroom. It was packed. The whispering buzz stopped for what seemed like an eternity the moment she entered. Just when she thought the silence would deafen her, the loud whispers resumed. She felt the eyes watching her and an overwhelming sense of panic momentarily froze her in place. Run. Run. Run. She started to turn when her attorney stepped in front of her and commanded, "This way."

Sam stopped mid-pivot and took a deep breath. She focused on his back, walked to a bench on the front row, and sat down. Sam decided at that moment Mr. Snelling had just earned his money. If he had not walked ahead of her, she would have fled. He slid in beside her just as the bailiff announced, "Please rise for the Honorable Judge Seigler."

Just a few blocks away, Sally Simpson was learning that Samantha Jennings was in town and standing before a judge at that very moment. Sally twisted her hands nervously in her lap as she listened to the woman sitting across from her.

The woman—no, the lady—was wearing white gloves. Spotless white gloves, thought Sally, with little pearl buttons at the wrist. Her legs were crossed at the ankles and neatly folded at an angle. The room was so tiny that the lady's knees almost touched Sally's. The thought made Sally pull backwards in her own chair as if the touch would burn.

Sally hadn't recognized her when she'd first opened the door. The glossy blonde hair had been tucked back in a neat chaffon then covered with a chic oversized hat. She'd worn white-framed sunglasses to cover the top half of her face and an elegant black and white scarf was tucked into the neckline of a white Chanel suit. An image of Jackie O had flashed through Sally's mind when the lady had entered the tiny apartment.

The second thing Sally had noticed about the lady was that she wasn't sweating. The apartment was on the third floor, at the top of a long winding staircase. The owner of the building had converted the Charleston mansion into one-bedroom efficiency apartments. And although Sally loved her home, it needed an elevator. Sally hated that she was always wet with sweat by the time she reached her front door.

Awestruck by her visitor, she had smiled and invited her in, even pouring her a glass of ice tea. Now, the tea sat on the end table, untouched, with the melted ice forming a clear layer to float over the dark liquid below.

"Now, you understand what you're to do?" asked the lady in a tone Sally had heard when she cleaned the church for the women's auxiliary back home.

"Yes, ma'am."

"'Ma'am,' how quaint." The woman's eyes assessed in cold silence, and then she nodded. "Yes, I think you do."

She stood and brushed her gloved hands down her skirt to erase any imagined wrinkles. She pulled her floppy brimmed hat low over her shades and walked to the door, waiting for Sally to open it. Sweat soaked the armpits of Sally's sleeveless, cotton dress as she held the door open. The lady stepped through the open passage, paused, and turned back, pinning Sally in place with the power of her stare through the darkness of the glasses.

"Remember, dear, I will be watching—and listening. You wouldn't want the police to learn where you were that night."

Sally paled. She nodded, too afraid to speak. The Jackie O look-a-like smiled a politician smile, then turned and walked down the spiral staircase with her gloved hand hovering just a fraction of an inch above the handrail the entire journey down.

Sally closed the door and slid the chain in place. She walked across the room and picked up the watery ice tea. She felt the cold drink travel down her throat and tried to still her shaking hand, but failed. The glass tipped over as she went to replace it. Ignoring the spilled tea as it spread across the table and slid over the edge, Sally walked over, picked up the telephone, and dialed.

"Mama?" said Sally.

CHAPTER FOUR

Caleb couldn't take his eyes off her. She stood just inside the courtroom doors like a deer caught in headlights. He searched her face but could see no sign of the carefree teenager he had known, but his heart skipped a beat as he watched her. Her pale blue eyes were wide and her pupils dilated. The normally tan skin was colorless. Her hair looked dark, plastered to her head and pulled back in a severe bun. But the severe style only made the vulnerability more vivid. Fear radiated from her and made his heart ache. He was certain if she blinked, she would turn and flee.

For a moment, she pivoted, but just as Caleb rose to chase her, a stiff and blushing young man walked around her, pausing to mutter a few inaudible words next to her ear. She blinked and followed him without question, keeping her eyes focused forward. Her posture was so stiff, he was sure she would shatter like fine china if someone touched her.

That must be Snelling, thought Caleb with disgust. He'd heard the deputies spitting out his name earlier that morning in the break room. Snelling, the "Yankee vulture" who had migrated south to set up his law practice after finishing Yale last year—a lawyer who liked seeing his name in the newspaper. How he had hooked Sam was unknown, but the speculation was rampant. Word had it that Snelling had offended the judge with publicity leaks that threatened to turn the courtroom into a circus. Caleb came to make sure the fallout would not harm Sam. Whether Sam liked it or not, he was there to help her.

"All rise for the Honorable Judge Seigler."

Caleb stood with the crowd, which had grown silent now except for the shuffling of feet. The judge entered, but Caleb couldn't take his eyes off Sam's face. He had daydreamed about her many times over the years, picturing how her life had gone. He'd seen her photography and read her interviews. Her photographs were amazing, but he had pored over the articles and learned little about her. He didn't even know where she lived.

Judge Seigler began calling roll, his monotone voice slowly reading the names from his calendar. Normally, the law clerk called the roll, but today the judge enjoyed the tension in the air and wanted all attention on his face. After all, it was an election year and this was the biggest case to walk through the Charleston courts since a South-of-Broad-Street Beauregard had caught his wife in bed with the help and chased them down the street with his great granddaddy's antique rifle. Luckily, the old gun's sights were off and the case turned into an assault with a deadly weapon trial instead of a murder trial.

"Samantha Jennings."

"Your honor, there has been a terrible mistake, I . . . ."

"Mr. Snelling, please inform your client that this is simply the roll call and that the court has not addressed her at this time. If she interrupts again, I will find her in contempt."

"Yes, your honor. I apologize to the court for my client's unseemly behavior," said Snelling, pushing Sam's shoulder until she was seated.

Caleb almost laughed as he saw the change wash over Sam. Gone was the terrified girl. She was livid. She was looking at Snelling as if sizing him up for a coffin.

Finishing the roll call, Judge Seigler looked down from his bench, "Now, Mr. Snelling, I gather that you will be the attorney representing Miss Jennings in the matter of The State of South Carolina versus Samantha Jennings."

"Yes, your Honor, I am . . ."

"Excuse me, your honor, but I beg to differ with Mr. Snelling. I will be representing Miss Jennings," said Caleb as he stood and faced the judge. His expression never changed as Sam turned her shocked face toward him.

"Mr. McCloud," said the judge with a raised eyebrow and thoughtful pause. "I must say I am surprised to see you in my courtroom. If the newspapers are correct, aren't you a fancy Atlanta attorney these days? From what I've read, you should be too busy to bother with the daily events of your old hometown."

"Your honor, I am based in Atlanta, but I am still a member of the Bar in South Carolina, and I am never too busy when justice calls."

Judge Seigler lifted a second bushy eyebrow. This high profile case was just the type of case to launch Caleb McCloud's already thriving political ambitions, but it wouldn't hurt the judge's ambitions either to have a high profile murder case defended by one of the most respected attorneys in the country. With McCloud involved, the case would receive national attention.

Sam's brain was finally over the shock and her anger was on the rise as she jumped up to speak, but Snelling regained his composure first and stole the spotlight.

"Your honor, I object. Miss Jennings hired me to represent her."

"Your honor, I did not hire . . ."

"Order in this court," yelled Judge Seigler, banging his gavel. "Mr. McCloud, I suggest you, Mr. Snelling, and Miss Jennings adjourn to the conference room and resolve this conflict. I will not tolerate any further disruptions in my courtroom. I will see all three of you back in my courtroom in ten minutes, and no one will speak unless recognized by this court. Bailiff."

"Yes, your Honor," responded Caleb.

"This way," stated the bailiff, opening a side door.

Sam opened her mouth to speak and then clamped her lips shut as she read the silent warning in Caleb's eyes. She glared at his back as she followed him through the door.

She shouted at him the moment the door shut. "Damn it, Caleb, you are not my attorney."

Snelling smiled smugly. "You heard my client. Miss Jennings, I instruct you to no longer address this man. From this point forward, I will speak for you."

Caleb had trouble hiding his smile as Sam spun back toward Snelling.

"I can speak for myself, you idiot. And as for you, I have just one thing to say to you," began Sam.

Snelling flushed red with anger, but Caleb calmed the situation smoothly. "Sam, if I could just speak to you in private, I can explain. I've been trying to contact you for weeks but I couldn't find you. Please, put aside your feelings about me for a minute and listen to me as an attorney—a much-needed attorney," he added, glancing at Snelling and raising one eyebrow. "Then, if you still want me to leave, I will walk out and never darken your door again."

Sam's eyes involuntarily looked at the door, and she felt such an ache of panic that she froze.

"Sam," Caleb began, gently touching her elbow.

Sam looked into his eyes and a pain that had nothing to do with Ben's murder pierced her heart. It was insane—it shouldn't still hurt. She had been a teenager, young and stupid, but the pain felt fresh and new.

* * * * * * * *

Sam had been standing between two large sand dunes when she saw him. The sun was setting and he was cast in shadows, but she would recognize that body anywhere. A long, lean body with washboard abs. He didn't walk like most men. His bare feet skimmed across the wet sand like skates on ice, a grace that seemed almost comical in a man of his size. She smiled and, watching him, her heart skipped. He was gorgeous and he was hers. He glided closer to her hidden spot—then suddenly spun back toward the sea. Sam started to run forward to greet him, but skidded to a stop. She stared in disbelief. The man gliding along the surf was Caleb, beautiful Caleb, but he was not alone.

A painful emptiness swept through Samantha's chest, and her heart dropped into her stomach. She watched in stunned silence as a petite, beautiful girl with dark black hair emerged from behind Caleb's shadowed frame. She was laughing as she jumped on his back, wrapping her bare legs around his naked waist. Her lips skimmed across his ear and her small pink tongue darted out. Sam felt the intimacy of their contact burn into the pit of her stomach.

Laura. The girl that boys desired above all others. Except Caleb, her heart cried, not Caleb. The first day she and her friends had arrived at the beach three months before, Caleb had noticed Sam, not Laura. Caleb had approached Sam as she was stretched out on the beach reading a book. He had actually stepped over Laura as if she didn't exist, stretching out on the sand beside Sam instead and teasing her about her romance novel.

"Okay, he's tall, blonde, and beautiful, right? You're into those gorgeous blonde lifeguard types and I don't have a chance, right?" His black hair shone like the wings of a raven, falling in messy curls into emerald green eyes that glittered with flecks of gold.

"Maybe," Sam quipped, after her initial shock, "or maybe he's tall, dark, and handsome."

"I love the tall, dark, and gorgeous myself," interrupted Laura as her eyes slowly roamed his lanky muscular body from top to bottom with an open invitation. "I'm Laura. And you are gorgeous."

His eyes never left Sam's. "Caleb. The name's Caleb. Hey, Laura, now that we know each other so well, could you introduce me to this exquisite mermaid next to you? I think I'm in love."

Sam's eyes reflected shock as she stared into eyes straight off the cover of a romance novel. Maybe she had conjured him up. The sun was hot today, and she thought about the amazingly realistic hallucinations people have after days in the desert. A deep-throated laugh escaped her lips as she glanced at Laura. Anger flashed in Laura's eyes, though the seductive smile never left her face as she stared at Caleb.

"Oh, you mean Samantha? Caleb, this is Sam; Sam, Caleb."

"Hi, Sam. You want to get married?"

Sam laughed again. "Could I have a few days to think it over?"

"Okay, but don't wait too long. I'm a great catch, you know."

Laura rolled her eyes as she stood up. "Well, it's too hot to be lying around. Let's go get a drink, Sam."

Sam looked back toward the shore at Laura and Caleb. Laura arched her back riding Caleb through the surf, her tinkling laughs ringing out in perfect harmony with the deep rumbles of Caleb's voice. He spun her around in circles then ran into the ocean. Her protesting screams were quickly muffled as he pulled her around and covered her lips with his own. Then, he swung the girl over his powerful shoulders and strode across the walkway just a few yards from where Sam sat frozen on her knees.

Sam was not sure how long she sat crouched on her knees cursing some god she knew could not exist. She could still hear the haunting melody of their laughter. Her soul ached; she felt hollow. Used. Her tears finally escaped, trailing salty paths down her cheeks.

A full moon rose above the water casting a bright beam of light across the ocean waves. Sam stood up slowly and ran. Down the empty beach, running faster and faster. Away from the scene playing over and over in her mind. The warm salty air engulfed her soul, mingling with the salt on her cheeks until they were one. Foolish, foolish soul. She ran until her legs could carry her no further. Collapsing on the sand, Sam curled into a ball until exhaustion and numbness overwhelmed her. Then, she slept.

* * * * * *

"Sam," Caleb said again, compassion filling the word as he stared into her glazed expression, "we don't have much time."

Sam blinked and pushed the childhood hurt back into the dark corner of her heart. She stared back up at Caleb and studied the older Caleb in silence.

"Sam?" he asked after several more seconds passed and she said nothing.

"Okay," Sam replied with no emotion. "Say what you need to say."

"Mr. Snelling, leave us alone for a few minutes."

"I'm not going anywhere. I was retained by Miss Jennings, and you are not to talk to my client without her attorney present."

Sam sighed and turned to Mr. Snelling, speaking softly, "You're fired."

"What?!"

"You heard me, you're fired. You weren't even interested in hearing my side of the story when I hired you. I'd be better off representing myself."

"What . . . you . . . "

Sam and Caleb stared silently at the red faced, sputtering boy.

"Well, you won't be getting your retainer back," he yelled as he opened the door and stomped out.

"Thank you, Sam."

"What the hell are you doing here?"

"I read about you in the paper. I knew you didn't kill anyone. I just wanted to help."

"How do you know I didn't kill Ben? After all, the paper made it clear that I acted as a jealous lover. I'm not a

33

spineless teenager any longer. Maybe I don't just turn the other cheek any more."

Caleb winced. "Sam, in my heart, I know you—whether you believe me or not. I know the kind of person who can kill; I've met hundreds of them. You could never be that kind of person."

Sam started to argue just for the hell of it, but he cut her off.

"Look, there's no time. Just think about yourself right now. You've got to appear before Judge Seigler in two minutes. Now, he's never been known as a hanging judge, but he might relish that kind of reputation during an election year. Either way, he will definitely find an excuse to throw you in jail if you go back in there and try to represent yourself. Please let me help you. Believe it or not, I'm a decent attorney, even though I'm not always a decent human being." He paused when she said nothing. "And you can always fire me later."

Sam stared at Caleb. Why was she arguing? He wasn't just a decent attorney—he was a great attorney. And she should know. She had clipped every article documenting his career. He had graduated law school in South Carolina and quickly become one of the most successful prosecutors in Atlanta. Two years ago, he had left the prosecutor's office and opened a small law office defending accused criminals and attending fund-raising events with the model-of-the-year draped across his arm. But he had an amazing knack for picking only innocent defendants, and his movie-worthy cases won him national attention as the defender of innocents and a future senatorial candidate with an eye toward the presidency. Although it would be the ultimate revenge, Sam hoped she didn't ruin his perfect record.

"Okay."

"Okay?"

"I'm not a fool, Caleb. Well, not anymore."

Caleb held his tongue and grabbed her elbow to lead her to the door. But he released her immediately when he felt her stiffen.

"Sorry," he muttered and opened the door the courtroom.

CHAPTER FIVE

Caleb wanted to place his hand on the small of Sam's back. She swayed on her feet as he spoke to the judge. Fortunately, the hearing was brief, and the two exited through a side door before the judge proceeded with his calendar.

"Jim, we're ready to leave," said Caleb.

"Sure thing, Mr. McCloud. Just follow me."

Surprised, Sam looked up into the face of the kind man who had helped her earlier.

"You know each other?"

"Mr. McCloud asked me to look out for you. Now, we're going out the way the judges leave so the press won't hound you, miss."

"Thank you, Jim. You're very kind."

"You're welcome, Miss Jennings."

"It's Sam."

A broad smile creased his face. "You're welcome, Sam."

Caleb was silent during the exchange but his eyes twinkled as they met Jim's over the top of Sam's head. Nope, Sam was not your typical Southern lady, and she unknowingly had just endeared herself to the head of courthouse security and the future sheriff of Charleston County.

Jim led them through a maze of hallways and staircases to the basement of the building. Another door opened to a narrow tunnel.

"Just follow the tunnel. It opens into the parking garage across the street. The elevator is on the opposite side as you walk out."

"Thanks again. You've been a great help."

"Anything for you, Mr. McCloud." Before Sam could question the slight humor she heard behind the comment, Jim turned to Sam and added, "I was gonna tell you 'good luck,' but you won't need luck with this guy on your side."

He chuckled and shut the door before Sam could respond.

"What'd you do to earn his worship? Pay him?"

Anger sparked his eyes as he glanced down at Sam. Instead of responding, he jerked his head toward the parked cars and said, "We should hurry."

The stony look twisted Sam's stomach. She wanted to take back the flippant remark, but her pride clamped her lips shut. She turned and walked toward the exit. Caleb paused only a second before catching up with her.

The silence filled the air as the two walked. Finally, Caleb sighed, grabbed Sam's upper arms and turned her to face him, ignoring the instant tension at his touch.

"You don't think very much of me do you?" He didn't bother waiting for an answer. "Jim's from Atlanta. He was the first defendant that I was hired to put away for life. The bottom line—he didn't do it. I got lucky and happened upon some evidence that proved him innocent. His own defense attorney hadn't even bothered to investigate all the facts. He became a friend."

Sam's eyes widened, not because he had helped Jim, but because he had volunteered the information

When she didn't respond, Caleb ran a frustrated hand through his thick black hair, pushing it away from his eyes.

"Look, Sam, I'm sorry about our past. I was young and if I could go back, I would . . . . Anyway, it doesn't matter. I can't change it. But I can help you with the future if you'll let me."

Old emotions churned in her stomach as Sam studied his face. Did he really wish he could change the past? Probably not. He probably didn't even understand why she was still so angry. It was obviously just a silly teenage fling to him. She knew that her hurt and anger would seem ridiculous to others, but the pain was there nonetheless. She thought it was gone, but it had just been hiding below the surface. She would die before letting him know that he could still hurt her.

"Okay."

Caleb watched the play of emotions cross her face. He saw confusion, pain, and determination, but her face was blank now.

"You can represent me. I need a good lawyer." And that's all he would be to her. She would never let him close to her heart again.

Caleb nodded, but for some strange reason, he felt he had just lost. They walked the rest of the way in silence.

Caleb's car was on the third floor of the parking garage. It was a navy Ford Explorer with darkened windows. He opened the passenger door and ushered her in.

"You can come back later for your car."

"I walked."

"Walked? From where?"

"I'm staying in a carriage house behind a small B&B down on the waterfront. I thought walking would be easier than trying to find a parking place."

Caleb shook his head as he got behind the wheel. "What were you going to do when you left the courthouse with a stream of reporters hounding you?"

Sam shrugged. "I wasn't expecting reporters. I thought I would go inside, explain to the judge that it was all a big mistake, and then go on with my life."

Caleb was at a loss for words. And Sam suddenly realized how naive she sounded. A faint blush crossed her cheeks.

"Okay, maybe it was a stupid assumption. But since Ben died, I haven't been able to think straight. The whole thing is just surreal. I keep thinking he'll walk up behind me, pull me into a big bear hold, and tell me it was all just a stupid misunderstanding."

Tears had filled her eyes and her voice trembled when she spoke of Ben. The sear of jealousy cutting through Caleb took him by surprise. He was jealous of a dead man. Of course she had moved on and found love; he had been the one to break it off. Caleb winced at the memory of what had happened. He had made a muck of the entire affair, but at the time, he'd been desperate.

* * * * * * * *

He was 24 years old. He had just finished law school and taken the Bar exam. He'd decided to enjoy one last relaxing summer, taking a job at a small beach resort working as a lifeguard before beginning his legal career as a prosecutor. He had graduated valedictorian, nearly at the cost of his sanity, and desperately needed a carefree summer before setting his career goals in motion.

He'd noticed Sam immediately. She seemed shy and serious next to her friends. She was always reading while her friends flirted and giggled over their secretly spiked drinks. Completely unaware of the stares her lanky body drew, she walked down the beach in her white bikini staring straight out to sea. Her youthful body was a golden brown, outlined by muscular legs and a firm torso. He wondered what sport kept her body so toned, yet graceful. He was acutely aware that she attracted the stares of older men; the high school boys talked mostly to her friends. Probably because Sam was fairly flat chested, while the other two had large chests and pushed their cleavage almost to their chins with skimpy bikini tops. Eighteen-year-old boys had an inordinate fascination with that particular part of the female anatomy.

Caleb made his move one day when her nose was stuck in a book. He smiled, relishing the look of pure astonishment in her eyes when she realized he was interested in her, not her friends. He had loved coaxing her out of her shell and watching her self-confidence bloom over the next three months. But it hadn't taken long to realize that he was no longer in control. He didn't realize how much danger he was in until the summer was almost over and the damage irreversible.

He had been seven years older and cocky. He'd romanced her with moonlight walks and picnics on nearby islands. At first, it was the pure challenge that lured him. She barely spoke in the beginning, but as the summer wore on, she relaxed. She was smart as well as beautiful, with a quick wit that kept him desperate for more. She saw the world with a wonderful innocence that made him regret his cynical side, born out of years of studying law and internships with the D.A.'s office. He suddenly remembered why he had gone to law school in the first place—his desire to help the world. She made him believe in that fairytale again. He found himself unconsciously drawing her name with his finger in the sand, calling her during work breaks, and spending every waking moment at her side.

Three months after meeting her and a week before they were to part, he was alone with her in his one-room apartment. They had just come back from a swim to grab lunch. His swim trunks were wet and clung to his hips as he pulled her into his arms. With a swift movement, her bikini top fell to the floor and he pulled her under him as he fell on his bed. He kissed her, lightly touching his lips to her eyelids, her cheeks, and down her throat. His lips closed over her small pink nipple and she moaned. His hands roamed over her flat belly and under her small white bikini bottoms. She stiffened, but he returned his lips to hers and felt her body melt under the assault. His fingers gently rubbed her as she instinctively raised her hips. Hot moisture flowed around his finger as he gently inserted it into the warm opening. She moaned and her hips rose again.

She was ready and he drew her bikini bottoms slowly down to her ankles. Her body was even more beautiful than he had imaged. A small triangle of dark blonde curls seemed to invite his hand downward. He drew his finger slowly through the curls and parted her. He moved his long index finger in and out as she moaned and swayed in embarrassed excitement. He pulled away from her long enough to pull off his swim trunks and reach for the top drawer of the bedside table.

"Caleb, don't go." Her voice had cracked; her eyes cloudy.

Quickly, he had found the condom and leaned over to kiss her again. He entered her slowly, feeling her stiffen as he stretched her wider. Holding himself still, he kissed her deep and long. She opened around him and he drove in, but froze buried deep within her clinging warmth when she cried out. His arms trembled as he held himself still and rained kisses along her face until she relaxed again.

Gently, he placed his hand between their joined bodies and slowly rotated his finger until she squirmed beneath him, calling his name in confusion. He held her close, going fast and strong until he heard her cry out in release, his own shout mixing with hers.

He rolled over and pulled her in his arms. She was a constant surprise and no one had ever felt so perfect in his arms. She was full of innocence and passion and never thought to conceal either from him. He could have held her in his arms forever. If she just hadn't spoken those frightening words.

"I love you, Caleb. And if the proposal you gave me the first day we met still stands, I've thought it over and my answer is yes." She promptly fell asleep.

He had not been so lucky. It was as if she had poured cold water over his head. He stared down at the mass of curls across his chest and the sleeping face. She wore no makeup and suddenly looked very childlike. Seventeen years old. She didn't fit in his future. What had he done? His career started in two weeks and here he was playing lifeguard and sleeping with a high schooler. He had to end this immediately before someone got hurt.

He'd been a coward. He couldn't drum up the courage to break it off with her. He'd tried to distance himself from her the next couple of days, making work excuses when she tried to meet. She was oblivious to his turmoil. Why didn't she understand the rules of a summer fling?

Her eyes glowed when he looked at her, and for once in his life, he was incapable of voicing his thoughts. The opportunity for an easy out was unexpected. He'd spotted her lurking in the dunes about the same time Laura, one of her so-called friends, walked up to him on the beach, flirting as usual. It was pure survival instinct that made him play along with the flirting as Sam watched. He even kissed Laura for good measure.

He'd felt guilty immediately. Still, he didn't go look for her. He waited for the confrontation, drinking an entire twelve-pack of Bud. When it became obvious that she wasn't coming, he'd tried to sleep. But when he closed his eyes, he was filled with guilt and a strange longing. He had just met Sam. It wasn't as if he had promised her anything more than a summer romance. He'd finally fallen asleep around five in the morning and awoken after one that afternoon. He could not deal with not knowing. He went in search of her. But she was gone. She'd checked out that morning. She hadn't even left him a note. Laura was the one to tell him Sam had left. She had run her finger down his arm and grinned up at him. To Caleb, her finger was like a razor cutting open his vein, but he had simply nodded and walked away.

* * * * * *

Caleb looked over at Sam as she sat in the passenger seat of his car staring straight ahead. He turned the keys and drove out of the parking garage.

"Where are we going?" asked Sam, glancing his way. Her tone was now calm and emotionless, and for some reason, it irritated Caleb.

"We need to talk. I rented a house at the end of the Dunes Resort on Isle of Palms. It's down a private road in a separate gated community. No reporters should find us there."

Caleb looked over to see if she would object. When she said nothing, he decided to push a little further. "And take your hair out of that stupid bun. The only pictures in the paper have your hair like that and you are less likely to draw attention if you get rid of the pinched look. We are going to a resort island, you know."

"Stupid bun! Asshole. You can't tell me how to wear my hair; I'll wear it any way I like. If you think, you can . . . . Why are you stopping?"

"Wait here." Caleb pulled up to what looked like a beach quickie mart. He jumped out and pressed the automatic lock on his key ring as he shut the door. Five minutes later, he returned with a brown bag and tossed it in her lap. "There. That should complete the disguise."

Sam shook like a kettle, feeling the steam in her chest expand. What had she ever seen in the overbearing brute? She opened the bag and was rendered speechless when she pulled out an extremely short pair of pink gym shorts and a skimpy halter-top with very interestingly placed large white flowers. A pair of mirror-reflecting sunglasses and black flip-flops completed the outfit.

"Go ahead and change while I drive us to the house. I won't look."

"You've got to be kidding."

"Sam, a dozen reporters saw you this morning. Your picture with your hair in a bun in that black suit is currently hitting the wire services as we speak. Do you really feel like facing those reporters now?"

Sam started to argue. She knew he was getting some unspoken pleasure out of the whole situation, but was unsure why. Well, two could play at this game.

"Fine. Pull over to that gas station across the street."

When he just stared at her, she added, "There's an outdoor restroom on the side of the building. I'm not changing in the car."

When Caleb watched Sam walk out of the restroom, he decided the joke was on him. A mass of unruly blonde curls cascaded down her back. And how could he have forgotten those legs? And, dear God, the flowers. That part of her anatomy had definitely developed over the last ten years. He hoped she got in the car quickly. She was only five feet away, and she was already drawing attention from passing cars. He was clearly deluding himself when he bought this so-called disguise.

Sam opened the door and hopped in just as some random guy drove by and yelled, "Holy shit, baby!" and howled like a wolf at the moon. Sam actually laughed as she shut and locked the door. Caleb muttered a few choice words until she pierced him with a raised eyebrow.

"Not a word," he said, throwing the car in drive and leaving a long tread mark as he pealed into traffic. Neither spoke as he drove over the East Cooper Bridge. He was crossing a second island bridge when Sam finally spoke.

"What's your problem? You picked the outfit."

Caleb gave a strained laugh as he glimpsed her way. "I know. I'd forgotten the legs. Just keep the sunglasses on and let your hair fall in front of your face when I pull up to the gatehouse. Oh, and throw that over your lap." He reached behind his seat, pulled out a damp beach towel and threw it at her.

"Hey, it's wet!"

"You'll live." Slowing to a stop, Caleb lowered his window halfway and held out a pass card. "Morning."

"Morning, sir," replied the guard as he leaned forward and peered through the window over to the passenger side of the car. "You two enjoy your stay."

"Thanks. We will." Caleb rolled the window up as he slowly drove past the gate and continued down a long narrow street lined with palm trees and perfectly manicured sidewalks. "I'm on the last street." He turned right and at the end of a cul-de-sac pulled under a large house that stood on pilings. "We can go in the back door."

Sam jumped out of the car and followed him to the steps at the back of the house. The steps lead to a huge deck that overlooked the Atlantic Ocean. Half a dozen weathered rocking chairs formed a semicircle facing the sea. In another corner, a hammock was stretched across a handcrafted redwood frame. Closer to the house, a white wicker table was surrounded by four wicker chairs lined with overstuffed green and white striped cushions.

Sam suddenly had an overwhelming desire to crawl up into the hammock and sleep until sunset. Caleb sensed the change in her mood when he glanced over his shoulder as he unlocked the door. She looked exhausted. Caleb suddenly remembered how terrified and lost she had appeared when she walked into the courtroom earlier. He had an almost uncontrollable urge to walk over and gather her in his arms, but he knew she wouldn't welcome him.

"Sam, you look like you need a break. Why don't you stretch out on that hammock, and I'll bring you a glass of tea?"

She jumped when he spoke. Good lord, she was so weary that she'd forgotten where she was.

"No, no. We should get this over with so you can get back to work."

"Sam, I really need about an hour to call the office. Would you mind sitting out here while I do that?" When she hesitated, he added, "I'm sorry, I know it's an inconvenience, but the Atlanta office wasn't open when I left this morning."

"All right. Fine. Maybe I could use just a little rest. I haven't been sleeping very well."

"Great. I'll be right back."

Caleb went inside and opened the refrigerator. Damn, there was nothing to drink. He put on a pot of water and turned on the stovetop. Almost fifteen minutes had passed by the time he poured freshly brewed tea over ice in two tall glasses. He opened the door and walked out on the porch.

Sam was sound asleep in the hammock. She had pulled her legs up to one side and her chin had fallen forward over her collarbone. Caleb set the tea on the table and grabbed a small cushion. He gently lifted her head and slid the cushion underneath. Then, he picked up a rocking chair and placed it beside the hammock. Tea in hand, he rocked slowly as he watched her sleep.

She looked like an angel. He glanced down her body and added, okay, she looked like what a guy thought an angel should be. His eyes returned to her sleeping face. Faint dark circles formed under her eyes making her look vulnerable. A faint breath whispered through the slight part in her rosy, plump lips. She still moved him, and she still scared him. He studied her for the next two hours, slowly reaching his conclusion. He couldn't let her go this time. No matter the cost. He drifted into sleep with a faint smile lifting the corners of his lips.

That smile was the first thing Sam saw when she opened her eyes.

CHAPTER SIX

Sam studied Caleb's smile as he slept. It was not a Cheshire cat grin. It was subtle—more like the cat that swallowed the canary. Sam wondered what dreams brought such contentment.

How long had she slept? She pushed up on her elbows. From the location of the sun, it must be early afternoon. At least the top of the hammock was in the shade or she would have looked like a one-sided lobster.

Sam stared at Caleb. He must have finished his work, come out to join her, and fallen asleep waiting. She felt a little guilty for wasting his time and knew she should wake him, but he was the dream she was afraid of dreaming. She was sick of reality. She held her breath as she studied the face that haunted her. Caleb had a few wrinkles around the outer edges of his eyes and his face was a bit leaner, but his black curls reached down to tickle the top of dark eyebrows. If anything, he'd grown sexier with age. She still wanted him, she thought, burning with humiliation. He was six-foot-four and all muscle. She wanted to crawl into his lap and trace her tongue over those lips. She stared at his lips. Would that smile vanish if he woke up and discovered it was her mouth on his?

Her gaze traveled slowly back up to his eyes. She gasped when she saw that they were open. His emerald eyes were intense as he watched her, and she felt the blushing heat creep across her face.

"Oh. Sorry. Didn't mean to sleep so long. I hope I didn't waste your time," Sam blurted as she pushed herself upward.

"No," he stated simply. He didn't move. He just watched her with an intensity that stirred the very air around her lips.

Sam was unnerved. She tried to flee, catching her foot in the ropes of the hammock. She would have fallen flat on her face if Caleb had not caught her. He moved with the grace of a large cat, pulling her up and into his arms. Her face was inches from his and she couldn't seem to move. His warmth seeped through her body. His eyes locked on hers for what seemed an eternity until, tilting his head to her lips, he leaned closer.

The break in eye contact allowed her brain to shift into gear. "No," she whispered. He stopped so close that she felt his warm breath on her lips and returned her eyes to his. "Please, no," she repeated though she was unsure she had spoken aloud.

Something fierce sparked in his eyes for a brief moment and then all was calm. He stepped back. His hands followed his body reluctantly, drawing slowly down her back with the movement and then clasping her hands so gently that it seemed surreal. Sam wanted to pull her hands back, but she couldn't move. The two stood unmoving until Caleb simply let go and turned to the patio door. She gazed at her now cold hands and almost called him back.

"It will be easier to discuss your case inside."

The case. It was like having cold water splashed in her still sleepy face. Their contact obviously had no effect on him; his eyes were a blank slate as he held the door open for her to enter. Sam silently followed him inside, though all she really wanted to do was run in the opposite direction. She'd felt prickles of renewed life when she awoke. Now, she was numb again.

Caleb sat down at the kitchen table with a notepad and pen and motioned for her to join him. "Okay, why don't you start by telling me when you met Ben and work up to the present?"

"What? Why? It's not relevant. The only thing that matters is that I didn't kill him. I wasn't even here when he died."

"Where were you?"

"At home."

"Do you have witnesses that can support your story?"

"No. I was alone," Sam sighed. "Well, except for Wallie."

"Wallie?"

"My dog."

Caleb let out a breath he didn't know he was holding. Another lover would have been an alibi, a perfect defense, so he shouldn't be relieved that her only companion was a dog. He frowned as he wondered about Wallie's namesake, but stopped short of asking the question; best to keep this impersonal.

"What about neighbors? Did anyone see you?"

"No, there are no neighbors."

Caleb raised a questioning eyebrow.

"I live on a small island off the South Carolina coast. It can only be reached by boat since half of the island is a federal park. A ferry takes visitors and campers back and forth several times a week. A park ranger sometimes lives on the island, but otherwise only campers are allowed."

"So the ferry company would know you were on the island."

"Well, not necessarily. I don't always take my car off the island when I go on assignment. I have a fifteen-foot Boston Whaler that I take inland sometimes. I just leave it at an acquaintance's work dock until I come back."

"Wouldn't he know that it was gone?"

"No," said Sam, casting Caleb a sheepish look. "Boston Whalers are a dime a dozen, and it's a busy marina. He lets me dock for free as long as I move it to different spots so no one notices that it's around too much. In exchange, I do free portraits of his family every Christmas."

Caleb frowned.

"I know, I know. But, it's not hurting anyone, and I'm not some rich defense attorney. Photographers don't make a lot of money."

"Just enough to buy their own private island."

Sam blushed and had the grace to look a little embarrassed. "I didn't buy the whole island. Just a house and a little bit of land. The island was deeded to slaves and their descendants after the Civil War. At the time, it was considered pretty worthless land. All the houses there were built decades ago. Today, except for my house, the island is a protected federal nature preserve. No future development is allowed. A couple dozen homes used to be located in a little village area on the Intracoastal Waterway where the ranger station is now, but those were sold to the government and torn down years ago. My home is the only house still standing, and it's miles from the campsites on the opposite end of the island. That's why I have no neighbors."

"Are you trying to tell me that you're the descendant of a slave?" Caleb asked incredulously.

"No." She rolled her eyes. "I did a documentary photo shoot of the island about five years ago. I camped on the island for months working on the project. During that time, I met an elderly man who lived alone at the end of the island. His ancestors had been outcasts. Look, it's a long story, but in short, he wanted to live the rest of his days in a sunny high rise in Florida, and I wanted to live on the island. He sold me the house because he had no family, and I guess he liked me. I'll be paying the mortgage off until I'm old and gray, but it's wonderful, peaceful."

"And isolated," Caleb stated. It wasn't a question. "So who was the last person who saw you, and who would remember seeing you in the last two months?"

"Ben was the last person I saw before I went to the island about two months ago. Then, Maggie came to the house last Friday and told me Ben was dead."

"Who's Maggie?"

"My girlfriend. She lives on the island except when she travels for work. And no, I hadn't seen her before that Friday. She'd been out of the country for three months."

"What about the postman? The newspaper delivery boy? The TV repair guy? A plumber? Anyone?"

She sighed. "No. I pick up my mail from a post office box in Charleston every month or two. The box is usually crammed full of old newspapers and magazines and bills. I don't have a TV or the Internet. I'd rather buy a new lens than invest in a satellite dish right now. I do all the repairs myself if I can."

When Caleb looked at her in disbelief, she lost her temper. "Look, I like my solitude. It's my choice, my life. I don't need repair guys or anyone else knowing where my house is or where I am. My photography has threatened my privacy before, and I don't like the stupid publicity hassle. I even put the house under a fictitious name."

"All right, all right." Caleb held up his hands in surrender. "I didn't mean to make you angry. I'm just having a difficult time understanding how anyone can stand being so cut off from the world. I'm just different I guess, since I keep up with news on an hourly basis. You're a journalist for Christ's sake!"

Sam didn't bother to reply.

Caleb wanted to ask more, but her closed expression stopped him. They sat in silence as he stared at his blank notepad.

"Okay, let's go back to my first question. Tell me about when you met Ben and everything about your relationship up until two months ago."

When she opened her mouth to argue, Caleb interrupted, "Sam, if you want me to defend you, I need to know. Ben is the reason we're here. If you can't tell me everything, I can't help you. You might as well defend yourself."

Sam closed her mouth. She didn't want to tell him. Of all the people in the world, she didn't want Caleb to know the pitiful history of her love life. But he was right. Besides, he could care less about her personal life; he'd proven that a long time ago. He was only interested in adding another high-profile win to his perfect record. And she was the perfect client, high profile and innocent.

"I met Ben in my fourth year at the University of North Carolina in Chapel Hill. I was required to take a couple of science courses even though I was a journalism major. I had taken one off-campus, but I needed one more course so I picked chemistry. There's a lot of chemistry involved in the darkroom, and I thought it would be, I don't know, easier. Ben was a grad student in chemistry."

"And he was in your class?"

"No. He was the teacher."

"Oh. I see."

"No, you don't see," snapped Sam at his tone. "I was a senior, and, well, I hadn't dated."

"What do you mean you hadn't dated?" asked Caleb.

"I was busy with school and working. I had to pay my own way. Plus, I had the extra expenses required of cameras and equipment. I bought used stuff, but it was still expensive. I got a scholarship my sophomore year, but I had to maintain an A average to keep it. I never had the time to date. Until Ben."

"I know you never met your dad, but I'm sure your mom would have helped you. I remember you saying how supportive she was of everything you did."

"Yeah, well it's kinda hard to help when you're dead."

"Dead? I'm—" Damn, why hadn't he known? He remembered Sam speaking of her mother like she was a best friend instead of a parent. Her death would have crushed her. "I'm sorry. When? How?"

"She was killed in a car crash the spring before I started college."

"Why didn't you call me?"

Caleb saw her look and felt an unbearable guilt for what he had done to her. When her mom died, she would have been completely alone. But he would have been the last person she would turn to. He realized that if she hadn't been desperate today, and he had left her any other choice, she wouldn't be sitting in the same room with him now.

"Sorry, I . . . . Forget I said that," said Caleb. "What happened after she died?"

"At first, I almost dropped out of high school. I was having trouble sitting through class, and I just didn't see the point. Then my counselor, she helped. She reminded me of how excited my mom was when I was accepted to UNC. She had wanted to go there, you know. But then there was me so—"

"Sam—"

"Look, it doesn't matter. There was about $20,000 in equity in the house so I sold it and paid my first year of college. Then, I got the scholarship and worked for the rest of it. The point is, I was too busy for a stupid college social life. I was there for a degree." Sam took a deep breath before continuing.

"But my senior year, I met Ben and everything changed. I was terrible at chemistry so I used to go to his office and make him spend all his time trying to make me understand." Sam smiled. "I was hopeless. And Ben was such a geek, a cute geek, but a geek. To him, Chem 11 was like counting to ten. To me, it was a foreign language. But he never gave up on me."

"I can imagine," said Caleb, glancing at the deep V in her halter-top.

"It wasn't like that," explained Sam, puzzled by Caleb's mock jealousy. "He never crossed that student-teacher line until the class was over. I got a C+ in the class but I didn't lose my scholarship since all my other grades were A's. I baked him a cake to thank him for helping me pass the course and took it to the office. It was the last day of finals and the university was closing for Christmas break. I hugged him, one thing lead to another, and we ended up kissing. I guess we both felt it all along."

Caleb did not respond.

"Anyway, I always stayed in my apartment over break. I worked the ten to three a.m. shift at a bar nearby. That Christmas, he stayed to finish his dissertation so he could get his diploma in January, and we started dating."

"And this was the beginning of your love affair with Ben?"

Sam flushed. She didn't want to tell the truth. She didn't want Caleb to know what a pathetic excuse of a woman she really was.

"Does it matter?"

"Your entire case rests on it. Didn't you read the papers recounting your jealous lover's rage—because the rest of the world did."

Sam almost laughed, but she stopped herself. She knew it would turn into hysteria and she really wasn't interested in a plea of temporary insanity. It was almost worth going to jail for the lover label; the truth was so pitiful.

Caleb didn't understand the emotions fleeting across her face. He also wondered if he was strong enough to listen to the sordid details when he wanted to be the only man in her life. It was like the last ten years had never happened. He waited, his stare revealing none of his emotional turmoil. His poker face had gotten him far in the legal world.

"Ben and I dated the rest of the holiday. While I worked, he finished his research paper. He made his presentation the Friday before spring semester was to start. He passed with highest marks. He is—was brilliant. We took the weekend off to celebrate. We splurged and rented a small mountain cabin. We had champagne and pizza beside a warm fire. It was magical."

Sam stood up and walked to the window to stare at the sea. She needed to leave, to stop thinking. How could she tell the rest? She drifted away, listening to the rhythm of the waves crashing to shore.

"Sam?"

Oh, hell. Who cared anyway? She could just run into the sea instead of beside it.

"Sam? I'm not here to judge your past. Just to help you." The desolation and pain in her eyes when she turned back to him made him want to stop her but he had to know, and not just so he could defend her.

"I wanted to believe in magic. I wanted to believe that I could be normal. I didn't want to face the truth."

"What do you mean normal?"

Sam sighed and turned back to look out the window.

"The entire night had seemed magical until we started kissing and he took my top off. But I couldn't do it. I felt nothing. I tried. I wanted to feel again. But the harder I tried the more awkward I became. Ben didn't notice at first. His hands were roaming and he was looking at my—at me. Then he stopped. I think one of my tears landed on his hand because he suddenly froze and looked up at my face like a hurt puppy. Tears just kept coming. I couldn't stop them. I wasn't making a sound, but I couldn't stop the tears. I don't know why, but his touch repulsed me. Wonderful, loving Ben. I loved him but I couldn't stand his touch.

"I'll never forget the pain in his eyes. He reached over and handed me my t-shirt and walked out the door. I don't know how long he was gone. I fell asleep in front of the fireplace hugging the t-shirt. I realized that night that I wasn't meant to be with people. I didn't like being touched. I'd always thought that it was just because I was too busy to get close to anyone, too busy for a social life, but the truth is I'm just cold inside. I don't feel the things other people feel. I was born to be an observer, not a participant."

"Sam," Caleb said as he rose from his chair.

"No," said Sam thrusting out her arm to prevent his approach. She kept her head down to avoid facing his disgust. "Don't come near me. Let me finish. You said you had to know it all. I woke up in the middle of the night with Ben shaking my shoulders. I must have looked pretty pitiful because when I started to speak he put his finger on my lips and told me to shush. He pulled the t-shirt over my head and picked me up. He set me on the couch, added a few logs to the fire and sat beside me with his arm over my shoulder. We stayed that way the rest of the night.

"I woke up the next morning as he was pulling his arm away. I looked at him thinking that I had lost my only friend. My only contact to the world. But he grinned." She shook her head with a faint smile. "He actually smiled, a genuine, goofy, lopsided smile, and said, 'No chemistry, hmmm?'

"I was so shocked I just stared at him with my mouth wide open. Then, I started laughing, and he was laughing. We never talked about that night. We stayed friends. He left the next week anyway to begin a career in research with Briar Pharmaceuticals, and I finished my last semester at UNC. But Ben was only an hour away from UNC at the Research Triangle Park. We got together once or twice a month until I graduated and moved away. We stayed in touch, visited whenever possible, but we never crossed that line again."

Sam was silent for a moment, waiting for Caleb to speak. But he said nothing.

"I'm really tired," Sam mumbled, unable to look at him. "Do you think we could finish this tomorrow?"

When Caleb didn't respond, Sam turned and looked up into his face. His expression revealed nothing, but he nodded.

They both stood for a moment.

"Caleb, before we go, can I borrow your phone?"

"My phone?"

"I don't keep one. There's no service on the island. But I promised to call Maggie after the hearing. She's probably frantic."

Caleb pulled his phone out of his pocket and handed it to her. He stood at the window and watched her pace across the deck as she talked. She looked worn and distressed. Then she was still, listening and nodding. A carefree smile broke across her face as her laughter filled the air.

Not Ben, but a girlfriend, he thought, as he followed Sam to the car. The drive back to Charleston was quiet, both lost in thought.

CHAPTER SEVEN

Abby sat back against the plush bucket seat of her SUV and watched the upstairs window across the street. She glanced at her watch and noted the time on a yellow legal pad. Noon. She skimmed her notes. So far she had recorded twenty people in and out of the building. Most were college students and one woman who looked like she might work for the Welcome Wagon.

The curtain moved and Abby picked up her binoculars. Her target was scanning the sidewalk below, her eyes darting from side to side. Abby lowered the binoculars but kept her eyes on the girl. The curtain dropped back in place, and Abby added a note. Picking up a carrot, she munched as she scanned the area but saw nothing new. Minutes later, the girl walked out the front door and hurried to her car. Abby turned the key in her ignition and followed. When the car pulled into the parking lot of a local moving company, Abby kept driving. She circled around and drove through the drive-through across the street.

As she paid for her large fries, she watched the girl throw boxes into her trunk, glance nervously around, and head back the way she had come. Abby followed from a distance, hitting the speed dial on her phone.

"She's on the run and very nervous."

"She's gone?"

"Not yet. She just picked up packing boxes and is headed back to her apartment. Want me to talk to her?"

There was a brief pause. "No. Not unless she looks like she's splitting for good. I'll be there before dark. Call me if anything changes."

"Damn, I'm sick of sitting. My carrots are gone, and I'm on to greasy fries. You know junk food leads to rash behavior."

"Don't make me fire you."

"I could wind this up if you'd trust me to do my job."

"I need to do this one myself."

"Making it personal is always a mistake."

"Well, it's my mistake. Gotta go."

The call disconnected in Abby's ear and she mumbled to herself as she grabbed the supersized fries. She licked the greasy salt off her fingers.

The steady stream of pedestrians continued through the afternoon. The carbs were lulling her to sleep, and she jumped at the loud rap on her window before lowering the glass to grab the large Starbucks cup.

"Grande cappuccino, lady. Don't want you falling asleep on the job."

"Asshole."

"Hey, is that any way to talk to your employer, sis?"

"The language is part of the deal with my cut rates."

Caleb laughed then glanced up at the window. "Anything change?"

"No. She took a load of boxes up with two trips and hasn't been back out. A couple of big guys went in but they left an hour ago. Don't know if they were hers."

"Okay, well, take off. I'll call you later."

"Maybe I should stick around or go with you."

"No."

"Dammit, Caleb, why don't you let me do my job?"

"You did. Go before she spots us together. I might need you to follow up later."

"Shit." Abby didn't want to drive off, but she knew he was right. She didn't really think he was in danger or she would just pretend to leave. After all, she was the licensed private detective; he was just the figurehead. She smiled, thinking of her brother's reaction to the figurehead label, and cranked the engine.

Caleb walked in the building and stopped to look up the sweeping staircase. He half expected to see Scarlett O'Hara gliding down, but the steps were deserted. Climbing slowly, he noted the various doors visible from the ascent. When he reached apartment 303, he rapped roughly.

"Who's there?" came an edgy feminine voice.

"Caleb McCloud, Miss Simpson. We just spoke on the phone."

He heard footsteps and felt the perusal through the peephole. There was a hesitation followed by the sound of turning locks and a sliding chain. The door opened slowly.

Caleb had seen her picture, but in person, she was fairytale pretty. Petite—maybe five-foot-two or three and looked to weigh no more than a hundred pounds with pigtailed strawberry blonde hair, big blue eyes, and freckles. She looked like a terrified Raggedy Ann doll. And he suddenly felt like the big bad wolf.

"May I come in?" He spoke gently afraid she would slam the door in his face if he startled her.

She nodded, opening the door a little wider and stumbling over her words. "I don't know why you came. I told you on the phone that I have nothing to say."

Caleb looked around the room. Boxes were everywhere. Some opened and some taped closed.

"Going somewhere?"

"Home. I can't study. I can't think—I dropped out of school—I need to go home. I can't stay here." The words poured out without thought then halted abruptly when she glanced nervously back at Caleb. "I don't know why I'm telling you any of this. It's really none of your business. What do you want from me?"

"I'm sorry, Miss Simpson, as I explained when I called earlier, I need to ask you questions about Ben's death. But if you're uncomfortable talking to me here, we could sit down later for a formal deposition. As Miss Jennings' attorney, I need to question all the witnesses to defend her."

"Defend her! How can you defend her? She killed Ben. It was in the paper. If I hadn't decided to stay home and study that night, she could have killed me too." Her face had grown even whiter, making her freckles bolder.

"Maybe I should go and ask my questions later," Caleb said as he turned to leave.

"No, don't leave!" she blurted, grabbing his arm as he pivoted toward the door. He slowly turned to face her, raising one eyebrow, and she dropped his arm as if it had burned her.

"Sorry, it's just, umm, I'm leaving in about half an hour, and I'd rather talk to you now and get it over with. I don't know if I'll ever come back."

Caleb didn't bother to explain to her that as a material witness, she would be required to return. He hoped to clear Sam before it got to trial.

Sally stepped further into the room and sat down, waiting for him to join her. He walked to a chair directly across from her, sat, and waited. He noticed the wet carpet at the edge of his chair and slid his foot to the left.

She twisted her hands and looked at her lap but began talking. "I already told the police everything I know. I gave a statement. Why don't you just read that and leave me in peace?"

Leave, stay, leave—this was one messed up kid. "I've read it, but I need to ask my own questions. The police assume my client is guilty, and I believe she's innocent."

Sally's head jerked up, and Caleb could have sworn it was terror he saw in her eyes. "How can you say that? They found her lens and her fingerprints. She killed him. She wanted him and killed him because he was mine and we were going to have a baby."

"The papers said you miscarried."

Her eyes darted. "Yes. I went over to his apartment that morning. I'd picked up biscuits and coffee. His refrigerator was always empty. I always told him he'd starve without me." She smiled faintly a moment and then froze again.

"That's when I saw him." Sally stood up and began pacing, but continued talking, almost reciting. "The door wasn't closed so I just pushed it open and, and there was blood. Blood everywhere. His eyes were open—he was looking at me with those dead eyes."

Sally made eye contact before continuing. "Dead eyes look different, you know. But they still look—they still see. Do you think they know?"

"Know what, Miss Simpson?"

She hesitated. "What?" She seemed to focus again. "I don't know—I mean, all I can remember is seeing those eyes and then I was screaming and running down the steps. I thought it was someone else screaming until the old lady next door started shaking me and yelling, 'What's wrong?' I must have fainted because the next thing I remember was waking up in the hospital. A doctor told me that I had lost my baby."

She lowered herself in her chair and fisted her hand in the cloth covering her stomach. She whispered, "I would have loved the baby."

"I'm sorry, Miss Simpson, I know this is difficult, but I have to ask. Did you notice anything different about the room?"

"The hospital room?"

"No, Ben's room, his apartment."

"Just blood. Lots of blood."

"I gather you had been in his apartment often."

She shifted uneasily. "Of course, it was Ben's apartment, and we were going to get married. But you can't make me go in that apartment again."

"So how are Ben's parents handling his death and the loss of his baby?" asked Caleb.

Sally looked up, startled by his quick switch in topics. "What? Oh, well I—I actually never met his parents." She stood up and began packing as she spoke. "The truth is, I don't think Ben had told them about me. The baby wasn't planned—but he really did want to marry me."

"So you stopped wearing your ring after he died?" Caleb asked softly.

"The ring?" She glanced vaguely down at her ring finger. "Oh, yes, I mean, no. We had just found out I was pregnant. We hadn't gotten the ring yet."

She seemed to be pleading with him to believe her. He suddenly felt sympathy for this young insecure girl who apparently had pressured Ben to marry.

"I hadn't even told my mom about the baby. It was hard, you know. It wasn't planned, and I didn't know how to tell her. I thought maybe I'd tell her after we got married. But she found out like the rest of the world—from the newspaper. I wanted to die. I'm from a small town, and gossip—well she works for the church, you know. I didn't know what to do. I don't want to be alone. I can't sleep. There was so much blood. I need to go home. Mama said I could come home." Her voice cracked and she looked like a lost child again. She seemed to have forgotten his presence.

"How long had you dated Ben?"

Her head snapped up. She stared at Caleb a second then tilted her head and concentrated on her sleeve, attempting to brush away an imaginary fleck of dirt.

"Miss Simpson?" He waited. "Sally?"

"What? Oh, we met last November. I went to a seminar he was teaching. And I took a course under him that next semester."

Well, she wouldn't be the first student Ben had fallen for. "You're a science major?"

"Nursing major. I plan to be a nurse. This was my last semester, but I can't—I need a break."

"Did you and Ben talk about his work?"

"His work? You mean outside of class? No. Ben didn't like to talk about his work. He always said work should stay at the office."

"At the office?" asked Caleb, frowning.

"Yeah, he just wanted to be with me. Work just paid the bills, that was his motto."

Caleb didn't respond.

Sally became agitated by his silence. "Mr. McCloud, we met months ago. We dated, we fell in love, and we were going to have a baby. He was marrying me and then that girl killed him because he didn't want her. He never even mentioned her name. "

"What did you do with Ben on your dates?"

"What? What do you mean what did I do?" Sally began pacing as she talked. "We did what everyone does. We went to movies, went to eat, went to the beach. What everyone does."

Her pacing led her back to her chair ,and she sat down, clasping her hands together in her lap.

"What movies?"

"What?"

"What was the last movie you saw with him?"

"What a stupid question. I don't remember. It doesn't matter." Just then her buzzer rang again. She stood and looked out the window. "You can leave now. The movers are here. I don't have to answer any more of your stupid questions. I want you to just leave me alone. I can't bear to think of Ben right now."

"Just one more question, Miss Simpson. Is there any chance that Ben had another woman stay at his place that night? After all, you hadn't known him very long. You said he hadn't even mentioned Samantha Jennings to you."

She turned on him—angry this time. "That's ridiculous. There was no one else. He didn't mention that woman because she was an old college fling. It was all in the paper. Besides he knew I was coming over with breakfast that morning. She killed him and that's all I know. Now leave. I have nothing else to say to you."

"All right. I'm sorry if I upset you. But I plan to find Ben's killer, Miss Simpson, because I can tell you, without a shadow of a doubt, my client is innocent. And the best way to prove that is to catch the real killer." With those words, he saw the fear returned to her baby blue eyes. "If you remember anything else, here's my card."

Caleb walked out the door, passing two burly movers on the staircase. He could feel her eyes on his back.

CHAPTER EIGHT

After Caleb dropped her off, Sam sat with her head bowed and her back against the closed door of the carriage house. Her exhaustion seemed to have a life of its own. Caleb had not said a word on the drive back after she had told him the truth about her relationship with Ben. He'd parked, walked her to the door, took her keys from her shaking hands, and unlocked the bolt. He'd opened the door and pushed her inside. She had instinctively leaned back when the door clicked shut; then slowly slid down the door until her head rested on her knees.

Sometime later, she awoke as the setting sun poured through the panes of glass leading to the back porch. She rubbed her face; she had to snap out of it. She was who she was. It didn't matter if Caleb knew. It's not as if he cared; why did she? She needed to think. Or to stop thinking altogether.

She stood up and threw her shoulders back. She needed to run.

Changing into running shorts and a torn t-shirt, Sam stretched. She put her foot over the front porch rail and touched her head to her knee. Pulling a baseball cap low over her eyes, she ran down the steps toward the Battery.

Running along the waterside and through the park, down small brick side streets and along hidden gardens. Running and never once stumbling over the cobblestone pathways. Her mind was empty. She felt free.

Sam ended the run at Battery Park, sitting down on a rusty iron bench under the low branches of an ancient live oak that dripped with gray moss. She leaned her head back, taking a deep breath. The light filtered through the branches, and she wished she had her camera.

She smiled and welcomed the calm. Running did that. She could focus now; she wasn't important. Ben was the one that mattered. She had to find out who killed him. It made no sense; he'd spent his life buried in the lab—in work. It was difficult to believe he even had time for a girlfriend. Wouldn't he have told her?

Sam thought back to their last visit. He had been mysterious, yet excited. Perhaps even nervous. It was possible that his excitement was over a new girlfriend or a baby. But he would have just told her about Sally Simpson. Wouldn't he? But what if he was still waiting for a pregnancy test result? She frowned. But he never spoke dramatically about his personal life. No. His passion had always been science and discovery. He'd talked about science that night, not a girlfriend. Sam thought back to that last night she was with Ben.

* * * * * * * *

"Sam, I'm on the verge of something big. Not just big, huge. Herculean. And, if my assumptions prove true, I'm going to change the world. I just need to check out a few more things, and I'll tell you everything. I promise. Hell, I'll show you the lab results."

"Ben, what are you talking about? Come on, tell me. Who knows when we'll get to see each other again?"

Ben grinned. "I'll tell you soon enough. I'll need your help."

"Help you? How?"

"Not yet. I have to be absolutely positive. I'll know soon enough." Ben wasn't usually mysterious, and Sam had wondered if he was on the verge of a new scientific breakthrough. He had been working on some new drug research but he never told her the specifics. Frankly, her eyes tended to glaze over when he ranted about pharmaceuticals.

She had started to change the subject when he had lowered his voice to a whisper even though they had been alone in his apartment. He'd whispered, "Sam, I can't risk telling you now but if something happens just think organic chemistry." She had yelled, "Think organic chemistry! Very funny." He looked like he wanted to say more, but then laughed and changed the subject. She had let it go because part of her hadn't really wanted to know.

* * * * * *

Organic chemistry. Ben had known she hated the thought of organic chemistry. It was Greek to Sam. Had he simply been joking? Was it some elaborate attempt to say the pregnancy blood test was positive? That was chemistry, right? Nothing made sense.

The wind blew the moss hanging over the tree limbs, and shadows danced across Sam's face. The air was cooler now and carried the acrid scent of rain. Lightning flashed across the water followed by a clap of thunder that rattled the bench. Sam looked up just as the sky opened to a driving summer storm. Jumping up, she ran for the carriage house but was drenched by the time she reached her front door.

She was pulling her keys out of her pocket when a gruff voice barked at her from the far side of the porch.

"Where the hell have you been!?"

Sam jolted. She hadn't even seen Caleb standing on the porch as she ran up the steps. Water was streaming down her face into her eyes. She held a hand to her throat and waited for her heart to slow down before she spoke.

"Caleb, you scared the shit out of me! What the hell are you doing here?"

"I brought you food because you look half starved," he yelled back. "What are you doing outside in this rain? Don't you have a lick of sense?"

"According to Maggie, no. Good thing I'm her concern, not yours." Sam jammed her key in the lock. "Why don't you go home and call me during business hours? Surely you don't make it a habit of bringing dinner to your murder defendants."

Caleb sighed and backed off. "I'm sorry. I just got worried when you didn't answer your door. Remember there is a killer out there that would feel safer if you weren't in the picture to come up with an alibi. He, or she, could be watching you right now."

Sam couldn't stop herself. She glanced over her shoulder and a chill that had nothing to do with the rain went down her spine. She'd never stopped to consider her connection to the killer. Caleb made a valid point, and it terrified her.

"Look, can I come in? I've got dinner, and it's hot. We can eat, talk, and plan. I'll catch you up with the progress I made this afternoon." Caleb paused. "Please, Sam. I didn't mean to scare you."

Sam pushed the door open and nodded. Caleb followed her in, locking the door behind him.

"I'm freezing so I'm going to take a quick shower and get dry clothes. There's a table over there. I'll be out in a minute." She walked into the bedroom and shut the door without waiting for a reply.

As Sam stood under the pounding hot water, she wondered what the hell she had gotten herself into. If she were honest, she would admit that her heart was racing because it was Caleb on her front porch, the old Caleb—the one in low cut jeans and a faded green t-shirt. Dear God, how could she work with him when she became tongue tied at his mere presence? Angry at her thoughts, Sam slammed off the water and roughly toweled herself dry. She threw on a pair of sweats and wrapped a towel around her head. She glanced in the mirror at her baggy image and almost laughed. Well, at least she didn't look like she was trying to hit on her attorney.

Relaxed again, Sam walked back into the sitting room. But Caleb wasn't there. She heard a chair scrape on the back porch and followed the sound. Caleb was sitting in one of the wicker chairs and had placed a meal of half a dozen appetizers and wine on the outdoor coffee table. The rain had stopped and the night was cool and foggy.

"I remembered how you liked porches so I thought we might be more comfortable talking out here. Is this okay?"

More than okay, thought Sam as she took in the scene. The food smelled wonderful, and he had chosen foods they had shared that summer. Her stomach flip-flopped again, and she suddenly wished she hadn't dressed as a bag lady.

"It's fine." She reached up and pulled the towel off her hair, roughly dried her curls, and tossed the towel in the corner. She settled in the middle of the settee and pulled her feet up Indian style. She was hungry, but suddenly unsure if she could swallow, so she sipped the wine instead.

"Why were you out in the rain?"

"What?" She hadn't been listening.

"What were you doing in the rain?"

"Oh, I went running. It relaxes me. And give me a little credit, Caleb, I didn't go out in the rain. It surprised me."

He watched her without comment. The air between them crackled and Sam shifted her gaze to the night sky, checking for lingering lightning. She tensed when Caleb spoke, splashing her wine over the edge of her glass.

"I talked to the police today and filed a request for access to any evidence they collected. We can go tomorrow and look at the evidence. But first thing in the morning, we are going to Ben's apartment. The police have been through it completely so there shouldn't be any problems. It's no longer a secured crime scene, so it may not do us any good, but the landlady told me that since Ben paid six months rent upfront, she was unsure what to do with his belongings until his family came to get them. She hasn't touched the place. Said she would have to exorcize the spirits first."

Sam nodded unable to face him.

"Look, if it's too much I'll go alone, but I just thought you might notice something that I would miss."

"No, I need to go."

"Did he have family?"

"Hmmm? Oh, yes. His parents and a sister. She's married, has two small boys. Named one Ben," she added with a slight smile. "I've never met them. They live in Texas. He'd go home about every other Christmas. And they'd come to Charleston occasionally. But they were still close. He kept up by phone and email. They should know if there was a girlfriend." But she should know too.

"Okay, I'll check that angle."

"I just—I just can't believe he's dead." The tears started. She just couldn't stop them.

If Caleb hadn't looked up at the despair in her voice, he would never have known she was crying. She didn't make a sound as the tears flowed down her pale face.

"Oh God, Sam, I'm sorry."

He stood and reached for her, lifting her up in his arms. She was too numb to react. He walked into the bedroom and sat down on the bed with her in his lap, held tight against his chest. When the flow of tears finally stopped, Caleb tilted her chin up and stared down at her puffy red eyes and swollen lips. He reached down and wiped away her tears with the rough pad of his thumb. Slowly, he traced the fullness of her lips. No longer thinking, just needing, he leaned forward and replaced his thumb with his lips and sucked the swollen flesh. Sam gasped and his tongue surged through the part. Passion exploded and neither could think, only feel, as their tongues danced and mated. Close to losing control, Caleb jerked his head back and broke the kiss, placing his forehead against hers. She whimpered, and he tucked her head under his chin, wrapping her in his arms.

His voice rang gruff with passion when he said her name. He felt her stiffen in his arms at the realization of what had happened.

"Don't say anything. Just let me hold you tonight. I can't leave you like this. I should, but I can't. I promise, I'll just hold you. No more talking, no kissing, no thinking. Just sleep."

Sam was too numb to resist. The truth was she wanted him more than she had ever wanted anything. She nodded against his chest. He stretched out on the bed and pulled her close. She was asleep within seconds. Caleb was not so fortunate. He used his toes to kick off his shoes, pulled the edge of the comforter over them and, hours later, fell asleep with his lips pressed against the top of her head.

CHAPTER NINE

Ben's apartment was a small, one-room efficiency. But at the moment, there was nothing efficient about it. Pushed under the double windows on the back wall was a desk covered with scattered papers. It seemed like the source of the waterfall of papers and notebooks overflowing onto the floor. The wall space was lined with books stacked in haphazard piles, and more books formed leaning columns beneath the kitchen bar that separated the tiny kitchen from the rest of the room.

Sam glanced nervously around the room, stopping when her eyes rested on the taped outline of a person in front of Ben's futon. An outline of raised arms stretched above either side of a head and a wide dark stain on the hardwood floors reached beyond the taped border as if someone had tried to color outside the lines. Sam froze and her knees began to buckle. A soft keening sound escaped her lips.

"Sam!" Caleb spun her toward him, holding her upright as he stared down at her ghostly white face. "I'm sorry. It was a mistake to bring you here. I'll take you back down to the car. You wait there while I look the place over."

It took Sam another moment to step beyond the horror and focus on Caleb's face.

"Sam?" Caleb whispered, shaking her slightly to see if she was going into shock.

She stared into his eyes, slowly becoming aware of the warmth of his hands on her arms. She closed her eyes a moment and shook her head. "No, I'm okay. I'm sorry. It was just the initial shock. I'm okay now. I have to be here."

Caleb said nothing for a moment, then nodded and watched her warily as she turned back to face the apartment. Tilting her head up, Sam walked behind the futon that had been Ben's bed and faced the desk. Her voice shook slightly as she spoke.

"Ben's desk was always neat," she recited in a monotone voice. "The kitchen dishes would pile up until the palmetto bugs took over, but he was very careful with his work and his books. Someone has searched through all his notes, his bookshelves. He used to alphabetize his so-called scientific library."

"Probably the detectives."

"Why? I mean, I can see searching the place, but someone methodically looked at every single notebook, every single book. Ben kept his notebooks along the back of the desk, neat and labeled," continued Sam, pointing at the one remaining binder along the back of the desk. "All these notes were carefully filed and labeled and lined up in order. The notes contain chemical equations and writings only a chemist would understand. The police came in here believing a woman had killed Ben in the heat of passion. That's what the paper said anyway. A blonde woman was seen fleeing and a bloody lens was the murder weapon dropped beside the body. Why would they meticulously search his work notes and books?"

Caleb frowned and picked up a handful of the scattered notes. She was right. No cop would waste his time hunting through every notebook and loose sheet of paper. Although the papers were everywhere, the way they were strewn suggested that someone had taken the notes out and examined every single sheet of paper in the room.

"Can you tell if any pages are missing?"

"Oh sure, pages eighty through eighty-three," Sam replied sarcastically, rolling her eyes. "Please, I couldn't tell if a page was missing even if a series of pages contained the basic symbols for water. I told you, science is not my strong point."

Caleb glanced back at the compound doodles and had to admit they could have been written in a foreign language as far as he was concerned.

"Point well taken. Anything else out of the ordinary?"

Sam walked around the room, drawing her fingers along the long lines of books as she searched the shelves. Caleb thumbed through each piece of paper in case something looked out of place. Afterwards, he searched under every seat cushion and every piece of furniture.

"Everything's different. Anyway, Ben was always adding to his book collection, and he could never leave his work at the office," she began but inhaled sharply as her fingers trailed across the front of a large chemistry textbook.

"What is it?" asked Caleb, running to her side and peering over her shoulder at the book.

"I—I don't know. No, it's crazy. I just . . ." she paused again.

"What? Anything, no matter how farfetched. Even a crazy idea is better than nothing."

Sam looked over her shoulder at Caleb before pulling out the book beneath her hand.

"It's just," Sam hesitated, opening the cover and running her fingertips across her name printed in the upper left corner, "this is my organic chemistry book from college. I gave it to Ben after the class ended, telling him that I never wanted to see it again. He jokingly told me that he'd keep it for me because one day I might want to discover the origins of life."

"Anything else?"

"Well, I don't know. It's strange, but he mentioned organic chemistry the last time we were together."

"Take a minute, think back. What were his exact words?"

"He was excited about something, but he wouldn't tell me what. And he seemed nervous, anxious. I asked, well sort of asked, but he changed the subject, and I didn't pursue it. But he whispered something strange. He said, if something happened, just think organic chemistry."

"Why was that strange?"

"He whispered almost like he was spooked. And we were up here alone. I remember it being, I don't know, it was just strange."

Caleb reached across her shoulder and grabbed the book

"What are you . . . " began Sam, but he cut her off.

"It's your book, right?"

"Well, yeah, but . . . "

"We're taking it with us. Finish looking around and let me know if you notice anything else. Anything."

Sam frowned at Caleb but slowly walked around the room again. She shuddered when she approached the floor tape, but kept looking. She opened the few drawers and cabinets and looked through the bathroom. Ben's scent was strongest there, and her eyes misted over as she tried to swallow the lump forming in her throat.

She walked back to Caleb but avoided eye contact for fear that she would foolishly run into his arms. She felt so cold and alone.

"Except for the mess, it looks the same. Like he could walk through the door any minute."

Caleb simply nodded, touched her lower back, and guided her out the door.

Standing on the landing, she inhaled deeply and looked out. She noticed the man in the doorway.

"Caleb, I forgot. I saw that man in the doorway just the other night. We need to question him. He could have seen something." She started to run down the steps but Caleb had grabbed her arms from behind.

"What do you mean you saw him the other night?"

"I came down here night before last, but I didn't go in because of the police tape. That man was watching me, but he had a knife."

Caleb cursed under his breath.

"We're going."

"But he may have seen something."

"Or he could be just a crazy homeless guy with a knife. Dammit, Sam."

Caleb went down the stairs but didn't release his grip until he reached the passenger door. Unlocking the door, he said, "Get in."

"We need to question him."

"The police can do that. They probably already have. Give them a little credit."

Sam paused and looked at the man again. He smiled at her, flashing his knife again. The doorway seemed to be his home so she doubted he was going anywhere, and she didn't want Caleb to get hurt. She climbed into her seat and waited for Caleb to turn into traffic before facing him.

"Why did you take that book?"

"It's yours, isn't it? Says so right in it."

"You know what I mean."

"Call it a hunch. Someone was looking for something in his chemistry notes, and I don't think it was a crazy homeless man." He handed the book to Sam. "Look through this. See if anything is different. Ben told you to 'think organic chemistry' and from what you are telling me, this is the only link you have to organic chemistry."

Sam held the book in her lap staring at the hated text. Then, she slowly turned the pages. She frowned when she noticed a slight arrow beside Chapter 15 in the table of contents. Ben had made many notes in her book when she had come by his office with questions, but they had skipped this chapter in class and she didn't remember a notation there.

She flipped back to Chapter 15 with a puzzled look on her face.

"What is it?" asked Caleb.

"I'm not sure yet."

She slowly flipped through the chapter until she noticed a highlighted footnote that referenced another chemistry book. In Ben's handwriting was written, "Please refer to this reference in your usual study location!"

She turned a stunned face toward Caleb.

"I don't understand."

"What? What does it say?"

She told him. Caleb said nothing, just waited for her to continue.

"My class skipped Chapter 15, and Ben damn well didn't give me any work beyond what was required. He knew I hated it. But this note is in his handwriting, and it instructs me to go look up this book at my usual study location. Ben knew I always studied down in the basement stacks of the old Wilson Library on UNC's campus. We used to joke that I had to go down in the dungeons to do my penance. The third level below the first floor was filled with old chemistry books. It was dark and musty, and I hated it. But there were no distractions."

Caleb was silent as he considered the ramifications of this clue. "Ben knew he was in danger."

"What?"

"Why else did he leave a clue that only you could find and only you could understand?"

"But, he would have just told me. Ben wasn't the type to enjoy intrigue."

"Maybe he was protecting you."

"I don't know. It makes no sense," said Sam. She looked up from the book as Caleb parked the car. "Where are we?"

"We're at the police station. We'll ask about your homeless guy." He hesitated. "And Sam, you have to be booked. I got them to let me bring you in for the formal booking and then you are being released in my custody. I posted your bail."

"You what?! I . . . "

"Sam," said Caleb, gently touching her arm. "It was the easiest way to get you out for the smallest bond. You are being released in my custody, and as long as you don't run, I get my money back. Because I work out-of-state, as long as you stick with me, you can even cross state lines. You're not running, are you?"

"No, but. . . ."

"Good. Let's go in and get this over with." He reached for the door handle but stopped and looked her over with a frown. "Hey, do you have any makeup in that purse?"

"I don't think the police are after a glamour shot," Sam smirked sarcastically, hiding the instant of hurt that needled her chest.

Missing the hurt in her voice, Caleb continued, "Pull your hair back that tight bun and put on heavier makeup. We don't want the mug shot to look like you."

Sam flipped down the mirror on the visor and looked at the unsophisticated face staring back at her. Yeah, she thought, because no one would pay any attention to the real Samantha.

"After you're booked, they are going to let us look at all the evidence the state has against you. But other than the lens, your fingerprints, and crime scene photos, I don't think they have much. Oh, and don't mention your chemistry book or anything else about Ben. In fact, as your attorney, I am instructing you not to speak. I'll speak for you." Caleb remembered the angry sparks the last time a lawyer had said that to her and quickly added, "Just in the police office. It's standard legal procedure and believe me it's for your protection."

"Okay," snapped Sam, "but I'm getting pretty damn tired of people talking for me."

Sam and Caleb walked into the police station in silence and left an hour later the same way. Caleb glanced over at Sam as he drove to her carriage house. She was rubbing the ink stains that still lingered around her fingernails.

"Where's my lens cap?"

"What?"

"That was my lens, but the lens cap was missing. I never left my lens without a lens cap protecting it. That lens cost $2,500."

"If it cost so much, why did you leave it at Ben's?"

"I didn't." She frowned. "At least, I don't think I did. I've never left camera equipment at his house."

"When was the last time you saw that lens?"

Sam shrugged. "At Ben's," she admitted. "But it was packed in my camera bag with the other equipment. I took some pictures at sunset the last night I stayed at Ben's. I used that lens. When I got back to his place, I'm sure I packed it away in the bag. I remember stacking the photography bag with the rest of my stuff. Putting my lenses away is just instinct. I don't even think about it. I just do it. I remember we hadn't eaten, so we went out for a late night pizza. I left early the next morning."

"Where did you sleep?" barked Caleb, the words escaping before he could stop them. "I mean—I only saw one futon in the place."

Sam gave him a puzzled look, confused by his tone. "What does that matter?"

"Just trying to figure out where you were in relation to your camera equipment," Caleb lamely interjected without looking at her. No matter what she said about her relationship with Ben, Caleb couldn't control his imagination.

But Sam didn't notice. "Oh. Well, the chair in that room makes a single futon if you push the footstool up to it. I slept there in a sleeping bag that I keep in my Jeep. My equipment was stacked by the door so I could grab it without making a lot of noise the next morning. I left at five a.m. I started to wake Ben up, but decided he needed his sleep."

"So when did you notice it missing?"

"Not until I read about Ben's death. I hadn't needed it. The news article said it was my lens that killed Ben so I searched the bag. I opened the compartment where I stored it, and the lens was gone. The small leather bag that I always slipped the lens in was in the compartment standing up like it did when the lens was inside, but it was empty. The lens cap wasn't in there either."

"Could someone have gotten into your house and stolen it? "

"I guess. I never lock the doors when I'm home, but I don't think anyone knows I live there."

Caleb was silent for the last few minutes of the drive. He parked the car and hopped out to walk Sam to her door. "I've got a couple of stops to make while you pack."

"What do you mean pack? I plan to stay here and find out what happened to Ben and get some work done while I'm at it. I brought my equipment."

"I plan to find out what happened to Ben too, but not from here. We're headed to North Carolina. And you're going to stick with me. You're leaving your car and equipment here."

When Sam just stared incredulously, Caleb added, "Look, we know you didn't kill Ben, but we don't have a way to prove it yet. Someone set you up. The lens, the description of the tall, lanky blonde leaving the scene of the crime, the destruction without any theft, and you went into hiding right after the murder."

"I did not go into hiding!"

"I know, you were already there," said Caleb under his breath, quickly holding out his hand to stop her angry retort. "I'm just pointing out that our best defense is to find the killer or at least a reason for a killer, and Ben left us the book. The book is the first lead we've found. We should drive to North Carolina tonight and be there when the library opens."

Sam fought her natural instinct not to follow orders. "Okay, that makes sense, but I can drive myself to Chapel Hill."

"Sam, be reasonable. Someone killed Ben, and they went to a great deal of trouble to make it look like you did it. If they killed once, they could kill again and for some reason they wanted you out of the way. You're staying with me or I'll withdraw the bond and keep you safely behind bars while I go search the library for clues."

Sam fumed, even as she understood his reasoning. She hated being crowded, and she had never felt more crowded than she did in a car with Caleb a simple touch away.

"Fine!" she shouted. "You can follow me in your car, but I'm not leaving my equipment, it's too valuable."

Caleb stared at the stubborn woman beside him. He sighed, "Well, pack it all up, and I'll think of something. Be ready to go when I get back. And don't go anywhere or open the door for anyone."

When they reached the B&B, he opened the door of the carriage house, did a quick search, and left without another word.

Sam went to her room and noticed her shoes by the foot of the bed. She sat down slowly on the edge of the mattress, feeling a small shiver run through her. She squeezed her eyes shut a moment and took a deep breath then changed into her running shorts. The hell with Caleb. She knew how to look after herself, and she wasn't about to count on anyone, especially Caleb. Besides, if she didn't clear her mind of that taped image, she was going to fall apart. She left down the back stairs on the off chance someone was watching her. And this time she double-checked that the door was locked. Pulling her baseball cap low over her eyes, she bolted down the steps.

CHAPTER TEN

Jim threw open his apartment door before Caleb had a chance to knock.

Noting that the door lacked a peephole, Caleb joked, "Listening by the door just for me?"

"Nope," grinned Jim, "a red-headed imp warned me."

"Is she here?"

"Yep, but she's threatening to leave. Mumbling something about a thick-skulled older brother treating a professional like a little sister instead of the brilliant detective she is."

"She is my little sister."

"Hey, you ain't gonna get any arguments from me. So what's going on?"

"I'll fill you both in, and I could use a beer."

Thirty minutes later, Jim was laughing at Caleb. "So, you're getting personally involved with your clients again?"

"You don't know the half of it," said Abby. "She's the only one that ever got away."

"Do tell," quipped Jim. "If you're pulling me into this, I need to know if those instincts are coming from your skull or your pants. I got a future to protect."

"Shut up, Abby." The tone of Caleb's voice had an underlying brittleness that surprised them both. They studied him in silence a few seconds then let the subject drop, listening to the details of his day in silence.

Abby spoke first. "Okay, I'll head over and question Mr. Orange Shirt."

"Be careful. The cops said when they interviewed him that night that they think he's schizophrenic. Talks to his damn liquor bottle like it's his best friend."

"I know how to question a witness, Caleb."

"He's got a knife. Maybe Jim should go with you."

"No, dammit, let me do my job. The homeless guys in Savannah have guns, for Christ's sake, and they're my best informants. He won't talk with some cop hanging around."

Caleb frowned. How had his little sister ever become so tough? He was going to go with her himself, but he knew she was right. And though she looked fragile, she had a black belt and a .38-snubbed nose revolver. Plus, the cops said the guy was harmless as long as you didn't touch his bottle.

"Call me as soon as you finish with him."

"Yes, big brother." She stood to leave but couldn't resist one last jab. "Oh, and I checked you out of your rental house. Your stuff's in Jim's room. Maybe you should change. Could have sworn you had that outfit on yesterday."

Caleb glared. Jim cleared his throat over a laugh and stood to hug Abby goodbye. "You're pushing it, imp," he said as he pushed her out the front door.

"I know," she laughed. "But it's such a rare treat." She kissed Jim's cheek and left, adding, "Bye, Caleb, love ya!"

Caleb stood and walked back to the bedroom to change, mumbling under his breath about pesky little sisters always poking their noses where they don't belong. Probably the reason she had become a detective. She'd always been a world-class snoop.

Lucky for Jim, he had his laughter under control by the time Caleb appeared with his suitcase in hand. Caleb still looked miffed so Jim decided now was not the time to ask him just how he knew Samantha. While Caleb was changing, he had called his office and taken a few days annual leave.

"Okay," said Jim. "I'm free to take Sam's jeep, but Caleb, that gal looked pretty headstrong to me. Saw her chop her lawyer off at the knees in the courthouse hallway yesterday. Based on what you just told me, maybe you should call before you drag me over there."

Caleb looked a little sheepish because Jim was right, but he had worked out that issue. "She'll ride with me. I knew she was broke when I paid her bond, and I threatened to have her hauled back to jail while I searched alone if she didn't cooperate."

Jim laughed. "Oh, that's gonna be some fun ride. Sure you don't want me along? I think you need me more to protect your back than to baby-sit her property."

"Let's go, smart ass," Caleb said. "Just be careful when she throws those keys at you, according to the local paper, she's got killer aim."

Sam was just unlacing her running shoes when she heard the knock on her door. Swinging it open, she glanced at Caleb and said, "Hi, come in. I need another thirty minutes to get ready, but don't feel you need to wait for me. I'll catch up."

Caleb was incredulous. She had been out of the house running when he had specifically ordered her to stay put. "Where the hell have you been? I told you to stay behind locked doors until I came back for you."

The run had refreshed Sam and she was in control again. She stood on her tiptoes and looked him straight in the eye. She was so furious that for a minute she almost punched him. "Listen, you jerk, no one tells me what to do. I know how to take care of myself. Being my lawyer does not give you the right to tell me what I can or cannot do! Got that?"

Jim smothered at laugh behind a discreet cough. When neither Sam nor Caleb noticed, he coughed a little louder before they had time to start throwing punches. "Hey, maybe I should come back later."

Sam took a step back and peered around Caleb's body to see Jim standing a few steps behind him. His hands were in his pockets and he was glancing at his feet. She got the distinct impression that he was more amused than embarrassed.

Her face instantly flushed with anger and humiliation. Not only was Caleb standing at her door yelling at her as if she were a child, but he'd brought his friend to witness the whole scene. She straightened and stared at Caleb, waiting.

Caleb took another minute. When he finally spoke, he sounded like the calm, rational man she had hired as an attorney but his eyes spoke of things to come.

"Sorry. Jim's here to take your Jeep and camera equipment. He'll watch over your things until we return."

"I told you that I'm driving myself," she hissed, lowering her voice to avoid more embarrassment.

Caleb acted as if she had never spoken. Glancing over her head, he saw her car keys on the coffee table. Most of her equipment was in neat cases by the door. Pushing her to the side, he picked up the keys and tossed them to Jim as he stepped into the open doorway. "Here, Jim. It's the orange Jeep out front. Those cases need to go too."

"No one is taking my Jeep," yelled Sam.

Jim didn't move. His grin widened and showed a set of beautiful straight white teeth. He glanced at Caleb and raised his eyebrows in question.

"Go ahead and start loading her equipment," Caleb called as he grabbed Sam's arm and pulled her toward the bedroom. "Sam and I are going to have a quick chat."

Sam was so angry at being manhandled that she jerked her arm away and punched him in the shoulder the minute he shut the bedroom door. It felt so wonderful; she decided to do it again.

Caleb caught her fist as she swung the second time. "Stop it! Look, I'm not going to argue with you. You are riding with me. One car, that's final. You can go with me and try to find Ben's killer or you can sit in the Charleston jail for the next six months while I do my own investigation. Hell, I'm beginning to think that you'd be safer in jail. And so would I," he added, rubbing his shoulder.

"You asshole, you can't do that."

"Can't I? The judge remanded you into my custody so I'm responsible for you until this case is over, like it or not."

"Then you're fired."

"Fine. Hope you like prison food. I hear chicken nugget night is pretty edible."

"I'll post my own bond."

"More power to you, lady. I'll just be wishing you good-bye and good luck." He opened the door to leave. "But, you should know," he said, turning back to face Sam, a little wary of her next explosion—damn, that girl could pack a punch, "the judge set your bond at half a mil."

"Half a million? Dollars? That's absurd!"

He actually had the nerve to lean back against the doorframe, cross his arms over his chest, and grin. She now knew why he never lost in court and she hated him for it.

"Judge trusts me not to ruin my political career by letting you go. Thinks my word is worth more than money, and as long as I stick by your side, you're free to help investigate. But you've been a fugitive for over a month, so you're considered a flight risk if I'm not around."

Sam started to argue again but suddenly she was just too tired. Besides, it was a losing battle. There was no way she was sitting in a jail cell. She really would go crazy. Besides, she had to find Ben's killer, and if that meant swallowing her pride and spending the next six months being dictated to by this Neanderthal, she would just grin and bear it. Well, maybe without the grin.

"Fine!" she snapped, and tried to push him aside to open the door.

"Not so fast," he said grabbing her shoulders. "Let's define 'fine.' From now until the trial, you do as I say. Our best chance is to find the truth and we are going to need to work together. I need to be free to track down information without worrying that you're gonna run off every time I leave the room. First time you ignore me and go off on your own, you're off to jail. That's the deal."

It was too much. Sam desperately wanted to punch him again. Caleb must have noticed, she thought with a smirk, because he was suddenly protecting the spot her knuckles had hammered. She'd never let him know her hand was throbbing.

"I'll agree not to go anywhere without telling you first, and to listen to you if it's within reason. But only if you'll agree to listen to what I have to say and agree not to go following any leads without including me. It's my life on the line, not yours, and I have every right to be involved in every step of this investigation."

Caleb stared at her in silence. She knew he didn't have to agree to anything because he held all the cards, so she cringed when a slow smile suddenly erased the tension from his face and she braced herself for another autocratic demand, trying to convince herself not to get angry but just to agree. At least she'd be free to duck out and find her own answers if the time came. She couldn't do anything from a jail cell.

"Deal," he said, sticking out his hand.

Sam stared at his hand in disbelief and was still standing there with her mouth open when he reached down, grabbed her hand for a quick shake, opened the bedroom door, and stepped out.

"Oh, and one more thing," she called after him. "I'm keeping one camera bag with me. Jim can deliver my Jeep and equipment to my house. Maggie can let him in."

"Okay." It was what he had planned, but he wasn't going to tell her that. He suddenly stopped, frowned, and turned back to face her.

"Sam, where was Maggie when all this happened? Wouldn't she have seen you during those months?"

"She was on a research vessel for work. She came straight to the house after docking in Charleston and seeing the headlines."

Caleb nodded. He would have to grill Jim about Maggie. He wondered what about this girl was so special that Sam had given up men. And there had been that kiss.

CHAPTER ELEVEN

Jim gripped the hood of the Jeep like a lifeline. His body leaned left, then right. His eyes were round with fear, and he cursed Caleb with what could very well be his last breath. Behind him, he heard the laugh of a madman.

"Hey, boy, you're gonna leave fingerprints in that hood," yelled the ferry captain from the pilot's box at Jim's back.

Under any other circumstance, Jim would have taken offense at the term "boy," but his mind was on other things. Like, would this Jeep's big wheels float?

The captain laughed again as a wave splashed over the front bow of the boat sending water under Jim's shoes. Jim decided that the captain better have his superman cape in that phone booth he called a helm. This six-foot-six-inch "boy" was gonna wrap his long fingers around that scrawny neck and hold on for dear life when this tub of scrap metal sank.

It took thirty minutes to reach the island and back the Jeep out onto solid ground. The longest thirty minutes of his life. The captain stayed on board, a little wary now that Jim's knees were steady and his fists were balled up like sledgehammers. The wise man touched the brim of his cap in a small salute and backed away from the ramp.

Jim stood watching the ferry putter back toward the mainland. He took a deep calming breath. He refused to think about how he would get off this damn island.

"Well, appears as if Sam was right," said a voice behind him.

The voice was sultry and lilting at the same time. A musical gravely sound that brought the blood pumping back through Jim's veins and made him forget the rusty tub motoring out of site. He turned slowly to face a different kind of threat and was rendered speechless. His grin was slow as his eyes burned a trail slowly down the length of the woman facing him. Well, he'd just solved one problem. With God's Eve already on the island, there was no need to leave.

She was a light mocha color with plump full lips that quirked up on one side. She raised one perfectly arched eyebrow as she watched his eyes come to life. She wore a one-piece black Speedo that on any other woman would have been a conservative swimsuit. On this island goddess, it accented an hourglass figure that put Wonder Woman to shame. Tan khaki shorts hugged low on her hips and high on her endless legs. The masculine hiking sandals should have spoiled the image but instead made her feet look delicate with high arches and long pink-tipped toes.

"Holy Mother of God." The words rushed out of Jim's lips without thought as the image before him sizzled his corneas.

She laughed, and Jim knew he had landed in the Garden of Eden. "Nope, I'm the park ranger."

He gawked.

"Not what you expected?" she asked.

He shook his head and forced his vocal cords to respond. "Actually, I had pictured more of a Deputy Dog with Harry Potter glasses."

"Sorry, to disappoint," she laughed, stretching out her hand. "I'm Maggie Fletcher."

Damn, thought Jim. He looked at the outstretched hand and expected to see a shiny red apple resting in the palm, but he took it and let go before he could feel the burn. But he frowned slightly as the name registered in his brain.

"Sam's Maggie." He said it as a statement, not a question. What puzzled Maggie was the hint of resignation in his voice.

"Well, that's a new one, but, yeah, I guess I am. Sam called and said that she was sending someone with the Jeep today."

"Oh, sorry. I'm Jim Johnson."

She watched as he shoved his hands in his pocket and shifted away just ever so slightly. Interesting. It had been a long time since she'd had a challenge. And he was worth it. His broad shoulders and huge biceps gave him the look of a NFL linebacker. And his face was too cute for words.

"How about giving me a ride back to my station so I can get my truck? Then you can follow me to Samantha's to leave her Jeep."

"What? Oh, okay." His body may have stepped back, but his mind was still stalled.

When he turned to walk around the Jeep to the driver's door, Maggie's eyes did some traveling of their own. On second thought, he'd make a great tight end. She laughed and hauled herself up into the passenger seat.

Half an hour later, Jim followed Maggie's truck across a narrow sandy path that tunneled through endless live oaks. He wiped sweat from his brow and laughed. She was a touchy little thing—literally. With each question, she had casually brushed her hand down his arm. At one point, while he was talking, she had reached over and plucked a small briar from the inside leg of his shorts, and he had almost broken the steering wheel with his grip. When he had glanced over to see if the touch had been intentional, she was simply looking straight ahead while she rolled the tiny briar between her forefinger and thumb. Jim shook his head.

If God was testing him, he wasn't so sure he was going to pass.

The trees gave way and they continued to follow the path across several sand dunes in the bright sunlight until they dead-ended in front of a small cottage. Maggie jumped from her truck, motioned for Jim to follow, and bounced up the steps.

She hesitated for just a second. The door was ajar. She frowned before a spurt of anger had her pushing inside.

"Who the hell is in here?"

She only had a second to scream and throw her arm up as she saw the bright blue vase swing at her head. With the impact, she collapsed in a small puddle just inside the door and her mind went dark.

Jim ran the second he heard her scream, but he was too late to catch her. He saw a figure in shorts and a ragged t-shirt dash out the backdoor. He bent, felt her pulse, and leaped over her to peer out just as the man disappeared over a sand dune. Jim turned and quickly checked the rest of the house before crouching at Maggie's side.

He was scooping her up off the floor when her eyelids fluttered open only inches from his. She moaned. He stood up and carried her to the sofa, shifting pillows to cushion her head.

"Did you get the bastard?" She tried to push herself up and the pain shot through her temples sending her back into the down pillows with another deep moan.

Jim pushed against her shoulders. "Lie still," he said as a small motor hummed in the background. "No, he's gone. I'll get you some ice."

"Damn it, you should've gone after him. I thought you were some kind of cop."

Jim walked around the kitchen counter and opened the freezer. Grabbing a dishtowel off a side hook, he filled it with ice, dampened it, and dropped down on the edge of the sofa to hold it to Maggie's head.

"Deputy. I'm a deputy."

"Not the sheriff?"

"Next year."

"What?"

"I'll be the sheriff next year."

"Well, I wouldn't be so cocky if I were you. You couldn't run down one little scrawny camper."

"I figured I should make sure you were safe first."

"I wasn't going anywhere. You should have chased that bastard down."

"I could have but thought the prudent thing to do was to make sure he didn't leave a friend behind to finish off his handy work."

Damn. Maggie's heart skipped a little beat. She hadn't thought of that. She tried to glance around the room without moving her head but it took too much effort.

"Did he?"

"Did he what?" Jim was holding the ice to her head but he could feel the heat of her breath on his skin with each word she spoke. She shifted her head, and her cheek rested against the inside of his wrist. He felt the tingle all the way to his gut. When he had seen her crumple to the floor, his heart had almost stopped.

Her eyes shifted to his with speculation. She would have laughed, but the adrenaline flow hadn't stopped. She was feeling shaky.

"Did he have a friend?"

"Oh. No." He felt her began to tremble ever so slightly, and before he could stop, he leaned in and kissed her. Gently at first, testing. Her response had him deepening the kiss, his mind forgetting everything but the woman beneath him. He reached with his other hand to caress her face, but the movement brought a gasp of pain from her and a swift kick of realty to him. He jumped off the couch as if he had been burned.

"Damn, I'm sorry, Maggie. I don't know what came over me. It won't happen again."

It was the first time he'd ever said her name and she was amazed that butterflies fluttered in her stomach. She watched him a few seconds then closed her eyes, adding softly, "Well, that's too bad."

CHAPTER TWELVE

Caleb glanced over at Sam as he merged onto Interstate 95 North. She was staring straight ahead in silence. Just like she had been since she stepped into the car, buckled her seat belt, and folded her hands in her lap. The frost emanating from her body was so cold he was surprised the windows weren't iced over.

Shit. He hadn't meant to bark at her back at the carriage house. But when he'd opened the door and saw the sweat running down her face and the running shoes, he'd had this vision of a yellow taped outline of her body on the streets of Charleston. She refused to acknowledge that she could be in danger and that she needed protection. Her recklessness scared the hell out of him.

He winced remembering Jim's parting comment. "Got a thing for that gal, huh? Glad to see someone crack that shell of yours. Sure you don't want me along as a bodyguard? I need a fun vacation." Jim had driven away laughing before Caleb could retaliate.

Okay, so maybe he was being a little unreasonable. But as her lawyer, he had a duty to protect her. He sighed. Be honest with your own subconscious, you idiot. You never got over her and you want a chance to be with her. You're taking advantage of the situation, and she is going to hate you when she finds out the truth.

He must have sighed out loud because when he glanced back at her, she was looking at him with a question in her eyes.

"Hey, Sam, I'm sorry."

"For what?" she asked calmly, though her eyes still sparked with brooding resentment.

She wasn't going to make it easy. "For getting so angry and threatening you with jail."

She refused to respond.

"Sam, it just scared me when I saw that you'd been out jogging again. I got an image in my head of you lying dead on the side of the road, and I took it out on you. I—I just need to know you're safe. We'll get to the bottom of this and clear your name, and then your life can return to normal. When it's over, I promise not to bother you any more."

His about change shocked her. One minute he sounded like he really cared about her and the next minute he sounded like he couldn't wait to be rid of her. Maybe she really was just another career case, another trial he had to win to keep his important record. She would just think of Ben. If she had to work closely with Caleb to help Ben, she could do that. It was nothing compared to the awful pain Ben must have suffered.

"Please, Sam," Caleb said when she didn't respond.

"Yeah, okay, maybe you were right. Not about the threats," she added quickly, "but about the danger. I even had the feeling someone was watching me as I ran. I kept glancing over my shoulder, but I didn't see anyone that seemed out of place. But I got a little creeped out, cut the run short, and went back. I was just about to shower when you arrived. I had already decided not to run alone again for a while when you barged in and started yelling."

"Well, shit. My career depends on my knowing when to keep my mouth shut. But around you, I just seem to put my foot in it." He grinned at her. "So you just let me think I won that argument and here I thought I'd played my strategy card brilliantly."

"Don't push it. I'm still furious that you didn't let me drive my Jeep."

"Sorry, honey. It's a jacked-up gold monster. Someone could follow that car from fifty miles away."

"Follow?" she peered nervously out the back window, scanning the cars. "Is someone following us?"

Maybe. He shook his head. "Nah, sorry, didn't mean to scare you. Just taking precautions. Look, you're exhausted. If you're going to help with this investigation, you need some sleep. We've got another four hours. Why don't you stretch out and get some rest?"

Sam hesitated before nodding. She had to stop fighting with him and think about the reason she was here. Ben. She was usually so logical and calm, but he made her angry just looking her way. Maybe she was just exhausted. She leaned the seat back, and rested her head against the window. Caleb flipped the radio to a country station and within ten minutes she was asleep.

Caleb glanced in the rearview mirror. He hadn't meant it when he had told her they could be followed, but now he wondered. The white Bronco several cars behind them had been there since they left the city. He shook his head. Damn, maybe he was just getting paranoid.

But three hours later, he was beginning to believe that he was not so paranoid. When he slowed down, so did the Bronco. When he sped up, so did the Bronco. It kept a three-car distance at all times. He decided on a little experiment and took the next exit, pulling into the first gas station.

He parked by the pumps and saw the Bronco turn in and pull to the side of the station just as Sam woke up and pushed her hair out of her face.

"Hey, do we need gas? I must have slept a long time."

"About three hours. Just thought I'd top it off before we reached Chapel Hill."

"Okay," said Sam, unbuckling her seat belt. "I'll run hit the ladies room."

"Wait," blurted Caleb, grabbing her arm. "I'll go with you."

"To the ladies room? Caleb, I get the 'don't-go-anywhere-without-me' command but isn't that taking it a little too far?" she said with a laugh.

Caleb blushed. Actually blushed. Shit. "I mean, I need to go in too. Let's just go together."

"Whatever floats your boat. Speaking of floating boats, I'm in a bit of a hurry," she said as she pushed the door open, hopped out, and strutted toward the glass door.

"Sam, wait." Caleb was by her side in three quick strides.

"Caleb, you're being ridiculous."

Forget not scaring her, the truth was crucial. He grabbed her hand and leaned over to whisper as he dragged her into the front of the store. "Sam, don't look over your shoulder, but I think we are being followed."

"What?" she squeaked, wheeling around to look through the wall of glass.

He jerked her hand to spin her back around. "Damn, you're bad at this. My sister would be rolling her eyes. What part of *don't look now*, didn't you understand? I'll explain it all when we are safely back in the car."

"You said we weren't being followed, and what does your sister have to do with this?" she asked suspiciously.

"Look—dammit, Sam—I mean *don't* look! Listen. I mean listen," he clarified quickly. "A white Bronco's parked on the side. It has stayed exactly three car lengths behind us for the last three hours and it followed us here. Just run to the bathroom, and I'll grab us some food and watch the front. We'll get ten dollars of gas and leave. Just act normal, and do not, do you hear me, do not look at the Bronco. If it is following us, I don't want the driver to know we suspect."

She looked at Caleb. Her life couldn't get more surreal. Maybe she would wake up soon. But if she did, Caleb would be gone.

Sam nodded and walked to the restroom. He was waiting with a small bag and two coffees when she returned. He put his arm around her to walk back to the car, refusing to let go when she stiffened. In less than five minutes, they were back on the road.

Sam turned sideways in her seat, sitting Indian style and facing Caleb. Turning her head slightly, she gasped when she saw a white Bronco pull from the side of the building and follow them back on the interstate.

"What is going on?" exclaimed Sam. She was suddenly very afraid.

He reached across and grasped her hand. Her fingers were cold. "It's going to be okay, honey. I promise." She simply nodded, wondering what Ben had been involved in, and wondering why warmth spread through her insides when Caleb called her honey.

The white Bronco followed them all the way to the Carolina Inn. Caleb parked on the street in front of the hotel. It was dark now but he saw the Bronco park about a block away. He waited a few seconds but no one emerged, and he couldn't see the driver through the tinted car windows.

"Stay put while I get the bags," Caleb grabbed the bags and opened Sam's door. Putting his arm around her shoulders, he started to lead her away from the car.

"Wait," she said. She pulled the door open again and grabbed her camera bag from the floor. Securing her bag over her shoulder, she allowed him to engulf her again as they hurried toward the hotel entrance. If she hadn't been trapped in his arms she would have turned when she heard a car door open behind them.

"Don't turn," he said, squeezing her shoulder. "Wait till we are at the front desk. You lean your back against the counter and watch the door while I check us in. But don't stare."

He was a nondescript man. Average height, brown hair. But he actually stood out in his brown suit. Everyone else in the hotel was in jeans and Carolina blue t-shirts. Most of the men had blue baseball caps on their heads. The man's glance rested on them a minute as he sat down in the lobby and opened a newspaper, effectively hiding behind it.

Sam glimpsed up at Caleb and nodded. He signed the credit card statement, grabbed her hand, and walked through the lobby toward the elevator. His hand engulfed hers with warmth and felt so natural. She knew it was just for show and somehow it made the touch painful, but she resisted pulling her hand back. Looking over her head as he spoke a little too loudly, "I got us a suite so you can have your privacy. We're in room 312."

The man never lowered the paper so Caleb never saw his face. The elevator opened and they stepped into an elevator full of rowdy college students. One young couple smiled silently at each other as the boy twirled a room key. They stepped out when the door opened on the second floor. Caleb tugged Sam out behind them.

"Hey, fellas," called Caleb, holding out his room key. "I know this sounds crazy, but my girl and I are trying to hide from our friends for a quiet night. We've got the suite on the third floor for the night. You wouldn't be willing to change rooms with us, would you? One friend has threatened to follow us when we leave the room, and we don't want to stay cooped in all night. If you switch with us, I'll even foot the bill for room service if you'll hide out in there all night."

"Three twelve," the boy exclaimed, seeing the key number. "That's the most expensive room in the hotel! There's even a two-person Jacuzzi. Sure!"

His girlfriend kicked his shin. "He forgot to tell you, we've got the cheapest room. We can't pay the difference."

"Oh, no, it's an even trade. We're going down memory lane, right Hon? We want that old college feel again."

Sam nodded and the keys were exchanged.

"Sweet!" shouted the young man as he pulled his girlfriend toward the stairs.

A small laugh escaped Sam's lips as she watched the two. But her laugh stopped abruptly when Caleb opened the door to their room. It had one double bed crammed in a corner too small for a bedside table. They stepped inside and the space seemed to shrink. Caleb filled the room. Every corner of the air she breathed filled her senses with Caleb. Suddenly, she was seventeen again.

"Caleb, I don't know if I can," she paused. "I don't think I can stay here. I just don't know if . . . ."

Oh, God. She felt so alone, so afraid. He was too large, too beautiful, too—too Caleb. She was still in love him. It was ridiculous. She didn't even know him. She had to get out of this room. She could not survive again. She should have chosen the jail cell.

"I need to go for a run," she blurted, looking back toward the door.

Caleb was baffled by the emotions flitting across her face. Humor. Shock. Pain. Followed by absolute terror. He quickly inspected the room but saw no cause for her fear. Yet, when he grabbed her upper arms to keep her from bolting back out the door, she was trembling.

"Sam, what is it? What did you see? Were we followed up here?"

Sam shook her head and took a deep breath. "No, no. I'm sorry. I just—I guess it's just the stress of everything. I'm okay, really." Just a little crazy, she thought.

"The guy downstairs, what did he look like? Did you see a gun?"

"A gun!" Sam exclaimed. Her panicked heart slowed down. Ironically, the thought of a man following her with a gun wasn't half as frightening as facing Caleb alone with one bed. She was so relieved that Caleb was totally unaware of her thoughts that she actually let a small laugh escape.

He watched her, looking for signs of hysteria, which only made her laugh again and hold up her hand. "I'm okay, really. I promise. No, I didn't see any weapons. He was medium height, brown hair, middle aged, and wore a brown suit. His chest was broad and looked like muscle not fat. You know, sort of a body builder type. No visible neck. He definitely looked at us before he hid behind that newspaper. Why do you think he's following us? Hey, maybe he's a cop."

"Doubt it. The cops think you're guilty so to them the case is over. But someone was looking for something at Ben's, and maybe they think we know where it is. Don't worry, Sam, I won't let this guy hurt you."

Sam nodded. No, Caleb was the one who was going to hurt her, not no-neck guy. And this time, she might never recover. She turned away to put her bag on the bed.

"Do you think we could go on a run? That nap in the car was great, but I need to get some kinks out of my body."

"No, sorry, Sam. It's safer to stay here. We can't risk being seen. We'll sneak out before dawn and lose him before he realizes it's not us in that room. And I really need some sleep. I tell you what. You take a long bath, and I'll order us room service. The bath should help the kinks."

Sam really needed to run, but water was the next best thing. She nodded and opened the bathroom door. Looking at the small tub, she wished they had the Jacuzzi suite, but it would do. And more important, they'd be in different rooms for a while.

"Okay."

Sam emerged from the bathroom in her baggy sweats and a towel wrapped around her head. The water had helped her to gather control of her emotions. And the smell of the food made her stomach growl as she noticed a rolling cart full of food sitting at the foot of the bed.

"Let's eat," said Caleb, as he pulled the only chair to the other side of the cart and held it for her. He caught a whiff of fresh soap and wished she didn't look so adorable.

Sam was suddenly starving and realized she hadn't eaten for days. Caleb had ordered a variety. Stuffed mushrooms, pasta, salads, steak, fruit, and desserts. The room was silent except for the clanging of silverware for the next thirty minutes as they devoured the food.

With one last bite of chocolate cake, Sam sighed and sat back to sip on a cup of hot tea. "Okay, I'm human again."

"You ate like you haven't had food in a week."

"Almost."

"Well, we'll have to make sure we keep you fed from now on."

"I won't argue with that. I know a great place that we can go for breakfast."

"Deal. We can hang out there until the library opens at eight o'clock."

"You've been busy," said Sam, noting the open phonebook. "Catch me up.

CHAPTER THIRTEEN

Abby stood in the morgue at the Charleston County medical examiner's office. The man on the table was a black male, mid-thirties, six feet tall, and 170 pounds. His body had been found in an alley off King Street with no sign of trauma. Drug overdose was suspected, but toxicology reports were pending.

"So, can you ID him?" asked the coroner.

"Not sure yet," said Abby. "What did you find on him?"

The coroner went to a cabinet and pulled out a large tray holding sealed and labeled plastic bags. "This was it."

Abby picked through the bags. The filthy orange shirt matched the description. A smaller bag held a hundred dollar bill and a small slip of paper with a number. She held it up and looked back at the coroner.

"Oh, that. Found it in his underwear, guarded by the family jewels. We called the number but it has been disconnected. Figure it might be a drug dealer since is was with the hundred."

"Did you do a trace?"

"Yeah. Stolen phone."

Abby nodded, but wrote down the number.

"So do you know him?"

"I've never seen him before, but I'm gonna ask around."

He frowned, looking at the petite woman. "Why don't you let the city detectives do their job? The streets around here can be dangerous."

"I know how to take care of myself. Besides, how much time are the cops going to spend on a dead homeless guy?"

None, he thought. "Why do you care?"

"I'm working a case, and I think this guy might have seen something."

"You think he was murdered?" He shook his head. "Didn't find any evidence of foul play at the scene. Just slumped up against a wall without a pulse. Looks like a typical homeless OD to me."

"There aren't any track marks?"

"Needles aren't the only method of pleasure for these guys."

She nodded and studied the dead man again. "Could you just look a little deeper? He might be the guy I'm looking for—witness to a murder. If he is, his death was awfully convenient. And I stopped believing in convenient a long time ago."

"Did you report that to the police?"

"I don't report hunches. Besides, the police were the only ones besides my client who knew I was planning to question the guy."

The coroner studied her, noting the implication without surprise. Well, no one had told him to put a rush on this guy. "It will take seventy-two hours to get all the toxicology reports back. I normally wait until I have all the results to turn the report over to the detectives."

She nodded and smiled. "Thanks. Here's my number if something changes. And I'll call you if I find something that you might want to add to your report."

Two hours later, Abby knew the homeless guy's name and much more. Money talked on the streets. They called him Charlie and he had been living in the doorway across from Ben Fuller's apartment for almost a year. According to the street people, they weren't homeless. They had squatting rights to their humble abodes. One man complained that Charlie's doorway was plenty big for two but he wouldn't share. Charlie threatened anyone who came too close and rarely wandered more than two blocks in either direction. Charlie's body was found six blocks away.

The cell phone number had been disconnected—for one damn day. The number was registered to a local abortion clinic. Apparently, a spin-off of a Planned Parenthood group supplied cell phones with limited minutes to abortion clinics. The phones were sent home with patients to use if complications arose. And of course, no one logged the phones in or out. This phone was disconnected the same day Samantha Jennings was booked. The last incoming call before the disconnect had been from a pay phone a block from Charlie's home.

Abby was going to have to visit the clinic. She didn't believe in coincidences.

CHAPTER FOURTEEN

Sam woke slowly just before sunrise. She was surrounded by warmth and snuggled deeper, not wanting to leave her dreams. She inhaled. A scent from her past had her lips slowly curling upwards, her eyes still closed. She rolled slightly then stiffened as her nose pressed against a warm hard chest and the cold wash of reality brought her fully awake.

Sam jerked her head back and opened her eyes. Sleepy green eyes stared down at her. She was suddenly aware of his arms surrounding her waist and tried to jerk away, but his arms tightened almost imperceptibly.

"Morning." The voice was deep, gravely. "How'd you sleep?"

"Oh, I, um." She tried to push away from his chest and felt the rumble of laughter beneath her palms.

His arms began drawing her into his warmth. Watching, waiting.

She was tempted, but pushed away from his chest.

"What happened to the pillows I piled between us?" Sam demanded suddenly suspicious of the laughing emerald eyes.

"Apparently, they weren't cuddly enough and you tossed them." Caleb rolled over on his back and crossed his arms under his head to prevent temptation.

Sam sat up, planting her feet on the floor and saw that the former pillow wall was scattered on her side of the bed. Color rose to her cheeks as she stood up, careful not to look back over her shoulder.

"Sorry. Didn't mean to crowd you. I tend to hog the middle of the bed."

"I remember," responded Caleb softly.

Sam's heart raced at the words and she walked quickly away.

"I'll take the first shower. I'll be quick," she called as she shut the door.

"Don't be sorry, Sam," he said to the closed door. "Best night's sleep I've had in years."

Caleb looked down the sheet at the giant tent and groaned. Damn, he thought, pulling the pillow over his face, she could have at least let him take the first shower. A long, cold shower.

The Carolina Coffee Shop was just as she remembered except there was no long line waiting outside this morning. But then again, no sane college student showed her face at seven-thirty a.m. on a Saturday morning. Walking in from the bright sun, Sam's eyes slowly adjusted to the low-lit room with the high-backed booths lining both walls. Down the middle were small round tables and what looked like a bar in the back. The floor was dark, distressed wood. The room resembled a jazz bar more than a coffee shop. A young sleepy woman met them with menus before the door bumped shut.

"We'll take a booth in the back," said Caleb.

Sam closed her eyes and inhaled. The smell of bacon and maple sugar filled the air. She was going to have a difficult time deciding between their famous omelets and a tall stack of pancakes covered with fresh fruit and thick syrup. She glanced at Caleb's back—maybe she could con him into sharing and then they could have both. She frowned slightly, wondering what about Caleb had made her appetite return.

"Sam!"

Sam heard the shout just before a warm body torpedoed into her. Instinct had her wrapping her arms around the small bundle as arms were flung around her neck and knobby-kneed legs circled her waist.

"Sam! Sam! I missed you."

"Tad! What are you doing here?" Sam exhaled in a rush and, once she was able to breathe again, laughed with pure joy. The carefree sound washed over Caleb and tugged at his heart. The small boy clinging like a baby chimp had brown hair, brown eyes, and flushed red checks. His body bounced slightly with excitement as chatter spilled from his lips.

"We are visiting Daddy's business for the week. And I get my own bed in the same room with Daddy. Guess what? I got a puppy. Daddy gave it to me. Step-mama doesn't like it so much because it piddles and wants it outside, but Daddy said no and I promised to clean up and it can't help it anyway 'cause it's so little, and I named him Eva—'cause he's a she—and 'cause Eva and Wallie would love each other when you came to visit but then I couldn't find you and that made Eva sad."

Sam laughed again and said, "Well, you found me now."

"Tad, get off Miss Jennings this minute. You are making a scene."

Tad's smile slipped and he looked embarrassed as he slid down Sam's body, landing with both feet on the floor, but he tucked his hand into Sam's as he turned.

"Sorry," he mumbled then brightened. "But look! I found Sam. Can she eat pancakes with us?" He tugged Sam toward the booth where his father and stepmother sat in the shadows.

"Good morning, Mr. and Mrs. Anderson. It's wonderful to see you again."

Mrs. Anderson did not speak but gave her husband a nudging look.

Anderson reached out and tugged at Tad's free hand, pulling him back into the booth. Tad struggled a moment but stopped his protest when Anderson snapped, "Tad, behave."

The boy looked into his father's stern face and bit his lip. "Daddy, can Sam eat with us?"

Anderson placed a firm arm over Tad's shoulder and faced Sam. "Hello, Miss Jennings. I apologize for my son's behavior. We were actually just finishing our meal and about to leave."

Sam saw the suspicion and wariness. It hurt. She understood his reasons, considering the stories, but it hurt.

"But, Daddy," argued Tad.

"It's okay, Tad." She smiled down at him and touched his cheek. She withdrew her hand slowly when she felt Anderson draw Tad away from her touch. Her eyes met Anderson's with a knowing expression. "I understand, Mr. Anderson. I was actually here on business myself and wouldn't be able to join you for breakfast."

Caleb, who'd been preoccupied making sure the patrons who turned to watch the little reunion didn't link Sam to the Samantha in the news, turned and concentrated on the man in the booth when he heard the hurt in Sam's voice. He stuck out his hand.

"Theodore Anderson, isn't it? I'm Caleb McCloud. I'm here with Miss Jennings. It's a pleasure to meet you." His handshake was perhaps a bit too firm, but he backed off just before conceding to a sudden adolescent desire to test Mr. Anderson's manliness. Well, maybe he didn't back off quite enough, he thought with a guilty pleasure when he noticed Anderson flex his released fingers. "I've read about your company and your amazing accomplishments. And this must be Tad; I remember your story in *Time* magazine. You're almost as famous as your daddy, Tad." This time he was gentle and his eyes softened as he reached over to shake Tad's hand. The boy beamed at being treated like a grown up.

"I'm gonna be just like Daddy when I grow up. He let me come with him this week so I could learn. But I miss Eva."

"I'm sorry you couldn't bring your puppy. Have you met Wallie?"

"Not yet, but I've seen pictures. Wallie is a boy so when Eva grows up, they can get married. And I'm gonna marry Sam so we'll all be a family."

"Smart boy." He smiled at Sam.

"So Mr. McCloud," Anderson interrupted, "I must say it's an honor to meet you too. I believe you've made the news much more often than I. Always on the side of justice." He stared at Sam and his eyes were speculative this time. "I believe the media describes you as a young Kennedy with a cape. "

"Only in the comics," Caleb laughed. "Besides it's well known that the press is notorious for romanticizing or villainizing its subjects based on little to no facts."

Anderson's expression didn't change as he glanced from Caleb to Sam and back, but with a slight tip of his head, he acknowledged the message. A waitress walked to the edge of the table, placed the check on the corner and backed off without interrupting the conversation. Anderson reached over and pulled it toward him.

Mrs. Anderson, who had been silently assessing the group, spoke for the first time, but her eyes never left Caleb. "Theodore, darling, we need to be going."

Caleb turned his head slightly toward Mrs. Anderson. She was easily fifteen years younger than her husband and as beautiful as any supermodel. So, thought Caleb, a trophy wife. He smiled and stuck out his hand and wondered if she would shake it or rub her cheek across it and purr. She seized her prize and held on just a few seconds too long while her eyes spoke to him in a seductive whisper before words pressed past her lips. "The pleasure is all mine, I assure you."

Caleb simply nodded and reclaimed his hand.

Mr. Anderson was counting bills from his wallet and missed the exchange.

"I apologize, Mr. McCloud, Miss Jennings, but we really must be going."

"But Daddy, wait. I gotta be able to talk to Sam. I want her to come visit."

"Son, I think Miss Jennings is too busy to visit you right now."

"But I will lose her again. How can I find her?"

"Wait," said Sam as she dug in her purse to pull out a card and pen. She flipped it over and wrote on it. "I get mail at that address and you can write me."

"What does 'P.O.' mean? I never did that kind of email."

"It's a post office box. I don't have email, just old fashioned letters that come to a post office."

"I don't know how to do that," said Tad, chewing on his bottom lip. "I just learned to email in my class. My teacher showed us, and we email letters to some soldiers who are lonely and they write us back. I wanted to email you too."

"I'm sorry, Tad, I guess I need to learn how."

"You could come home with me, and my teacher could show you," announced Tad.

"Now that's an idea," smiled Caleb, opening his own wallet and pulling out a card. "Here, Tad, this is my email. You can write Sam at my email and I'll give it to her, okay? I'll even teach her how to email."

"Gee thanks. You'll like email, Sam. It's fun. Daddy helps me write thank-you emails to all those people who helped me." He held up the cards to show his dad. "Look, Daddy, I got cards just like the kind you get."

"So I see. Why don't I keep them safe for you?" He said reaching forward.

Tad quickly hid the cards behind his back. "No, they're mine! I'm big and I won't lose them. See?" And he opened a pocket on the side of his pants, stuck the two cards inside, Velcroed it closed, and grinned.

Anderson started to argue but changed his mind.

"If that's settled, we had best be own our way. It was nice meeting you, Mr. McCloud. Miss Jennings." The three left with Mrs. Anderson aiming one last smile at Caleb.

"Bye, Sam!" shouted Tad as the front door closed behind them.

Settling into an empty booth, Caleb watched Sam in silence for a moment as she stared out the now empty glass door.

Finally, he spoke, "Wall-e?" He emphasized the E.

"What?"

"You named your dog after a cartoon robot?" he asked. The lost look left her eyes just as he hoped and was replaced with humor.

"Yeah, seemed to fit, living in our own little abandoned world."

"I like it. I'd have picked something like Crusoe."

"Really? I'd have pictured you with a Gilligan."

Caleb laughed, and the two lapsed into a comfortable silence as the waitress filled their coffee cups.

"You'd never met Theodore Anderson before today?" asked Sam.

"No, why would I?"

"He's big in political circles. So are you."

"Not that big." Caleb paused and studied her again. "Tell me about Tad."

"What about him?"

"I was impressed with your *Time* cover story on him."

"You were?"

"Of course. Even if I hadn't seen you with him today, the article and photographs told me you loved him."

Sam seemed startled but then conceded with a nod. "What's not to love?"

"He sure looks healthy now?"

"Yeah. It's a little hard to believe that was the same little boy I met a little over a year ago. He was so frail. Dying slowly, and very painfully, day by day."

"You saved him."

"That's ridiculous. I simply wrote a story. His father, jerk that he is, saved him."

"Mrs. Anderson is—interesting."

"Interesting? Is that the new word for stunning?"

"She is a looker." He noted the flash of jealousy and almost smiled before continuing, "Gorgeous is what I'd call her. Dumped the first wife for her?"

"No. Actually, word was he loved his first wife, but she was sick for a long time. Cancer. The new Mrs. Anderson was a lab tech, offering . . . comfort. Gossip at GloboHealth was that they were cozy long before the first Mrs. Anderson died."

"Gossip?"

"Oh, the research community was tight. Ben told me. Actually, he introduced me to Anderson after Tad got sick."

"Ben thought of the story for *Time*?"

"No, actually it was Mrs. Anderson. She may be a gold digger but she seemed to care about Tad in her own way. She was the one that convinced her husband to go public with Tad's story."

"So more than just a gorgeous body."

Sam frowned at him, thinking of the way Mrs. Anderson had studied Caleb. "A woman no man could resist."

"I wouldn't say that," said Caleb. He turned to the waitress before Sam could respond.

After much debate, they ordered pancakes, fruit, an omelet loaded with mushrooms and Brie, a side of bacon, and never-ending cups of coffee. By the time they finished, the table was littered with empty plates. Sam left the coffee shop wondering if it were possible to sneak back to the Carolina Inn for a nap before braving Wilson Library.

As they walked up the broad library steps to the front door, Sam turned to Caleb, "I hate this place. Let's go spread out a blanket in the quad, take a little nap, and then go down into the dungeon. My stomach's too full to face it. Rows of science books. I could lose my cookies—or pancakes."

Laughing, Caleb pushed her toward the door. "Then you shouldn't have made me order all that food. Let's get this over with. Besides I'm dying to find at least one clue in this mess."

Reality set in and Sam thought of Ben. Caleb watched as her eyes darkened with pain. She nodded and walked ahead in silence. Caleb could have kicked himself. He was so involved with being with her, he'd forgotten about Ben.

The library stacks were dark and musty. Most of the old chemistry books looked like they hadn't been touched for centuries. Books of odd sizes and drab colors lined the shelves down endless rows. The little white stickers at the base of each leather cover bearing the appropriate Dewey Decimal number created the only sense of order.

Sam's fingers traced the leather bindings as she scanned the numbers.

"This is it." She pulled an old, oversized tome off the second shelf.

Both Sam and Caleb glanced over their respective shoulders before sitting down on the floor and opening the book. Sam flipped briefly through the pages then turned the book upside down and shook it. Nothing fell out. Then she turned to Chapter 15. She turned every page of the chapter but found no notes from Ben. She studied the table of contents, but again no notes.

"I don't see anything that makes sense," she said to Caleb. "I thought there would be a message. But it would have been out of character for Ben to write in a valuable old book."

"Let's see your chemistry book again. "

Sam leaned over, dug through her backpack and pulled out her Chem 11 book, handing it to Caleb. In the table of contents, Ben had drawn a small arrow and written, "Review Chapter 15." Flipping through the chapter in her chemistry book, the only writing was beside the single footnote telling Sam to refer to the book in her usual place of study. The footnote read, "*History of Chemistry and Wartime Spies*, page 251."

"Try page 251."

Sam flipped to that page. "I still don't see anything."

Caleb looked at the page and back at the Chem 11 book, then grinned. He grabbed the old tome from Sam's hands, stood up, and held the open page up to the single light bulb dangling from the ceiling.

"What are you doing?" hissed Sam, scanning the aisle for lurking librarians. "That book's an antique. All I need is to get fingerprinted again for destroying some old chemistry book. My hate of chemistry is well-known in these parts."

Caleb laughed and held the book even closer to the bulb as she dangled from his bicep.

"I'm not kidding, you're going to burn it," exclaimed Sam. Caleb ignored her and slowly moved the book back and forth until the bulb had singed nearly every inch of the page.

"Take a look," he said pulling it back down. "Thought your boy wasn't into intrigue."

Handwriting had appeared in the margins. It was Ben's:

> *Sam, if you are here, guess there's trouble. Meet me at the place we celebrated my Ph.D. I bought it under a pseudonym. Learned that from you. We'll be safe and I'll explain.*

Caleb smirked in triumph, closed the book and reshelved it. Neither spoke as they walked out of the library and down the quad toward Franklin Street.

"How'd you know to do that?"

"What? Oh, just call me Bond, James Bond." He smiled.

She quirked her eyebrow, and he laughed.

"The name of the book referred to history and spies and that page deals with ancient methods of secret messages. I learned the invisible ink thing in an elementary school science project. Historically, it was one of the first means of passing covert communications. You use cornstarch melted in water and a toothpick, or in those days a bird feather, to write. It dries clear but heat turns it brown."

"I've never heard of that."

"Sam, it was basic knowledge in elementary school. Every boy I know tried it at some point. "

"Well, that explains it. I don't have the right body parts."

"And thank God for that."

She scowled at him. "Ben took a chance believing I could figure that one out."

"It was described on that page," said Caleb. "You would have eventually read the page."

She walked in silence a moment. Her voice was barely audible when she spoke again. "He thought he'd be safe. Whatever this is, he thought he was safe and we'd be together again." Her voice hitched.

Caleb's heart twisted, but he restrained from pulling her into his arms. "We'll find his killer, Sam. I promise."

Sam nodded and after a few minutes spoke again. "Where are we going now?"

"The friend I talked to last night said he'd leave a car for us in the parking garage just behind Franklin Street."

"What about your car?"

"The city will tow it. I'll pick it up when we get back. We can't risk Brown-Suit-Guy tracking us. And Sam there is something else I didn't tell you last night."

She waited.

"That homeless guy—" he began. "Well, he's dead."

Sam whirled to face him. "What? How do you know? Why didn't you tell me? We had a deal. I thought I could trust you."

"Damn it, Sam, I'm telling you now. You can trust me. I just got the call last night. He showed up at the morgue. Coroner thinks it was an overdose," he hesitated. "But I've got someone following up on it. A private investigator. She has her doubts and is digging a bit deeper. She'll let us know."

"Us?" The word dripped with sarcasm.

"Shit. Me. She'll let me know, and I'll tell you."

"And I'm supposed to believe that?"

"Sam, you needed some sleep and food. That's the only reason I waited to tell you. If you collapse, you won't be any help with all this."

"I won't collapse! And it's not your job to protect me; it's your job to defend me. I want to know everything the minute you know it. Got it? That was the deal."

Anger sparked in Caleb's eyes. "Fine. Got it. I tell you every gory detail as it unfolds."

She stared at him, saying nothing.

"I swear," he barked, angry that she didn't trust him.

Sam nodded and began walking again. "I need your phone. I want to call Maggie before we leave and fill her in. We trust each other."

Sam didn't catch the words Caleb muttered as he handed her his phone.

CHAPTER FIFTEEN

"Hey, Maggie, it's Sam."

"It's about time you called me. You need to buy a phone. You won't believe what's been going on here. Oh, and thanks."

"Thanks for what?"

"The six-foot-six mega hunk. Though he's not very good with the bad guys. But my moaning and playing up the guilt card has been tons of fun."

"Bad guys? Moaning? What the hell are you talking about?" Sam stopped in the middle of the sidewalk, and a lanky boy bumped into her back almost knocking her over. Caleb caught her and physically pulled her to a bench hidden under the limbs of an old oak before trying to grab the phone from her ear, demanding, "What's going on? Did something happen to Jim?"

Sam turned away from Caleb, shaking her head, "Shut up, Caleb, I can't hear! The connection is terrible. Maggie, what did you say? Are you all right? What the hell is going on?"

Caleb scowled, but let Sam keep the phone.

"Someone broke into your cottage and smacked me on the head with one of your gorgeous blue bottles. Oh, it's pretty much shattered, by the way—the vase, not my head. But I did clean up the mess before I left. Well, Jim did. I was busy moaning."

Sam would have jumped off the bench, but Caleb placed a firm hand on her shoulder, "Someone hit you? In my house? Are you okay? Who was it? I'm on my way right now."

"Whoa, girl. You don't need to come. In fact, I'll kill you if you do. It'd give mega hunk a chance to escape."

"Maggie!" Sam's tone was full of frustration and concern. She leaned back on the bench.

"Okay, okay. Well, Jim came to deliver your Jeep. And he was like—wow. That's all I can say—wow. But for some reason, one minute he's all over me, and the next he backs off like I've got the plague. I'm having a blast playing with his head."

"Maggie, the smack on *your* head?"

"Oh, yeah. Well, Jim shows up and we go to take your Jeep back. I go to the door and it's open. So I charge in yelling, but some guy smashes me with a bottle before I have a chance to duck. Next thing I know, I'm being carried to the couch like I'm as light as a loggerhead baby and this hunk is trying to kiss the hurt away."

"Are you okay?"

"Well, the kiss did leave me lightheaded."

"Damn it, Maggie, this is serious. Stop trying to protect me."

"Sorry. Thought I could distract you with the kissing part. I'm fine. Whopper of a headache, but nothing that a lot of tender love and care hasn't cured. Really, Sam, I've fine now. Just milking it. Jim took off the entire week to look after me."

"What about the intruder?"

"He got away. I'm sure it was just a camper trying for squatting rights and a dip in that swimming pool you call a tub. I think he just swung the vase to get away. We've not seen hide nor hair of anyone since and Jim has looked. He makes me keep a weapon and Wallie at my side at all times. I think I impressed him with my park ranger firearm. Nothing sexier than a curvy black woman that can shoot the pinecones off the local trees."

"Maggie, I really think I should come back tonight."

"Samantha, don't you dare. I'm perfectly safe, and I'm not alone, remember? Tell you what, you can come home when Jim leaves."

Sam sighed and gnawed her bottom lip. But before she could speak again, Maggie interrupted her thoughts. "Hey, Jim wants to talk to Caleb."

"Are you sure you don't want me to come back tonight?"

"Positive. Look Sam, I'm fine really—better than fine in a strange, twisted way. But he leaves Sunday. Come home then."

Sam took a deep breath and thought of the clue Ben had left. She needed to see that cabin. "Okay, Maggie, but if things change, you and Jim get off that island. I'm giving the phone to Caleb."

"Deal."

"Jim," Caleb barked into the phone.

"It's still Maggie. I just wanted to say that I know who you are and if you hurt her again, I've got a gun and know how to use it."

Caleb looked down at Sam with a surprised expression.

"What?" Sam asked anxiously, but this time Caleb shook his head.

"I'll keep that in mind," he said. "Now, put Jim on."

"Hold on I'll get him. Jim! Phone."

Caleb listened in silence as Jim repeated his version of the story. Satisfied that Jim would protect Maggie, he updated Jim and hung up. He glanced around to make sure their visitor from last night hadn't wandered onto campus.

"Okay, let's go," he said.

"But what did Jim say? Do you think we should go back? What if it's the guy who killed Ben? Maybe he even killed that homeless guy."

"Jim thinks it was a camper. He said nothing had been touched, but he'll check out your place every day and look after Maggie. Remember, the homeless guy was killed about the same time as the break-in so it can't be the same guy. Besides, according to the witnesses, a woman killed Ben, remember?"

"According to the witnesses, I killed Ben."

Caleb looked over at Sam and smiled. "Point taken." He stood up. "Regardless, the best way to make everyone safe is to find out who killed Ben. And based on that message he sent you, he knew about a threat. The cabin is the only clue we have right now."

Sam nodded and stood up, staring out in the distance before turning to walk toward Franklin Street. Caleb glanced sideways at his now silent partner, wanting to reassure her. Hold her. Instead, he simply walked to the parking garage and located the car. Within minutes, they were driving west. Before driving onto the interstate ramp, he broke the silence.

"So, where exactly is this cabin? I assume Ben was referring to the mountain cabin you told me about before."

"Yes," responded Sam, picturing the small house deep in the woods. She was surprised it was still standing. "It's near Asheville. I didn't know he bought it. There are so many things I didn't know." She stared out the window and studied the road ahead. "I thought I knew him so well. He was my friend, and I really didn't know anything about him. Maybe he stayed my friend all these years out of pity."

"Sam, don't be an idiot. Who did he trust with information when he thought he was in danger? You. Where did he plan to hide? In a place only you and he were aware of."

Sam nodded and lapsed into silence again. She was unsure if these observations made her feel better or worse. Ben was dead and she had no idea why.

Caleb wished he knew what she was thinking. Did she regret that she and Ben hadn't become lovers? Ben had all those years with her while he had only what he could gleam from her photography and vague articles about her life.

He decided to change the subject. "So I just head into Asheville?"

"You take the Ashville exit but you don't go into town. There's a small side road that goes up a mountain. I have to see it to remember. I didn't pay attention to the road signs back then."

Caleb frowned. "Are you sure you can find it?"

Sam rolled her eyes. "Yes, but I'm not so sure that we'll make it up those old mountain roads. Where did you get this thing anyway?"

Caleb laughed. *This thing* was an early 1970's VW Beetle. The tag said vintage, but the rusty outside said old. It sputtered like a riding lawn mower and refused to go over sixty miles an hour. Cars weaved around, passing them on both sides as they traveled down the interstate with all the windows down. The car was obviously built before air conditioning was invented.

"Belongs to a friend of mine who has an art studio just outside Chapel Hill. We knew each other as undergrads. Fact is this was his car back then. He says it's a work of art and he'll never let it go. Lucky for us, he has another car, and this thing is ours for as long as we need it."

"Yeah, lucky for us," said Sam, but she smiled and leaned her head back to let the wind blow in her face.

CHAPTER SIXTEEN

"Sam? Wake up, Sam. We're at the Asheville exit. Tell me where to turn."

Sam couldn't believe she'd actually fallen asleep again. But the fresh breeze, the sun, and the puttering of the engine had lulled her to sleep. And Caleb, if she were honest. She felt safe when he was around.

"Sam?"

"The road was about three miles before town. Look, see that old gas station?"

"That's a gas station?"

"Among other things. That pile of rusty tin and old tires hasn't changed a bit." The corner of her mouth curved upward just enough to reveal her dimple. "Well, maybe it's a bit taller. Go past and then take that second road."

Caleb turned on a narrow paved road. The signs along the way just showed wiggling snakes as they climbed, going around one hairpin turn after another. The gears were grinding and the car refused to go over twenty miles an hour up the steep incline.

"There's a dirt road just off the next corner or so."

It was the "or so" that had him concerned. By the time they found the small dirt road, the Beetle's engine was smoking. Fortunately, the last road was downhill, and Caleb coasted around the narrow curves in neutral using the emergency brake to slow their descent before coming to a halt in front of an old cabin.

"I think this is it."

"You think?!"

"I was only here once, but how many places like this could there be?" asked Sam, looking at the old building.

The cabin was weathered gray and white and almost hidden by clinging vines and weeds. The once green door had only small patches of cracked paint clinging to its surface. The ancient window frames were ridged with similar paint chips. The entire shack rested about a foot off the ground on stacks of smooth river stones at appropriate corners. Apparently the stacks were not very even because the entire building tilted slightly toward the right. The Appalachian version of the Leaning Tower of Pisa, thought Caleb.

Caleb shook his head as he stared at the house then back at the smoke steaming out from under the edges of the car hood.

"Well, we won't be going anywhere else anytime soon. I'll go check it out."

"We'll go check it out," Sam stated as she walked around Caleb and across the overgrown path to the front door and knocked.

No one answered. The door was securely locked although Caleb was fairly certain the wood would have caved in if he rammed his shoulder into the middle of the door. Hell, maybe all he needed to do was lean, but he was more than a little worried that the entire shack would collapse with the door. They walked around the house trying to peer in windows.

"This is it," said Sam, sitting on Caleb's shoulders to looking through the one back window that had no curtains.

"How can you be sure?"

"I remember the room," she explained as he lifted her off his shoulders and placed her feet on the ground. "And one of the photographs I gave Ben is hanging over the fireplace."

The back door was locked too, but Caleb quickly opened it with a credit card.

"Cool trick," Sam commented.

"My clients are full of interesting and useful facts for everyday life."

"I just bet."

The inside of the cabin was a stark juxtaposition to the exterior. The heart of pine floors were not polished, but smooth and clean. The walls were sanded planks that had been recently whitewashed. The planked ceiling was the same warm pine as the floors. A large headless black bear stretched out across the floor between a huge overstuffed cream couch and two matching cream chairs. There was no television, but a large stone fireplace. A roll top desk sat in the corner under the small window Sam had peered through. Beside the desk was a white bookshelf with a small printer and rows of neatly organized books and notebooks. But it was the artwork that captivated Sam.

Over the years, she had given prints to Ben. He had always acted pleased and thanked her, but the only two he had ever hung in his apartment were a photograph of the sunset she had taken when they were at the beach one day and one of the moon over the Charleston harbor. Deciding he was simply being polite, she had given him a lamp one Christmas. He had been so profoundly disappointed that she'd resumed her photography gifts and never questioned what he did with the pictures.

They were here. All of them. Matted in white and framed in simple black. The works of gray covered the walls like an art gallery. The only photograph not hanging was the one she had taken with a timer of her and Ben sitting in front of this fireplace. It was in a white frame and sat on the top of the bookshelf facing his desk.

Caleb moved from frame to frame with silent respect. The photos were of people, places, things, but mostly they were emotion. A mountain stream shrouded in fog. A spotlight of sunlight burning through dark clouds to highlight a steady flow of waves. A small child in ragged clothes reaching out to touch a small kitten's head poking out over the edge of a cardboard box.

Sam sat on the edge of the chair watching Caleb and holding her breath. He walked completely around the room.

"My God," he breathed, turning to face her. "You are amazing. I knew you were good, but these belong in a gallery. Obviously, Ben agreed."

She hadn't known how afraid she was for someone to review her work. Her work, not some assignment. She had shared her personal photographs only with Ben. He had never commented beyond the thank you, and she had been afraid to ask.

"I never knew. I wasn't sure he even liked them."

Caleb turned to look around the room again until his eyes came to rest on the portrait by the desk. Ben's grin was huge, his eyes crinkled at the corners. Sam's smile was soft, not quite reaching her eyes. She was looking at the camera but she was sitting slightly behind Ben and the small depth of field had made her slightly out of focus.

"When was this picture taken?"

"As soon as we got to the cabin that time I told you about. Ben wanted a photo of the two of us on our first vacation. I set up the tripod over there."

"He was in love with you."

"Then? No, I don't think he loved me, but he did want us to be together. And maybe even hoped one day that we'd fall in love. But—but no." She grimaced at the memory. "I told you what happened. Things changed that day. He was mad at first but later he was okay. We were just friends after that, and he never wanted that to change."

"Sam, how can you be so clueless? He was still in love with you. I'd say obsessed. Look at this place for God's sake!

It's beautiful, but it's like a damn shrine. Only the two of you knew about it, and hell, he left clues to make sure you met him here. Alone!" The thought suddenly terrified Caleb. "Sam, is it possible his obsession with you lead to his death somehow? Maybe his little Raggedy Ann girlfriend is not as helpless as she seems. Maybe she found out about his obsession and killed him and wanted to punish you at the same time."

"I'm telling you, Ben was not obsessed with me. It wasn't like that."

"This place says different."

Sam glanced around the room again. The place shone with sunny simplicity. She should love it, but she felt a cold chill creep down her back. The life of the room beamed from her photographs. Photographs she hadn't known he'd kept.

She had thought of Ben as a brother she never had—a friend—a true friend. But nothing more. Caleb's words echoed in her mind, and the light reflecting off the shades of gray suddenly seemed sinister.

"I need to get out of here," she exclaimed. Turning, she rushed out the back door and ran down a path toward the river. Caleb caught up with her almost immediately, clasping her shoulders and spinning her around into his arms. She couldn't stop herself. She wrapped her arms around his waist, buried her face in his neck, and sobbed.

Caleb held her close. He ran his free hand along the back of her head, smoothing her hair. "Don't cry, Sam. It's okay. Really, it's okay."

"Is it my fault? Is Ben dead because of me?"

"No, no. Don't ever think that."

"How do you know?" exclaimed Sam, pushing back in his arms to watch his eyes. "You saw that room. You've seen his notes and clues. Everything seems to be about me and now he's dead!"

"Sam, we don't know why he died. But it wasn't your fault."

She buried her face into his chest again and the tears returned. "If Sally Simpson went to such great lengths to kill him and frame me, then it has to be about me."

"We don't know for sure it was Sally. But I do know one thing. No matter why Ben died, it was not your fault." He placed his fingers under her chin and tilted her head up to stare into her eyes. "None of this is your fault."

He lowered his head and brushed his lips across hers, tasting the tears. "I'm going to find out what happened. We're going to find out together. I'm not leaving you. It will be okay. I promise."

He kissed her wet eyelids and used the tip of his tongue to trace the path of the wet kisses down to her chin. He gently nipped the edge of her jaw line.

He felt her surrender. He knew he was taking advantage of her vulnerability and he should stop. He knew he should, but his body refused to obey. It was like coming home. His arms surrounded her and his lips devoured hers. A sigh escaped her and his tongue slipped into the warmth. He was lost, but so was Sam. Her tongue matched his rhythm, and she wrapped her arms around his neck, digging her fingers into his loose curls. He broke the kiss for a second to inhale her very essence.

"Caleb," she breathed.

"No, don't speak," he whispered, slipping an arm under her knees and lifting her up. He kissed her to silence again and looked around. He dared not go back in the cabin, so he carried her down the path to the stream where lush green moss filled a small opening surrounded by giant boulders.

Setting her gently on the thick, mossy carpet, Caleb removed his t-shirt and jeans. Sitting down on his knees he pulled off her shirt and jeans, then lifted her and laid her on top of the clothes. She was braless beneath the shirt. He marveled at her perfection. Gently, he cupped one breast, then the other, rubbing his thumb across each nipple until they budded.

"You are so beautiful," he stated simply and lowered his lips to her nipple.

She whimpered and grabbed handfuls of his hair. Not to shove him aside, but to pull him closer. He moved to the other side and a moan escaped her lips as her hands moved down to his smooth muscular shoulders.

He kissed the side of one breast and with his tongue traveled up to her chin where he nipped a slow path until he could capture her full bottom lip between his teeth. His hand traveled between their bodies toward her panties. They were lacy and pink and very tiny. Blonde curls peaked out from beneath the thin triangle driving him mad.

Leaving her lips, he trailed a new path downward, between her breasts, and down along her tight abs. He rose on his knees between her legs and gazed at the lace-framed beauty before bending to trail wet kisses along each inch of lace.

Sam's hips lifted upward and she moaned tossing her head from side to side. At her movement, Caleb slid the bit of lace down her legs and tossed it aside along with his boxers. Unable to wait, he covered her body with his.

He chanted her name and kissed her swollen lips as he buried himself to the very heart of her being. She was slick and tight. She lifted to meet him time and time again until they both cried out in unison.

Caleb collapsed on top of her, then rolled, pulling her with him. He tucked her head under his chin. Neither spoke. They just held each other.

CHAPTER SEVENTEEN

Sam kept her eyes closed, living the dream. She could feel his warm body next to hers. The smell, musky and male, mingled with the fresh smells of rich black dirt, moss, and grass. The river splashed gently, rushing over its rocky bed. The sunlight touched her bare skin through dancing shadows and a breeze swayed with the leaves overhead. But the most welcoming sound was that of Caleb's heartbeat, steady and strong beneath her ear.

"Sam, we need to talk."

Sam cringed as the dream died. Reality reared its ugly head, vanquishing any lingering delusions.

"No. It's not necessary," said Sam, sitting up and pulling on her shirt. She stood and stepped into her jeans as Caleb watched. "We really should go search the cabin for clues."

"Sam," he said, jumping up and grabbing her arm before she could leave.

She turned to stare at him. She was bound and determined to hide her emotions, but that was difficult when all her emotions were aimed at a man who, at the moment, resembled a wrathful—and very naked—Greek god. She wanted to kiss him all over and tumble back to that dream. But he wanted to talk. She couldn't bear to hear the words.

"Sam, dammit, this is important."

"There's nothing to talk about." Her voice was calm and matter of fact. "I know what you're going to say, but you needn't worry. It just happened. Just like last time. No strings attached. It didn't mean anything. We're not kids anymore. So if you'll let me go, we can get back to what's important. I promise not to fall apart again."

Caleb dropped her arm as if it had stabbed him. *What's important?* he thought furiously. He couldn't believe the cold practical woman walking—no strolling—away from him was the same person he had just made love to. He turned and stared at his clothes, wondering how he had misjudged what had just happened. He'd had sex with many women over the years but made love to only one. And she was waltzing away as if it meant nothing.

He was seething by the time he had pulled his jeans back on. Then, he saw it. The small scrap of pink lace. He bent down and picked it up and a thought occurred to him, looking back up the now empty path. Maybe she wasn't so unaffected. He smiled to himself as he tucked the lace into his front pocket. How many women forget their underwear? And she really had no reason to trust him after what he'd done the last time they'd made love.

Shit, he thought rubbing his hand over his face. He wanted that loving, carefree girl back. He was willing to bide his time. After just one taste of her, he knew that whatever happened he would not lose her again. Hell, some day she might even forgive him. He whistled softy to himself and began climbing back up the old path.

Sam stood in the cabin again and stared at the room. It still unnerved her, but compared to walking smoothly away from Caleb, she felt she could handle anything. Shit—what had she been thinking? She hadn't been. That was the trouble. But then, she had to look at the positive side. She hadn't been frozen and cold with Caleb. She shifted slightly as an image crossed her mind. She actually smiled, thinking that if she wasn't standing there right that minute, she could have sworn she'd gone up in smoke down by the river. There was hope for her. If she met the right person, she could live again.

She looked up as Caleb walked into the room. Unless it was only with Caleb, she thought warily. His eyes were hooded but he behaved as if nothing had changed. The earth certainly hadn't moved for him, she thought, vowing not to let him know how she really felt.

"I was thinking that maybe we should just look around the rest of the cabin—then look through his desk, since that was the focus of the search in his apartment," said Sam, trying to take control of the situation.

Caleb nodded and stared hollowly at her. He almost sighed aloud but swallowed the small noise before it escaped. Her mask had a slight crack now that he looked at her closer. Her tone was businesslike and frank, but her hands fidgeted as she spoke. She seemed unaware of the slight quiver in her voice and her eyes were just a bit wary. She was not a very good actress. He wondered if he should push her.

Sam turned her head, but she observed Caleb from the corner of her eye. His behavior confused her. He just stared and actually seemed slightly amused. Her temper flared, and she bit her tongue as she walked around him to explore the rest of the house. Caleb followed in silence.

The cabin was tiny. There was a kitchen just off the family room with doors leading to a pantry and a half bath. The front hallway led straight into the family room. Beside the front door, very narrow wooden steps led to a loft. The loft had a dresser and a wrought iron bed plus a small bathroom.

Sam opened and closed the dresser drawers. One drawer had a change of clothes, but the rest were empty. The bathroom had a claw foot tub and a pedestal sink. Other than a few toiletry items and some towels, the room was empty.

Caleb leaned in the doorway and watched her search. Her body jolted when it brushed his as she walked out of the bedroom.

"Well, don't just stand in the way. Are you going to help me or not?"

He glanced at her then at the bed and smiled ever so slightly. Sam huffed and went back downstairs. Caleb's smile widened as he studied the bed. Yep, she was clearly flustered, and there was only one bed. Whether Sam liked it or not, they would talk. And he planned to make sure that talk ended up here.

Sam was already rummaging through the shelves by the desk when he walked in the room. Caleb opened the roll top desk and found a laptop computer. He turned it on only to be stopped by a password. He tried several potential passwords—Ben's date of birth, his girlfriend's name, Chem11. He looked up at Sam and around the room. He typed Sam. Nothing. He typed Samantha. The screen blinked and filled with small icons.

He started with the folder labeled "my documents." There were over forty files with cryptic signs. He methodically opened one file after another, scanning the contents. Some made sense, others did not. Many dealt with his research, but none seemed out of the ordinary.

Caleb decided to try a different angle. He logged onto the Internet. Immediately an icon popped up and the words "you've got mail" broke the silence of the room. Sam looked up.

"Did you find something?"

"Dunno."

Caleb was lucky. Ben had saved his password on this computer, and the mail inbox was full. Passing over about twenty junk mail messages, he found one, a reply message from a Dr. Naples labeled "as per request." He opened the message:

> *Hey Ben,*
>
> *How's life at the coast? Obviously not as exciting as RTP or you wouldn't be wasting your time looking up some old photograph and asking me questions about old files all the time. Don't you know all that sun will give you skin cancer? Come back. We could use your ugly mug around here.*
>
> *I attached the photo. Lucky for you, I had a copy stuck in the back of the desk drawer. Weber's copy didn't survive the explosion. Everyone's still in shock about Weber. Can't believe he would be so careless.*
>
> *Well, enough of the morbid. Paste the photo in your memory book and move on boy. Whatever ya'll were working on is ash now. And invite me to the beach. I could use some R&R. We'll drink a toast to his memory.*
>
> *Later,*
> *The Top Doc*

Caleb clicked on the attachment and watched as a large photograph of four smiling men filled the screen.

"Sam, do you recognize anyone in this photograph?"

Sam stood up and leaned over Caleb's shoulder to stare at the photograph.

The smell of the shampoo from the inn filled her senses, and she had to force herself not to lean her nose into the shiny curls. What was wrong with her? This was about Ben. She blinked and focused on the screen.

"Yeah," she said, touching the screen. "That's Dr. Naples, he was just a buddy of Ben's who worked with him at Briar Pharmaceuticals. He and a couple other lab techs joined us for lunch once and he looks almost the same as he did years ago. That one is Dr. Weber. He was Ben's supervisor just out of school. He died in a lab accident about four months ago. He was almost eighty, but Ben was really upset when he died. That's Ben. And, the guy in the background," she leaned closer and squinted. "Wait. Isn't that Anderson? What was he doing posing with a bunch of Briar employees?"

"Theodore Anderson? Are you sure?"

Sam stood up straight and leaned her hip against the bookshelf.

"I can't tell for sure from this photograph, but it sure looks like him. And he'd always turn away from the camera just like that if he ever saw me taking pictures near him."

"Is that when you were doing the story on Tad?"

"Yeah, I actually lived at his mountain house last summer, and Anderson was home a lot."

"Why would you be living at his house?" Caleb fought to keep the jealousy out of his voice, even remembering Anderson had already remarried the sex goddess then. Even knowing it was absurd, he still had trouble with the image of Sam living in any man's house. "Maybe you should tell me everything about that summer."

"Why? What does that have to do with anything?" demanded Sam. "I'm sure Ben just wanted a photograph of him and Dr. Weber. He loved that guy."

"Just humor me. We need to look at every angle, and I haven't seen any other angles." Caleb didn't look at her when he spoke; he knew his motives for squeezing information from her probably had nothing to do with her case.

"Sounds like a wild goose chase to me," she sighed and looked out the window. It was late, and she was tired and hungry. "Tell you what. You go through the rest of the stuff on the computer. I'll find something to cook in the kitchen. I'm just too tired and hungry to think right now."

Unfortunately, she was being reasonable.

CHAPTER EIGHTEEN

Abby was frustrated. She wanted to impress her big brother, but she was coming up empty handed. She had to face the fact that she had done everything she could with Caleb's case, but in her gut, she knew something was missing and she didn't want to give up.

The dead guy was definitely Charlie. Charlie Taylor. He'd been living on the streets for over five years. Periodically, he'd wave his little pocketknife at a tourist, ranting about the CIA or little green men. But he was basically harmless. The cops would haul him in to the public mental health facility for a 72-hour stay, but rarely longer. He'd been diagnosed as a paranoid schizophrenic, and after a few days of medication, he was always released back onto the streets of Charleston.

With this information in hand, Abby headed to the police station to confront the detective who had interviewed Charlie shortly after Ben Fuller's death.

"Hi, I'm Abby McCloud. We talked on the phone," she stretched out her arm and gripped the detective's hand.

"Come on back," he said. He smiled and a perfect row of white teeth flashed. He held her hand a second too long before nodding toward a desk in the back. "This way."

He was young, thought Abby, probably a year or two younger than she was. And cute—very cute. Problem was, he knew it. Well, he wouldn't be so cocky in a minute.

"So, Miss McCloud, you said you had some information for me?"

"I believe so, Detective Williams. You're one of the detectives on the Ben Fuller murder case, aren't you?"

"That's right. But you needn't worry. We booked the murderer."

"Did you?" Abby asked sarcastically, but he missed the implication.

"Yes, ma' am. Did you know the victim?"

"No." said Abby. It would be easy to play this guy. He was dying to brag about his accomplishments, but she pulled out her business card. Caleb would kill her if she didn't play by the rules. "I'm a private detective hired by that alleged murderer's attorney."

He looked at her card and leaned back in his chair to study her. She expected him to shut down, but to her surprise, he smiled. "I've got no beef with a woman detective. In fact, I find it sexy as hell. Just what can I do for you?"

Her smile was slow, sensual, and calculated. Her job had just gotten easier, but she decided to give him a break too. "You interviewed that homeless guy that lived in the doorway across from the murder site, right?"

"Yeah," he said, pulling open a drawer, shuffling through some files and pulling one out. He flipped through until he came to some handwritten notes. "Here it is— Charlie Taylor. He wasn't much of a witness. A true Looney Tune. Let's see. He said that a bat flew down the steps that night and swooped around and around the street lamp. He said the bat had been sucking blood and tried to suck his blood too but he chased her off."

"He said 'her'?"

"Yeah," he laughed. "Guess it was Batwoman."

Abby ignored the comment. "Did he say anything else?"

He looked back down at his notes. "He said the bat came back the next morning with a friend. I remember, he said he hid in his dark corner and listened to the bat scream, but when the alien ships with blue lights landed, he ran away. After that, he wouldn't answer any more questions. Just kept saying bat, bat, bat, bat. I finally slipped him a few bucks and left."

"Have you seen him since?"

"Nope, but then I didn't have a reason." He studied her face and raised one eyebrow. "Do I have a reason?"

She nodded. "Think maybe you should take a trip to the morgue with me."

He frowned but got the gist and stood. "Hey, Rick," he called, "I gotta go out for a while. Watch the phone."

His buddy looked up and his eyes traveled up and down Abby, "Sure thing, pretty boy."

Detective Williams rapped Rick on the back of the head as he exited.

The coroner rolled the body out and pulled the sheet back.

"Well, shit," said Williams. "Yep, that's Charlie. What happened to him?"

"Just got back all the lab tests," said the coroner. "Drug overdose."

"What drug?"

"Drugs actually. Some legal, some not. Heroin, antipsychotics, and booze—a depression cocktail. Probably went to sleep and never felt a thing."

"Heroin?" asked Williams with a frown. "Not his normal drug of choice."

"What do you mean?" asked Abby.

"He loved the bottle. Every extra penny went to booze. Don't remember him ever getting busted for heroin."

The coroner shrugged. "Who knows? An addict is an addict. Maybe the bottle wasn't enough any more. It's actually a normal pattern. But the thing is the heroin alone wouldn't have killed him. There was very little heroin in his blood stream, but add it to the booze and antipsychotic meds, and his heart probably just slowed down and stopped."

Williams nodded. "Thanks, man. Send me a copy of that report for my file."

Abby walked out with Williams. "Is that it?"

"Is that what?"

"Don't you think it screams foul play? A witness dies of a drug overdose from a drug he doesn't use."

He smiled at her and said, "You want to stay in town and discuss it in detail over dinner?"

She glared at him.

He held up his hands. "Okay, okay, but can't blame a guy for trying. No, I don't think there was foul play. He was a worthless witness and we'd already talked to him; so why kill him? If you've got something else, tell me and I'll follow up on it."

"No, I don't have anything else," Abby said with frustration. "Yet."

Williams handed her a card before she left. "That's my number if you decide dinner is a good idea."

He drove away, and Abby sat back in her car seat. Glancing at her watch, she thought she should head back to Savannah. She had other cases. She cranked her SUV, but turned left instead of right. She'd try to talk to someone at the abortion clinic with the stolen phone one last time. She'd gotten nowhere grilling them over the telephone, but she would try in person. That phone number was the only clue left.

Abby flashed her private detective badge at the receptionist behind the glass wall and hoped she wouldn't look closer. "Good morning, Miss. I'm Detective Abby

McCloud, and I have some questions about a stolen cell phone traced to this address."

The woman frowned at her. She wasn't a pushover, probably because abortion clinics had reason to be wary. "May I see that badge again?"

Abby cursed to herself and handed it over. The woman looked at it closely and glared when she pushed it back through the window. "I'm sorry, but if you have questions, you should ask at the local police department. All issues dealing with this clinic are confidential."

"Look the number for that cell was found on a dead man; maybe I could talk to your superior."

"No. I really must ask you to leave now."

"Listen, lady, I'm sure your boss will have a few seconds to answer my questions so the clinic doesn't become involved in a murder case."

The lady did not respond but slid the window closed. Abby smiled and waited, turning when the interior door to the office opened. Her smile disappeared when a large armed guard appeared.

"Miss, you will need to exit the premise."

He escorted Abby to her car and stood in the parking lot waiting for her to drive off.

Well, that had gone well, thought Abby. But she hadn't really expected to learn anything. Considering that the cell phones were handed out to patients like candy from a jar, there would be no way to determine who had had the phone last. It would be a simple matter for a drug dealer boyfriend to use it to deal drugs. After all, it would provide free minutes on a number that could never be traced to the dealer.

As Abby turned out of the parking lot, she glanced at the woman driving in. She drove a small white Mercedes and wore matching large framed sunglasses. Not the usual clientele for an abortion clinic but then she was probably a volunteer from the Charleston elite. Or the mother of a wayward spoiled child.

The woman's face nagged Abby all the way home. She was pulling in her driveway in Savannah when she remembered.

"Dammit!" she yelled, hitting her hand on the steering wheel.

Throwing her car in park, she pulled out the detective's number and dialed.

"Detective Williams, it's Abby McCloud."

"Change your mind about dinner?"

"Unfortunately, I'm already back in Savannah, but I do have a favor to ask."

"What's that?"

CHAPTER NINETEEN

Caleb insisted on helping Sam wash the dishes when they finished dinner. She'd found spaghetti noodles and a jar of sauce in the cabinet. The refrigerator had been empty except for a large screw top bottle of white wine. Ben was never the wine connoisseur.

Sam had had too much to drink. She kept sipping when the conversation lulled, and Caleb seemed content to say very little and just watch her. Now, his fingers kept caressing hers in the soapy water each time he added a new dish to the water. When a second glass almost slipped through her fingers to the floor, she threw the dishrag into the soapy water with such force it splashed water back in her face.

"I'm going for a run. You finish the dishes."

Caleb's expression never changed as he stepped forward to finish the chore. With his back to her, he said, "Just stay close to the cabin. It's not safe."

Sam was already annoyed and his dictatorial attitude just added to her mood. "There's no way in hell anyone followed us here, Caleb."

"Probably not, but I was thinking more of the bears."

"Oh," she hesitated. "Bears?"

Her gaze narrowed as she caught the laughter in his eyes when he turned to face her. Without another word, she stomped up the stairs and found her duffle bag that Caleb had tossed in the room earlier. She tried not to notice that it was spooning his bag. Unzipping it, she grabbed a tank top, shorts, socks, and shoes. She stepped into the bathroom to change. When she came out, tying her hair in a ponytail as she walked, she almost tripped when she saw Caleb lounging in the doorway across the room.

"You know, we could just get our exercise in here."

"Move." She shoved him out of the doorway, but not before he saw the fire flash in her eyes. She jogged down the stairs and out the front door.

He laughed. "I'll just cozy up the place while you're gone."

He thought about going after her. Even went so far as to pull out clothes and dump them on the floor. Then decided maybe he'd pushed her too far. He was kidding about the bears because they tended to avoid people. Plus, it wasn't dark outside yet, and four-legged creatures were the least of their problems right now. Caleb decided a long shower was better than a run with a woman who wanted to kick dirt in his face.

Pulling out his toiletry kit, he turned on the water to let it heat up while he brushed his teeth. The steam was rolling through the room by the time he stripped and stepped under the pounding stream of water.

The water hitting Sam was cold and hard. She had barely run ten minutes when the skies decided to dump pellets of cold, icy water on top of her head. In frustration, she shook her fist at the gods and muttered curse words under her breath. The only response she got was a rumble of thunder that sounded strangely like Caleb's laughter. She turned back toward the cabin. The cold rain hadn't even dulled the wine, but at least she had no headache.

He wasn't in the bedroom when she opened the door. His suitcase was open so he'd obviously changed before heading out to follow her. She decided to take a quick shower before he returned. The devil side of her brain had her smiling at the thought that he was walking around outside and was as cold and wet as she was. At least the rain would have hidden her path. She was braless so she tugged off her wet tank top and was using it to wipe her face as she opened the bathroom door. She walked straight into Caleb and shrieked, dropping her shirt and jumping back.

Caleb was standing before a steamy mirror shaving. Water glistened off his sleek chest. A rather small white towel was wrapped low around his hips. He turned and grinned as she opened the door. He was wet, but he was sure as hell not cold.

"Hey, I would have waited if I'd known you wanted to join me. But come on in, there's room for two in here."

Sam slammed the door and felt her face flush red at the muffled laughter from the other side. Angry at her own embarrassment, she jerked the door back open.

Caleb almost slit his own throat with the safety razor when he glanced in the mirror and saw Sam start to strip out of her remaining running clothes. She was naked from the waist up. And better than naked below. She had replaced the bit of pink lace with a blue one. As she bent over the tub to turn on the faucet, he saw that the back of the lace was a simple ribbon forming a T. The water splashed in the sink as he dropped the razor and turned to face her.

Sam looked over her shoulder. Gone was his mocking laughter. The intense heat of his smoldering eyes covered her body. A thrill shot through her, and she was emboldened by a sexual power she never knew existed.

"Caleb." Her voice was throaty and foreign to her own ears. She walked into his arms. Her lips locked with his, dueling, as they slowly slid to the floor

Twenty minutes later, Sam lay amidst wet towels on the cold tile floor and couldn't believe what had just happened. Caleb was nibbling her ear.

"One day, we're actually going to make it to a bed," he laughed.

Sam simply smiled.

Caleb suddenly stiffened and jumped up.

"Oh, shit!"

"What?"

"I stuck a frozen apple pie in the oven before I came up here."

Caleb yanked open the door and ran. Sam laughed as she watched the finest pair of buns she had ever seen vanish through the open bathroom door. Picking herself off the floor, she finished filling the tub and sank into the warmth.

CHAPTER TWENTY

They had dessert in bed. Caleb had spread a worn red-checkered tablecloth across the top, peeled the black crust off the very well done pie and stuck two forks in the middle. He had poured the rest of the wine in a large jelly jar to share. An old lantern's low light glowed from the end table. Sam's light laughter filled the air as Caleb told amusing stories about his three-year-old twin nephews. Sam's entire body and mind felt an at-home comfort she had never experienced before. She pushed her plate away and her hands circled the jelly jar tilting it back and forth to watch the lamplight's reflection against the wine.

Caleb watched Sam, wondering how he had ever walked away from her all those years ago. This was the Sam he remembered. Carefree and open. God, she was beautiful. He desperately racked his mind for just a bit more wit to make her laugh.

"So there I was pacing in the hallway stopping just short of the boys' bedroom door listening to the sobbing. But my big sister said I had to let them cry at least fifteen minutes before checking on them. She said at two they had to learn to sleep alone in their bedroom. But, hell, I was just the babysitter and the favorite uncle at that. I only lasted seven minutes. Checking my watch, I gave up and opened their bedroom door.

"And there they sat on the floor between the two twin beds. Matt had his diaper off and there were about a dozen balled up wet wipes surrounding him. Mark had another wipe in his hand and was about to pass it to his brother who was crying uncontrollably. My heart dropped to my stomach and I fell to my knees and began searching for injuries but found nothing. I pulled the sobbing boy into my lap and asked what was wrong.

"Matt just kept sobbing that he broke it, but I saw nothing broken. His brother chimed in explaining that Matt had broken his wee wee. That it was big and now it was broke. I looked around at all the cold wet wipes and suddenly understood. See, Matt was at that stage where boys sort of, well, umm, enjoy self exploration."

Sam's laughter filled the air.

"His mom was having a terrible time keeping his diaper on him at night. Here I was pacing the hall and my poor nephew thought he'd broken his most important body part," Caleb grinned.

"I quickly explained to the boys that it wasn't broken, it was just tired and it was supposed to look like that sometimes. I explained if he put his diaper back on and wore it all night, it would be fixed in the morning. And of course, his genius uncle was right. My sister couldn't understand why he was almost four before he would agree not to wear that diaper at night. He and I had to have another man-to-man."

Sam laughed so hard that light tears rained down her checks. Caleb pulled the wine jar out of her hands and set it on the table along side the empty pie plate. He traced her face with his fingertips, dipping a finger in her dimple. Her eyes darkened as he ran his thumbs across her eyebrows and pulled her forward, kissing her eyes, her nose, her lips. This time, the bed was close enough.

The next few days were surreal to Sam. By unspoken agreement, they didn't speak of their personal relationships, past or present. They just enjoyed each other's company. In the mornings, Caleb worked online while Sam went running. During the day, they went through Ben's notes looking for clues. In the late afternoon, Caleb worked on the car while Sam photographed the area around the cabin. Today, she was photographing him, he noted, rubbing dramatically at a spot of grease under his chin.

"How can I fix anything with you under foot photographing me every minute? I keep worrying about you getting my good side instead of fixing this engine."

Sam laughed. "What? There's a good side? Well, damn, I just wasted a roll of film. But then again, I can probably get a good price on these grease monkey photos of the future Senator from Georgia."

"You wouldn't dare."

"Hey, just doing my job."

Sam squealed as Caleb's arm snaked out and wrapped around her waist and the other grabbed her camera.

"Hey, no one touches my camera but me," she yelled, indignant.

"Yeah," said Caleb, holding her at arms link with one hand and putting the camera to his eye with the other. "Time I got some pictures of you." Pointing, he pushed the button and listened to the motor drive click off about ten shots before she managed to wrestle the camera back.

"Keep those greasy hands off my instruments."

He laughed, grabbing her from behind and placing one greasy hand on each breast.

"How about these instruments?"

She squealed, spinning out of his arms. She tried to act indignant, but Caleb starting laughing so hard that he sat on the ground. Glancing down at the perfect handprints encircling her breasts, she dissolved into a heap of laughter beside him.

She leaned over and kissed him on his laughing lips and then pushed him over on the ground and straddled him, leaning over to pin his arms to the ground. His laughter changed to a sensual smile and he lifted his hips upwards against the inside of her thighs. A small gasp escaped her lips.

Caleb's look turned smug. "Let's go inside and finish this."

Sam frowned at his arrogance, then with a self-confident smile of her own, leaned forward and kissed him until he trembled. She released his pinned arms and jumped up before he could grab her.

"When you finish fixing the car, we can finish this," laughed Sam, batting his hands away as he stood up and began stalking her. Peering under the hood of the car, she looked serious again, "Hey, how soon will you be finished? I mean, we exhausted our search of all Ben's papers two days ago."

The truth was Caleb had finished fixing the car three days ago. It really had just overheated. He had been using the car to spend more time alone with Sam. She was just starting to trust him, and he was afraid when they left she would withdrawal again. But the truth was they had to go. It was important that he find some way to prove to the court she was innocent.

Caleb sighed and shut the hood of the car. "It's finished," he said.

"Oh."

He read the disappointment and the fear of the future in that small word.

CHAPTER TWENTY-ONE

The ride out of the mountains toward Chapel Hill was quiet. Neither Sam nor Caleb wanted to talk about the magic of the cabin for fear the delicate bond they had created would shatter. So they rode in silence.

Sam looked out the window and saw a sign; Chapel Hill was fifty miles ahead. She sighed and Caleb gripped the steering wheel to keep from reaching out to her.

"Sam, I think . . . ."

"Where do we go from here?" interrupted Sam. She spoke quickly when his look showed he had misunderstood. "I mean, with my case. What do we do next?"

Caleb didn't want to talk about the case. He wanted to drive to Vegas then take her out of the country to safety. Even as the thought flashed across his mind, he felt the shock of it.

"Caleb? Did you hear me?"

"What? Oh, yeah." Focus he thought, as that knee jerk confirmed bachelor response kicked him in the gut, just focus. "Sorry. I was, um, thinking we should go visit that Dr. Naples and ask him if he knew what Ben had been working on lately. Maybe it'll give us a lead."

"Why Dr. Naples?"

"I don't know. That photo and email gave me an itch between my shoulder blades and that's an itch I've learned not to ignore."

Sam laughed. "Oh, sure, an itch. Growing a gypsy eye in the middle of your back?"

"Yeah," smiled Caleb, "something like that. It opened the first time I saw you."

Her smile drooped a little and he could have kicked himself.

"Sam," he tried again.

"So what does this itch tell you about Naples?"

He was silent a moment and sighed before answering her question. "I reread the email and it implied Ben had been asking a lot of questions just before he died. I looked for more emails to and from Naples but found none. Maybe Ben was erasing them."

"Hiding his tracks?"

"Maybe. I think we got the last one because Ben hadn't had a chance to open it."

"And you're thinking maybe Naples kept his emails or at least can tell us what Ben was asking."

"Exactly."

"Maybe. Naples and Ben could go on and on about minute project details. If they weren't involved in trade secrets, they did often bounce ideas off each other. I always zoned out when they started their science babble. They'd just go on and on until I'd remind them to eat and they'd laugh and return to a conversation down on my level."

Caleb nodded.

They decided not to warn Dr. Naples and arrived at his office just before lunch. To Sam's relief, Dr. Naples hugged her warmly and assured her that he never believed the press. He agreed quickly to lunch and to help in any way he could to find out what happened to Ben.

"I don't really know what I can tell you that might help. Last time I talked to Ben was at Weber's funeral. Ben was really upset. Kept going on and on about how it couldn't have been an accident. I just figured Ben was grieving."

"Did he ever explain why?" asked Caleb.

"Just that Weber was a stickler for safety on the job. And you know, it was weird. Weber was a sharp old bird, and I didn't see any sign of forgetfulness now that you mention it. Since Ben died, I've been giving Weber's death a little more thought." He paused, lips pursing before he continued.

"Ben had been visiting Weber's office a lot during those last months before Weber died. Maybe they were working on something together. Ben always respected the old man more than any other researcher, including me," he added with a laugh. "Weber was supposed to be retired but the company still used him for some small projects because his knowledge surpassed the young researchers. He was given free reign of the labs, night and day, as long as the company owned the rights to his discoveries. You know, there was one odd incident."

Caleb and Sam waited as Dr. Naples took another bite of his sandwich and washed it down with sweet tea. His brows wrinkled as he concentrated.

"I never mentioned it to Ben because, well the truth is, I just thought that Ben was being a little melodramatic about the accident and I didn't want to see him jeopardize his career by making crazy accusations. You know, he was doing some work for GloboHealth and they were paying him good money."

At the mention of GloboHealth, Sam jerked her head up and glanced at Caleb. Caleb's expression remained calm.

"Ben was working for GloboHealth?" asked Caleb.

"I don't think many people knew that," said Naples. "Everyone thought he was just teaching, but he was researching on the side. I knew and so did Weber. In fact, I always assumed Weber was helping him with something related to GloboHealth." Naples glanced at Sam. "Would have thought you knew this."

"Why would you think that?"

"I saw the *Time* article you did. Damn good piece, by the way. That kind of article always helps us researchers. You should do some more."

"I'm always looking out for a good story. But back to me knowing about Ben's work with GloboHealth. Why would I know that? What does my article have to do with it?"

"Oh, well, the story came out and I just figured Ben suggested Anderson hire you for that publicity stuff. Figured he would have told you about his work when you did the story. Big story for you and great publicity for Anderson."

"He never said anything to me. Ben, I mean. He never told me he worked for GloboHealth."

"Hmm, guess it was on the QT. The FDA's got too many rules to get research done fast and you don't want to taint the system with people doing favors. Anderson was probably desperate to buck every rule to save his son, but smart enough to cover his tracks."

"Cover his tracks?"

"You know, like a binding agreement with Ben to protect trade secrets. His paperwork probably extended to talking to reporters, including friend reporters. We sign them all the time. "

Naples looked a little sheepish when he added the last explanation.

"But you're sure he was working for GloboHealth?"

"Well, now, I could never say for sure, and to be honest, I hope you'll keep this between us. Truth is GloboHealth is the competition. And helping the competition is a terminating offense in this business. But most researchers are really more interested in cures and discoveries than the dollar bills. We often help each other out; sort of a silent brotherhood among scientists that no one ever talks about."

"Did you help Ben?" asked Sam.

"Oh, no, not me. I wasn't involved at all. Never even heard Ben mention the word GloboHealth. But you work with people long enough, you notice things and then just sort of ignore them." He took another sip of tea and seemed to hesitate before continuing.

"I saw some papers on Weber's desk once. I'd gone in to get him for lunch. Noticed the initials PUD and then a bunch of figures with red question marks—all of it on a spreadsheet with a GloboHealth logo in the left corner. Weber must have noticed because he quickly dropped a folder over it, grabbed my arm and said he was starving. We never mentioned it to each other. The unwritten code," he added with a crooked smile.

"When Ben died, I read in the papers about a girlfriend. Thought it was just a jealousy thing until the papers named you as the killer. Knew it had to be a lie, and I started thinking," he nervously glanced over his shoulder, relaxing when he saw the small deli was deserted except for a small soccer team with their parents. "The night Weber died, I worked late. I saw the light on in his office and was going to stop by and tease him about old men needing their sleep, but then I saw the main light go out and someone step out. At first, I thought it was Weber. But the guy was too tall, and walking like—I don't know—like he didn't want to make any noise. I dashed back behind the corner while his back was to me and listened to the man walk down the dark hall and out the front door."

"Did you know him?"

"Well," Naples began, looking uncertain and nervous, "I can't really say. I mean, it was dark in that hall and I really just saw him from the back, but I could have sworn it was Theodore Anderson."

"Mr. Anderson?" asked Sam.

"And you never told the cops?" Caleb demanded, shocked at this new information.

"It didn't mean anything. I mean, I just sort of figured that Weber was helping Anderson help his son, you know, helping him get that PUD drug through the FDA. I had no reason to ruin Weber's reputation with the company. Besides, his family wouldn't have gotten his company life insurance or pension if it looked like he was involved in helping the competition—no matter how legitimate the cause."

"What if Anderson turned on that gas burner?"

"What?! No, I don't believe that. That's crazy. It was just a stupid accident, and you'll never convince me otherwise. I'm sorry he died like that, and I'm even more sorry that Ben died, but you'd never convince me that one had anything to do with the other. Ben was hit in the head, and if you ask me, they should be questioning that pregnant girl. I don't believe for one minute Ben agreed to marry her. He would have said something—maybe, just maybe, she didn't like taking no for an answer."

"Or maybe it wasn't his," said Caleb.

"Damn straight. He may have said so, and she grabbed the closest thing and hit him with it. Bet she never meant to kill him," said Naples, turning to Sam. "Just your rotten luck that she picked up one of your camera lenses. But I'm sure it will all be straightened out." He sighed. "I really miss the boy."

"Me too," said Sam as tears filled her eyes. She leaned over in her chair and hugged Naples who patted her on the head.

"Sorry I don't know more that could help you, but Ben really never mentioned the girlfriend. That's what's so weird about it."

Sam grasped his hand. "It's okay. Someone has to know her."

They stood to leave and Caleb handed him a business card. "Call me if you think of anything else. It was nice to meet you."

"Hey, don't mention that Anderson encounter either. Don't know why I brought it up. Becoming a rambling old man. But the boss doesn't need to know a competitor was in the building. I could get fired or Weber's widow could lose the pension."

"Your secret's safe," promised Sam, giving the old man one last hug and they left.

Caleb was fuming when he got in the car. "What the hell do you mean his secret's safe? I'm an officer of the law. I'm required to turn over any information that may help in a murder investigation unless it's my client."

"Well, I am your client."

"Not Ben's murder. Weber's."

"There is no murder investigation for Weber."

Caleb started to argue then clamped his mouth shut. She was right. At least for now.

"Okay. I'll keep this under wraps unless I need it to help defend you."

"No," Sam snapped. "You will keep this under wraps, regardless. I will not have someone else die because of me!"

"Sam, that's ridiculous. No one died because of you."

"How do you know? It all seems connected to me and GloboHealth. Ben had said he was onto something big and he needed my help. Looks now like the only thing I helped him with was GloboHealth. And if Dr. Weber was killed because of GloboHealth then it all goes back to my story. I will not have Dr. Naples's life at risk because he tried to help me. Do you understand me?"

Caleb heard the fear and the pain in her voice and sighed. He knew none of it was her fault but he also knew she wasn't ready to hear that now.

"Here's the deal," he began. "I promise to say nothing unless I must to help you." He held up his hand when she started to object. "And I promise that, even at that point, I won't say anything until I've talked to you. Deal?"

Sam's body relaxed and she nodded.

Several minutes passed before either spoke again.

"So what do you think it all means?" asked Sam. "Why was Anderson in Dr. Weber's office?"

"I don't know. You know Anderson. Is he capable of murder?"

Sam thought back to the time she spent at the Anderson home.

"He was harsh and a bit cold. But murder, I just can't imagine it. Tad seemed a little intimidated by him, but I always thought it was because he was a strict parent. Very upper class and snobby; went strictly by the rules with everything. I figured Anderson must really love his son to allow me into his private sanctuary to take photographs. Tad was definitely lonely. I never felt there was a warm and fuzzy relationship between father and son. But never violence."

"What about his mother?"

"Oh, she died when Tad was only about two years old. I don't think he really remembers her. Anderson married one of the lab techs about six months later. The new Mrs. Anderson that you met at the coffee shop."

"How was her relationship with Tad?"

"In public, very attentive. When I was there, she mostly ignored him. They had housekeepers, nannies, and drivers to deal with Tad, and she spent her days doing whatever she wanted: tennis, hairdresser, shopping, lunch with friends. I always got the feeling that sometimes she simply forgot Tad existed—unless she was posing for photographs. Unlike her husband, she liked the media attention. I've got to admit, I was secretly happy when *Time* magazine chose a father-and-son photo for the spread and didn't include the new Mrs. Anderson. I heard she called and demanded that she have approval of which photos appeared in the article so the editor just edited her out"

"Could Anderson have killed his first wife?"

"What?! I don't—This is crazy. She had cancer."

"Such things have happened before. Young mistress, lots of money. And hadn't she been sick for years. Death may have been taking too long."

"No. It's just too crazy. You're thinking all this is because he killed his wife and somehow Ben found out and told Weber. No, you're just making up shit now. I still come back to that Sally Simpson and that it was an accident. We need to find more facts."

"You're right. Let's return this car and regroup."

CHAPTER TWENTY-TWO

"So you're the mermaid." Those were the first words out of John Greyson's mouth when he opened the back door and grinned down at Sam.

"What?"

"John!" growled Caleb.

"Body of a sea goddess. Blue heaven eyes. Sun kissed cascade of curls. The one that got away. Caleb, you were right, you were a fool."

"Oh, Lord," Caleb groaned and put his face in his hands. "John, have pity for Pete's sake. I did bring back your beloved heap of junk. I even tuned the engine."

Sam looked from one to the other in confusion.

"Heard all about you for years," continued John, grabbing her forearm and pulling her forward into a sunny yellow kitchen. He grinned, looking her up and down before he released her. "Yep, you're the one. But, I must admit, I thought you were a pink elephant. Only came out during drunken all-nighters."

Sam looked at Caleb who just grinned and shrugged.

"Oh, the stories I will tell you." John laughed and winked at Sam.

Caleb punched his friend. "John, dammit, you're breaking that bros-before-hos oath."

"Hey," said John throwing up his arms as he caught Sam's expression. "He said it, I didn't."

John laughed and lifted Sam's suitcase out of her hand. "You know, honey, you and I should talk. Photographers and artists mesh well together. I'll pose for you; you pose for me. You two want separate rooms, right? You know, Sam, Caleb here is a love 'em and leave 'em kinda guy. The kind with a little black book full of steamy names like FiFi and Lola. Me on the other hand, I'm a hopeless romantic looking for love."

"Shut up, John."

Sam simply raised her eyebrows and followed a laughing John. Caleb mumbled something about backstabbing best friends and followed the two down the hall. John laughed even louder when Caleb followed Sam into her room and threw his suitcase on the bed, turned, and slammed the door in John's face.

Caleb had taken two steps toward Sam when the door opened again. "Now, you two take all the time you want getting settled. I'll be in the kitchen. There's a phone by the bed if you need it. And kids, the second guest bedroom is just across the hall if you're feeling crowded. Or, Sam, I've got a wonderful king-sized bed at the end of the hall."

"I just don't know how I can repay your thoughtfulness, John Boy, but I'm sure I'll think of something," said Caleb dryly, shoving his friend out of the room and turning the lock. John's laughter drifted down the hall.

Back to the door, Caleb ran his fingers through his hair and searched for a way to explain John and the little black book. Sam's back was to him and she was pulling a change of clothes out of her suitcase.

"Is it okay if I take a shower and make a call?" asked Sam, turning with a smile.

The question threw him off guard. "Yeah, but about John and his babbling."

"What about it?" she asked with an innocent expression on her face.

"Um, nothing, nothing."

"Okay, see you in the kitchen."

Caleb walked out and closed the door behind him, shaking his head.

"Thrown out?" asked John when Caleb walked into the room and grabbed a beer out of the refrigerator.

"Nope."

"Damn, losing my touch. So is she the mermaid? What's the scoop between you two?"

"Like I'd tell you."

"Oh, come on, Caleb, where's your sense of humor? She's the one, isn't she? And all these years, I really thought she was just a drunken dream. I couldn't believe it when she walked through that door. If you'd warned me, I would've kept my mouth shut."

"Yeah, right."

John laughed. "Okay, maybe not. You got it bad, don't you?"

"Not that you deserve to know, but yeah. I'm gonna marry her. She just doesn't know it yet and you'd better keep your mouth shut."

"Damn. So can I have the black book?"

"You're not funny. And quit telling her that shit. She might believe you. I'm having enough trouble convincing her I care with all the chaos in her life right now."

"Hey, I just call it like I see it. But what is up with this case? After you took the car, I read about her case in the paper. She doesn't look like the black widow type. Or should I post Rocky at your bedside to protect you?"

Hearing his name, Rocky bounded into the kitchen and pounced on Caleb.

"Yeah, that'd be some protection," said Caleb as he leaned over and picked up a yipping Yorkie puppy that fit neatly in the palm of his hand. "He could annoy her to death."

Taking no offense, Rocky licked his thumb to clean the drops of beer that had sprayed when the top was popped. Caleb pulled out a chair and straddled it.

Sam let the warm water pour over her head, smiling as she thought of Caleb's baffled expression. Good to keep them guessing. But mostly what she felt was all warm and fuzzy. All these years, she'd thought he'd just used her and never given her a second thought. Summer fling. To learn she had haunted him, at least in his drunken dreams, meant that he had cared. Stupid ass, she frowned, why had he never called? Moreover, why had he cheated?

Remembering the cheating, she thought about the little-black-book comment, and the fuzzy feeling evaporated. She sighed. Well, she wasn't a mooning teen any longer; she was an adult enjoying a fling and discovering the big O.

She toweled dry and chose her ripped jean shorts and a sweatshirt, sans bra. Maybe she'd get him drunk and they'd forget their worries for a night. Apparently, she could learn a lot if she plied him with liquor. The thought made her smile. But her happiness dimmed with a twinge of guilt as she thought about Ben.

Walking back into the bedroom, she looked at the phone. Sitting on the edge of the bed, she picked up the receiver and dialed.

"Hey, Maggie, it's Sam."

"Sam!"

Sam listened to Maggie and soon she was dishing her own intimate details. Laughing and making mental notes of Maggie's suggestions, Sam decided to change her top and shorts. It was almost an hour later when she walked into the kitchen.

Caleb almost dropped his beer, letting it spill over the sides as he caught it. Sam loved Maggie. John snorted under his breath and winked at her. Who would have thought a thin t-shirt—sans bra—teamed with a pair of tiny gym shorts would elicit such a response?

A miniature dog darted across the floor to lap up the spilt beer. It looked like a large gerbil, and Sam laughed at the sight and scooped up the pup, bringing it to eye level.

"Hey, fella. What are you? You look like a snack for Wallie."

"Who the hell is Wallie?" asked John, as he snatched Rocky and cradled him safely against his chest.

"It's a cute little robot," commented Caleb dryly.

"Wallie is my mutt," laughed Sam. "But I promise, he really wouldn't eat your baby. At least, he wouldn't if he realized that little critter is a dog."

"Don't worry, Rocky, I'll protect you from this crazy woman and her cannibalistic dog."

"Rocky!" Sam laughed as John set the toy puppy beside a toy bowl full of food. "So what's going on?"

John glanced at Caleb and laughed when Caleb rushed to speak before John could comment.

"Nothing. Nothing. Just deciding what's for dinner."

"Yep. How do veggie burgers sound?"

"Gross, but beggars can't be choosers," said Caleb.

"I'll help," said Sam.

The evening was relaxed and fun. The three sat around the kitchen table eating veggie burgers, salsa, and chips and drinking margaritas. Sam laughed until tears rolled down her face at the stories the two told. Dueling stories. Each one more outrageous than the next. Before long, Sam realized her plan to get Caleb drunk had backfired. Since she was drunk by the second drink, it became obvious she'd be under the table before he reached the point of spilling his guts. But it didn't matter. She couldn't remember the last time she had been this relaxed or happy.

"Hey, guys, it's after midnight and some of us have work tomorrow. So good-night. Make yourselves at home." John affectionately slapped Caleb on the back almost knocking him off the chair. Then leaned down and gave Sam a loud smacking kiss on the lips.

"Lips off my girl, man!" yelled Caleb as he kicked out and missed.

John laughed and headed off to bed.

Caleb stood and then swung Sam up in his arms, making her world spin. The night was like a dizzy dream. As she drifted to sleep in his arms, she could have sworn he whispered, "I love you, Sam."

CHAPTER TWENTY-THREE

Sam rolled over in bed and her head exploded with pain. She groaned and cradled her head to steady it. What had she done? Tequila was the devil.

"Morning, gorgeous."

Sam groaned and pried open her eyes to growl at the voice. But she saw the voice had a breakfast tray with steaming coffee and a bottle of aspirin.

"Oh, thank God."

Caleb laughed as he handed her a mug and two aspirin. He crossed his arms and watched as she swallowed the pills and the entire cup of coffee in one long gulp. She then munched on a piece of dry toast, careful to chew very softly.

"Better?"

"Well, I may stop begging for death."

"Glad to hear it." Caleb threw back the covers, lifted a very naked Sam up in his arms and walked to the bathroom where he lowered her into a tub of hot water. Stripping off his boxers, he stepped in behind her and pulled her back against his chest.

"Okay, I guess death isn't so bad, because I think I made it to heaven."

Caleb laughed, hit the Jacuzzi button and held her as the circling steam filled the air.

An hour later, Sam laughed as she toweled dry. "Now that's a hangover cure I never read about in Cosmo."

"Always ready to show you new things." Caleb smiled and popped her with his towel. Before she could retaliate, he pulled her against his body and gave her one more lingering kiss. "I gotta make some calls. You get rid of that morning breath."

"Hey!"

He was propped on the bed with the phone tucked on his shoulder when she finished drying off and brushing her cottonmouth. His chest was bare and forehead wrinkled in concentration as he took notes. Sam's heart flipped, but she couldn't help but ask herself, what she was doing? She needed some lessons from Maggie to keep that fling line from crossing over.

She quickly dressed and went to the kitchen in search of more coffee. As she sat at the table staring at her coffee mug, she thought about Ben and felt a wave of sadness.

"Hey, I thought you were feeling better?"

Sam looked up. Caleb was leaning against the doorframe studying her.

A wistful smile flittered across her face.

"I was, but coffee returned me to reality and Ben."

"Yeah," commented Caleb as he walked over and poured himself a cup of coffee. "I just talked to the office. I'm getting a background check on Anderson to investigate the connection between him and Ben. We've got some time and at least what may be a lead."

He sat across from her, cradling his mug. "Sam, I've got to go back to Atlanta for a few days. Another case hit a snag, but I want you to come with me."

"No." Sam needed to return to her own life, and to distance herself from Caleb before she forgot who he was.

"Sam, don't make me pull the bail card again."

Anger flashed across her face. "Go ahead. I don't believe you. Besides I have a trump card of my own now. Something about lawyers sleeping with their clients."

Caleb's face flushed with anger, and he stormed over, slamming his fists on the table. "That's not what this is and you know it, damn it."

Sam raised her eyebrows but remained silent.

"This is such bullshit." Caleb paced and kicked his chair to the floor. Sam refused to budge, matching his angry stare with her own.

Caleb stared down at the chair as he gathered his emotions. Reaching down, he set it upright and straddled it, facing Sam. He raked his hand through his damp hair and changed tactics.

"Sam, I need to keep you safe, but I have to go to Atlanta. Just help me out for once."

She stared at him a moment then shook her head. "I need to go home. I have a life and job too, Caleb. And I've been taking care of myself for a long time—I don't need you to keep me safe."

When he said nothing, Sam sighed and continued, "I have no intention of telling anyone what is between us unless you force me to. You can't sit there and blackmail me and think I'll just meekly do what you say. I'm safe at home. I have Wallie and Maggie. Besides, no one knows where my home is. You couldn't even find it." She was glad he didn't bring up the break-in. She didn't want a new argument over why she couldn't go home.

Caleb knew she was right but it didn't lessen the anger boiling just under the surface. She made their relationship seem cheap. But he had no choice and she knew it.

"Fine. But I'm driving you."

"There's no bridge, remember?" Before he began shouting again, she added, "But you can drive me to my boat, and I'll have Maggie and Wallie meet me at the dock. I won't be alone."

"Sam —"

"Caleb," she said in the same mocking tone of frustration. Then, she decided she was pushing too far and softened her tone. "Caleb, I know how to take care of myself. My island is the safest haven I know. I haven't run into a pirate yet."

No response.

Sam sighed and tried again. "Caleb, I need some alone time. For me. And I need time to think, for Ben's sake. Please. I can't think around you."

Caleb knew he had lost. "Take a phone. Call me if anything even feels wrong. Call me if everything feels right. Just call me."

"Cell phones don't work on the island, no towers, but believe it or not, there is a radio phone at the park ranger station I can use. I'll call you when I get on the island so you won't think I skipped bail." At his angry look, she quickly added, "And I'll call you if I need help and to let you know I'm okay."

He nodded.

CHAPTER TWENTY-FOUR

She opened the passenger door and stepped out of Caleb's car. He walked her to her boat and fastened her life jacket. Wrapping his arms around the life vest, he pulled her close, kissing her until her head was spinning.

"Dammit, I'd feel better if you'd at least let me take you all the way to the house."

"Caleb, I do this all the time. It's the inland waterway, not the Atlantic Ocean. Besides if the water was any calmer, I could swim home."

"We could wait for the ferry."

"That's not until tomorrow afternoon. Besides, I thought you had a hearing in Atlanta."

Caleb was not happy, but he knew he was being overprotective. He felt her pulling away, and he needed time with her. He looked around the empty dock and conceded.

"Call me the second you get to the dock. If you don't call in 30 minutes, I'm turning around."

"Caleb, it takes 30 minutes to boat over to the island. Afterwards, Maggie's got to drive me to the station to use the phone and that's a good ten minutes. Make it an hour."

"Forty-five."

Sam rolled her eyes. "Bye, Caleb."

He pulled her in and kissed her hard before lowering her down into the small Boston Whaler. He stood and watched as she motored away and had to admit she knew how to handle a boat.

She waved and shouted, "Talk to you in an hour."

"Hell." But he laughed and headed back to his car.

Sam leaned her head back and closed her eyes, filling her lungs with thick salty air. She smiled and throttled up. She pulled up to the dock in less than twenty-five minutes and threw her line to Maggie who was waiting. Consequently, she almost went overboard when a 95-pound ball of energy landed with one leap into the center of the boat, knocking Sam off her seat into the hull.

"Wallie!"

"That's some well trained dog you got there," Maggie said dryly.

"He's perfectly trained," laughed Sam. "Doggie Lesson Number One: Love your master above all else."

She hugged him tighter before smacking his rump. "Okay, mutt. Out! Out, before you drown me."

With one last tongue lashing from chin to forehead, Wallie jumped back on the dock, sending the tiny skiff rocking violently. He sat and watched with his head tilted to the side while Sam gripped the sides for balance and laughed.

"Reckless mutt." She grabbed her two small bags, tossed them to Maggie, and leaped to the dock before Wallie decided to join her again. Sam tousled his head, and he looked up at her with his tongue drooping out the side of a gapping grin.

"About time you hauled that skinny ass home." Maggie bumped Wallie out of the way and almost knocked Sam down again with her hug. With a firm grip on Sam's shoulders, she leaned back for a closer look. "Well, my, my, don't we glow."

"Look who's talking," Sam grinned.

"Baby, I always glow. Now, let's head to your house and you can tell all over the bucket of crabs I've got in the back of the truck."

"Sounds like a plan, but first I need to swing by your place and call my bond master."

"Kinky."

Sam laughed.

"Caleb, we've already had this discussion. It's a deserted island for Pete's sake. Even has its own armed park ranger." Sam rolled her eyes as she held the phone to her ear. "Yes, she's right here as a matter of fact. Yeah. Okay, let me know what you find out. I'll check in every few days."

Sam blushed when Maggie laughed. "Okay, okay, every day, but I gotta go. Yes, yes. Okay, bye."

"That man's a goner!" said Maggie. She frowned as she studied Sam's red face. "And from that mushy look in your eyes, you're right behind him."

"That's ridiculous."

"Sam, I've known you a long time and that's a new look for you." Maggie shook her head before Sam could argue. "Hold that denial until I get you plastered. I've got two jumbo bottles of truth serum snuggled next to those crabs and time's a wasting. We'll take the short cut. It's low tide."

Sam grinned. "Fabulous plan."

With the windows down and Wallie safely surfing in the bed of the truck, Maggie flew across the edge of the surf sending a spray of salt water through the open passenger window. The beach was wide, flat, and endless, and the hard-packed sand made the world's best redneck racetrack. The radio boomed, rattling the dashboard as they belted out the latest angry chick song at the top of their lungs. Wallie provided the bass with his deep, happy barks. Sam was wet, happy, and relaxed by the time they bounced over a sand dune and into her driveway.

"Home," she sighed.

"Girl, you left out all the good parts," Maggie complained two hours later.

She lounged on the sofa with her bare feet draped over one arm, keeping beat with the music. Sam sat Indian style on the floor facing the distressed trunk that served as a coffee table. Wallie lay spread-eagled on the floor beside her, snoring softly. The table was littered with crab shells and two empty wine bottles. Sam sipped her fifth glass of wine and thought about the headache she would have in the morning, but an image of a naked Caleb and his hangover cure flashed through her mind making her blush and blurt out a denial that sounded fake even to her own ears.

"I did not."

Maggie's laugh was deep and contagious. "Don't worry. I looked up his picture on the Internet and I've got a great imagination. Still, you are not keeping with the spirit of a girl tell all. And I want to know if my imagination . . . measures up."

Sam threw a pillow at her and changed the subject. "What about you?"

"I'd tell if there was something to tell. It was like playing musical chairs all week with me always one step behind. He wouldn't even let me sit in his lap."

Sam laughed. "Never say it. Maggie finally met a guy who didn't swoon at her feet."

Maggie pouted. "Seriously, Sam. When I met him, he looked like he would swoon. Ate me up with his eyes. I let him know I was interested, and Lord knows, I'm not subtle, but I only got to first base once and he apologized for that."

Maggie took a large gulp of wine before continuing. "Shit, but he's gorgeous. Got this kinda shy bumbling thing going too. And I swear I heard him talking to God under his breath all week. But he spent the whole time keeping me at arm's length." She studied Sam. "Come to think of it, the minute I mentioned your name, he stepped back. I mean literally stepped back. It's a wonder he didn't step off the dock."

"Hey, don't even give me that look. He's not into me. I saw him a total of ten minutes."

"Doesn't mean he wasn't star struck. I've seen it happen to more than one guy who looked at you and started stuttering. You're just too oblivious to notice."

"Yeah, right. No really, Maggie. He's Caleb's friend and, if anything, he treated me like a funny little sister."

"How?"

"Okay. Well, he had my Jeep, right? I told you how Caleb bullied me into leaving the equipment with Jim. Well, I leaned in the open window to give him explicit directions about taking care of my stuff. I was kinda pissed at the time."

Sam frowned, recalling the conversation. Caleb had been watching from the porch of the carriage house, resting against the post with his arms crossed as she talked to Jim. "I was bitching about Caleb being an overbearing control freak, and I should be taking my own car and my own stuff. Jim laughed and patted my head like I was some two-year old babbling, and he yelled at Caleb just before he left."

"Exactly what did he say?" asked Maggie.

"Jim yelled, 'So that's the way the wind blows' and Caleb yelled back, 'There is no wind. Not even a breeze.' Come to think of it, I don't know what the hell they were talking about. I just wanted my Jeep."

"What else?"

"Jim said he'd been waiting almost ten years for someone to get to Mr. Cool, Calm, and Collected. And he laughed saying pay back was a bitch but now Caleb knew how all those women felt wanting something that they could never have. He cranked the Jeep and said he couldn't wait to meet my Maggie—that she must really be something special. He peeled out of the parking lot like he owned my Jeep. I could hear him laughing, but I couldn't figure out what was so funny."

"He mentioned my name?"

"Yeah. I told him to turn over the Jeep and my camera equipment to you. I think Caleb told him about you too but I don't know what he said."

"So you told him my name?"

"Well, duh. I told him to give my stuff to my girlfriend Maggie. He asked how to find you and I told him I'd let you know he was coming and, besides, we lived there alone so it shouldn't be difficult. And he said something about Caleb mentioning I had a girlfriend."

"Wait, you said it just like that? 'My girlfriend Maggie'?"

Maggie started laughing until tears were streaming down her face.

"What? Did I miss something? What's so funny?"

Maggie stood up, leaned over, and kissed Sam on the lips, making a loud smacking noise.

"Don't worry, girlfriend, everything's great. Look out, Jim."

CHAPTER TWENTY-FIVE

John opened the door and laughed. Caleb's little sister stood on his doorstep looking like a drowned tabby kitten.

"Well, if it isn't Little Orphan Annie."

"Move aside, Daddy Warbucks."

He ruffled her curly red hair as she ducked under his arm into the kitchen. Abby was mortified.

When Caleb had called and asked her to investigate a possible connection between GloboHealth and Briar Pharmaceuticals, it should have been just another step in the ongoing investigation. But no, overprotective big brother had made the job contingent on her staying with John. Adding insult to injury, he'd insisted John accompany her to Briar Pharmaceuticals. She worked better alone. Besides, what good was a hippie trust-fund artist who resembled a tall, perfect Robert Redford. Dammit. She hadn't seen John since she was a mooning teenager.

She flushed redder as she thought about how she had forgotten that she was no longer a teenager and had dressed for the reunion. A sexy green dress with a scooped cowl neck, revealing just enough to pique interest, and a hemline falling just a couple of inches above her knees to add maturity. She had wrapped a multi-colored Italian scarf from under her breasts to the waist showing off the figure of a woman, not a girl. The final touch—strappy, grown-up high heels. But ergo, the damned flat tire just two miles from his house.

She had stepped out of the car and her heel had snapped. Tossing the ruined sex shoes in the back of the SUV, she had pulled on her favorite shoes. Just as she had gotten the old tire off, the skies had opened up. She could swear the thunder sounded like a deep chesty laugh from the gods. Her carefully ironed hair had sprung back to its heritage. Now, she stood in John's kitchen, water dripping from her fingertips and puddling around her plaid Keds. The sexy cowl neck of her dress sagged like old lady boobs and the once beautiful pale emerald green was tie-dyed in bright streaks.

John grabbed a soft white dishcloth and ran it across her face before she could do more than stammer. The top of her head came just to his shoulder, and she looked like she weighed about a hundred pounds completely wet. Her freckles stood out against her pale white complexion and he saw her shiver. Her giant green eyes dared him to laugh again. He did.

"Kid, you're freezing." He wrapped his arm around her, pulling her against his warm, hard body. "And very wet."

She shivered again. But this time, it was not from the cold.

"Come on," he continued. "Let's get you out of those wet clothes and into a warm bath."

The words had heat infusing her body. "My suitcase's in the car," she began, pulling out of his embrace before she further humiliated herself.

"I'll get it, you go start the water. Last door at the end of the hall. Go ahead," he urged with a small shove. "Start the water. I'll put your things in your room." He watched her leave and noted how the wet dress clung to her well-defined ass. He shook his head at the wayward thought and headed outside to grab her suitcase.

Abby stood for a second. It was a wonder he hadn't patted her on the butt. How did he do it? She was a successful private investigator with a legal, loaded handgun stuffed in her brand new Kate Spade purse. She'd brought down a 200-pound, armed and crazed ex-con in a Savannah alley just this week. Why did he make her feel like a five-year-old carrot-top with a skinned knee?

In self-defense, Abby decided to find the tub and regroup. She stepped into the hallway and looked left, then right. She frowned and went left. The bedroom was large and mono-toned but comfortable. A brown down comforter covered the bed and there was a herringbone couch in front of a fireplace. The floors had plush, plaid rugs scattered over polished heart of pine planks.

French doors at the back of the room opened to a bathroom that dreams were made of. The tub was a small swimming pool with too many jets to count. The walls were a mosaic of green glass and the cabinets, a rich coffee brown. A thick, white guest robe hung between the tub and the shower. And the shower—there were no words. Jets on three walls and a two-foot rain showerhead hanging from the middle of the ceiling. The glass door met the ceiling creating a perfect steam room. Abby was hard pressed to choose between the tub and the shower. But the colored glass jars filled with bath salts were the deciding factor.

John entered the guest room and tossed Abby's suitcase on the bed. He frowned at the silence in the bathroom. He walked over and listened at the door and then knocked softly and cracked the door.

"Abby?"

Silence. He pushed the door open and stepped in. "Abby?" Empty. Now where did that girl go? He walked out of the room and opened the remaining guest room. Empty. He frowned.

Stepping back out into the hallway, he focused on his bedroom door and smiled. Could be an interesting week. He debated a second.

"Caleb's sister, Caleb's sister," he mumbled the mantra to himself and left her suitcase in the guest bedroom, walking back to the kitchen to make hot tea and a late night snack.

Abby sighed in relief. The bath salts had turned the water blue and silky. She ducked her head under the water and shampooed, filling the room with the smell of fresh lemons. She was reluctant to leave the warmth but knew she had to face John again. She toweled dry and wrapped herself in the robe that swallowed her and brushed her toes.

Abby stared at herself in the robe and decided she looked five again! No way was she facing him in this robe. She walked out into the bedroom to dress. Her suitcase was not there. Forgetting her looks, she stormed out to find John.

He was sitting at his kitchen table sipping tea and homemade muffins. He looked so granola, she thought.

"Was my suitcase too heavy for you? Where the hell are my clothes?"

He looked up from his tea and choked. She should have looked ridiculously childish in his robe. But she didn't. She was the sexiest thing he had ever seen. Her hair had been towel dried and hung in ringlets halfway down her back. Her skin was no longer pale but a delicate rose. And her lips—plump and ruby red. The fact that she was wrapped in his robe made his mind conjure fascinating images of her naked body underneath.

When he choked, Abby blushed deeper. She knew she looked ridiculous, but twice in one night was almost too much to bear. She fisted her hands on her hips and glared.

The movement had John swallowing his tongue. The robe gapped open to just below her belly button. He could see the sides of firm white breasts. A distinct line down her flat belly begged to be traced with his index finger to the small mole just at her bikini line.

Abby saw the fire flash in his eyes and glanced down to follow their path. She gasped and pulled the two sides of the robe back together all the way to her nose. She inhaled deeply to steady her nerves and she was overwhelmed. The combination of Irish Spring and Old Spice assailed her nostrils and the realization struck her.

"It's your robe."

"Yeah. I'd be happy to take it back," he said, regaining his composure. Slowly, he stood, stalking her. Before she could react, he was on her. His hands slipped under the robe and tugged her against him. He bent over and nibbled her lips, testing.

Her world exploded. His hands were warm, running down her back and cupping her bare bottom as he pulled her up to his body. She responded without thought to the kiss she had dreamed of half her life.

John was lost when he heard the moan deep in her throat. Her lips parted and he sank into the kiss. Lost. The smell of fresh lemons and soap.

"John," she whispered when he lifted his head to rain kisses across her eyes, her checks. Her hands slid up his chest to his face. He moved his hands up to push the robe off her shoulders and leaned back to look at her face. Reality hit.

"Abby." He practically shouted the word and jumped away, turning his back on her. "Oh, shit! I'm sorry. Caleb will castrate me."

It took Abby a second to regroup. Her head was spinning.

John turned back around, pulled the two sides of the robe closed, and tied the belt tightly. He stepped back again and put his hands in the front pockets of his jeans. He looked at her red, swollen lips and almost stepped forward again.

"Caleb's sister," he mumbled under his breath.

"What?"

"Nothing, nothing. Ummm, your clothes are in the guest room at the other end of the hall. Maybe you should put something on before joining me for tea."

Abby had recovered from the kiss. Just barely. Looking at John, she was amazed. She suddenly felt her self-confidence return. Her shrug was lost in the volume of the robe.

"Your robe. Your room," she stated and smiled, pulling out a chair and sitting down. "Sorry, you should have come in and dragged me out. But I must admit I wouldn't have gone easily. Thanks for the wonderful bath."

John needed to run from the room before he did something foolish again, but he saw the impish grin and regained some of his own composure. Two could play at this game.

"No problem, sweetheart. You're welcome in my tub anytime. I happen to know that there's plenty of room for two."

Abby felt the conflict in her stomach that fluttered at the word 'sweetheart' while jealousy stabbed at the image of another woman in his tub. Maybe she was out of her league. Her lips still throbbed from the kiss and she touched them absently.

The innocence of the movement rushed through John and he felt his body respond. He turned quickly and poured her a cup of tea and threw a muffin on a plate. Setting the food in front of her, he stepped to safety and sat down across the table.

Abby picked at the muffin. John watched silently. He could behave himself for a few days. He just had to picture her as the sixteen-year-old with the clown clothes she called high fashion. He remembered her at his college graduation. She still had braces and wore leggings instead of hose. They were striped and reminded him of the ones worn by the Wicked Witch of the West when Dorothy made that crash landing. The image relaxed him and the hunger had vanished from his eyes when he glanced back up. She was just John's little sister again.

Abby saw the change but didn't know what had changed. Her insecurity sparked her anger again.

"I guess I'll head to bed. I've got a lot of work to do in the morning. I'm going to spend the day checking out a few facts before I head to Briar Pharmaceuticals."

John felt the brush off and held on to it like a lifeline. "Fine. What time are we going?"

"I really don't need you to go with me. Caleb forgets I'm all grown up."

John wasn't having that problem. He was working on it though. It would help if she'd stop leaning over in that oversized robe.

"I promised Caleb I'd go with you; so what time are we going?"

"Look, it'd be a lot easier for me if you just stayed here and tinkered with your toys. Caleb will never know."

"But I will. What time?"

Abby rolled her eyes and stood up. "Fine. Caleb is paying me enough to deal with you too. We leave at nine a.m."

Abby stood and left. John's eyes traveled down her back. The thick robe covered her beautiful derriere—if only his fingers didn't have such a wonderful memory. Then, he grinned. Tomorrow should be interesting.

CHAPTER TWENTY-SIX

Caleb signed his name to the brief and tossed it in the out box on the corner of his desk. He checked his watch. Midnight. Rubbing his eyes with his palms, he sighed and swiveled his chair around to face the Atlanta skyline. A full moon silhouetted the tall buildings that twinkled with intermittent lights.

He'd been back a week, but Atlanta no longer felt like home. He had to face the fact that no place felt like home without Sam. He swiveled back and pulled out a folder and opened it. The words swam before his eyes. Sam's trial was set to begin in one month. Talk about a speedy trial. He still had no clue who had killed Ben Fuller or why.

The phone rang, and he glanced down at the blinking light. His first thought was Sam—until he remembered how late it was and that she had no phone. He let it ring three more times before he picked up the receiver.

"McCloud."

"Hey, big brother, thought you'd still be at the office."

Caleb smiled. "Hey, Abby Girl, looks like I'm not the only one working late. Tell me you found something."

"Nope, sorry. I went through the file cabinets at Briar Pharmaceuticals and couldn't find anything relating to Ben

195

Fuller, Theodore Anderson, or GloboHealth. Even took your worthless friend John with me to distract Naples so I could plant a couple of spy cameras. John's been helping me monitor them for a couple of days, but we've found nothing."

Caleb sighed. "Damn. Thanks for trying, sis. You can drop it for now. I think the Anderson link was probably just a wild goose chase, but it was the only clue we found."

"Caleb, I've been giving a lot of thought to those clues."

"Yeah?"

"Maybe they weren't murder clues?"

"What?"

"Maybe they were just clues to lead Sam to Ben like you said. You know a treasure-map-marriage-proposal kind of thing."

"I told you, he and Sam were just friends. Nothing romantic."

"To Samantha maybe, but you said the mountain cabin convinced you that he was obsessed with her."

"Yeah." Caleb frowned and leaned back in his chair. "You might be right. But that doesn't change the fact he was murdered."

"No, but I'm thinking maybe you should look at the pregnant girl again."

"The formerly pregnant girl."

"Whatever. But she's running and scared. I saw it in her face that day in Charleston. And another thing—I told you that I saw that lady, you know the one that came out of Sally's building the day you paid me to spy. Well, I saw the same lady at the abortion clinic where that stolen phone originated—the one homeless Charlie had the number for."

"Yeah. You got an ID on her? Are they linked?"

"No, dammit. Sorry. I could kick myself for not recognizing her that day, but I've got someone posted in case she ever returns. They'll call me with tag numbers, and

I've got a Charleston detective who promised to run the number."

"I don't even want to know how you got that promise."

"No, you don't. But listen, Caleb, I don't like the fact that the woman was in Sally's building and the abortion clinic. And the phone number on the dead guy links the three somehow. I really don't believe in coincidences. Maybe Sally and Ben were not headed down the happily-ever-after path, but the abortion path. Maybe the clinic gave Sally a phone and she was paying the homeless guy to spy on Ben."

"I don't know, Abby. The Sally Simpson I met was a skittish little mouse and the homeless guy had a knife."

"But she was in nursing school. Who knows, she could have worked at the clinic where he was being treated. I'll check that angle. But let's just say Ben wanted her to abort and she went so far as to schedule an abortion. She could have had a fight with him and hit him with the lens because it was handy. Maybe she ran out and didn't know he was dead. If she found him the next morning, the shock of what she'd done could've made her miscarry. And that woman I saw, well, she looked high society. Maybe she does charity work with unwed mothers and came to see her because of the miscarriage or a follow-up of some kind."

"It does make sense in a convoluted way," he admitted. "If Ben wanted more than friendship from Sam, an unwanted child by another woman would end that dream. And when I talked to Sally that day she acted scared when I told her that I was going to find the killer."

"Here's her mom's address and phone number. I'll email some background information in a minute. I'd go myself but I've got to get home to protect another client. She's an abused wife and the husband is getting volatile. I should have enough to get him arrested in a week or two."

"Damn, now I'm going to worry about you *and* Sam. Why don't you go back to art school?"

"Nope. I love my job. And don't worry, I know how to handle myself whether you believe it or not."

"You know, John mentioned that he was enjoying your visit and that he kinda enjoyed the spy business. I could suggest he take a vacation in Savannah and hang around for a week or two until that guy is booked."

Abby was glad he couldn't see her blush through the phone line. "No!" she barked.

Caleb laughed at her adamant response. "Abby, some day you and John have to stop this rivalry. He's my best friend, and he can be a lot of fun. You let grad school turn you off to the artsy types, but he's different. Think of him as a laid back virtual brother."

Brother! Abby almost snorted. That was the last thing he would ever be. "I gotta go, Caleb. Be careful when you talk to Sally. She may be tiny, but when cornered even a kitten can be dangerous. And if we're right, this one could be deadly. Keep me in the loop."

"You got it. And if you change your mind about John, I'm sure he will tag along with you back to Savannah."

That time she did snort—just before she disconnected.

Caleb fiddled with the notepad and switched his computer back on. Sally Simpson's hometown was Ware Shoals, South Carolina. Talk about small. Looked like the population was less than three thousand. Caleb studied the photograph on the driver's license of her mother, Sarah Simpson, in one of the attachments Abby forwarded. As an attorney, he didn't want to know how she got it. His sister tended to respect justice more than the law. The woman resembled her daughter. Tiny, frail with giant blue eyes. She was only thirty-seven. A young mother.

Her wedding date showed that Sally was born six months later and divorce papers showed that her father stepped out of the picture six months after that.

He'd go to her home Sunday morning. Maybe Sally didn't attend church and he'd catch her at home alone. Then again, questioning her in front of her mother might yield more answers. Either way, he needed answers or a new lead—he glanced at the file again—and soon. But for now, he thought eyeing the couch, he needed a few hours sleep.

"Mr. McCloud? Mr. McCloud?"

Caleb opened his eyes, a little disoriented. Looked down at his shoes and remembered he'd decided to catch a few hours sleep on his office couch. His secretary was shouting his name as she set a cup of steaming coffee on his desk. He swung his legs over the side of the couch and sat up to face the woman who took better care of him than his own mother. She was a short, sixty-year-old woman with a messy grey cap of curls and just a bit rounded at the middle.

"It's eight a.m., Mr. McCloud. Lucky for you, I start my day early. You've got a hearing at 10 a.m. in Judge Harper's courtroom for the Sutton appeal. I picked up your suit from the cleaners on my way home last night. It's hanging on the back of your door." She put her hands on her hips and turned to stare at him for a moment before shaking her head. "You know, you need a wife."

"Miss Sarah Mae, you've got to learn to breathe between sentences." *Miss* before the first name of a Southern woman was a requirement in the South. "And it's a sad but true fact of life that today's wives refuse to pick up their husbands' dry cleaning. I for one thank the Lord every day for wonderful Southern secretaries."

Caleb stood and walked over to his desk, dropping down into his chair and cradling the coffee cup. He sighed in pure pleasure with the first sip.

"Don't I know it," she grumbled. "But if you had a wife, she'd make sure you picked up your own dry cleaning on your way home to a real bed."

"But I love waking up to your pretty face every morning. And until that husband of yours kicks off, I'm stuck with the couch."

Sarah Mae laughed. "Those Irish genes run deep in your soul with all that blarney. Oh, and your new client, Miss Jennings, is holding on line one."

"Why didn't you say so?!" yelped Caleb as he slapped his coffee down on the desk hard enough to have it sloshing over the edges. He hit the blinking button with unneeded force and grabbed the receiver.

Sarah Mae's eyebrows rose with interest, and she pulled his door shut behind her at the wave of his hand.

"Sam!"

"Oh, Caleb. I was about to hang up. Sorry, I didn't mean to disturb you. I could have just left a message with your secretary."

"You wouldn't dare."

Sam grinned.

"I just called to see if you had any news."

"As of last night, no. Abby suggested I talk to Sally Simpson again."

"Abby?" Sam hated herself for the spurt of jealously that rippled through her veins.

"You know, Abigail. My kid sister. Glow in the dark red curls, green eyes, turned up nose. Five-foot nothing. Kinda resembles a Christmas elf."

Sam laughed. "Caleb! I remember you talked about your sister a little, but I never met her, remember? You complained she followed you and your friends around. I don't think you ever used her name—just grumbled about The Pest."

"Ha. Ha. Yeah, I was a little harsh back then. She's all grown up now with her own detective agency. She's fierce. More like a sprite than an elf."

"So you told her about my case?" Sam's spirits dipped at the thought of what Caleb's little sister must think of her.

"I hired her to look into some things. She was just with John checking out Briar Pharmaceuticals again. She said it was a dead end. Seems to think Ben's clues were more a way to get you alone in the cabin and maybe Sally found out. You know, the jealous lover scenario."

"I still think that's ridiculous. Didn't the eyewitness tell the police they saw a tall woman with blonde hair running away from Ben's apartment that night? And why would she come back the next morning?"

"It was night and Sally does have strawberry blonde hair. More red, than blonde, but who knows what it'd look like at night under street lamps. Witnesses are often wrong, and the old lady next door doesn't impress me as a great witness. Maybe Sally saw the lens, argued, hit him with it, and stormed out. Maybe she didn't even know she hit him that hard. She shows up the next morning with make-up breakfast treats, finds him dead in a pool of blood and runs, screaming. She didn't hit me as the premeditated type."

"But why blame me?"

"Well, technically, she didn't. The cops did. But here's a new twist; Abby said she saw a South-of-Broad type coming out of Sally's apartment building just before Sally hightailed it down to the local moving company. She saw that same woman at a Charleston abortion clinic a few days later."

"What does that have to do with anything? Who was the woman?"

"Abby's working on that, but she suggested maybe she was doing charity work with unwed mothers, and Sally had visited the abortion clinic at some point."

"I see where you're going. Things weren't so peachy keen with Ben and Sally. So maybe they weren't thinking marriage, but abortion. That makes so much more sense! Ben would have kept the abortion thing a secret from me to protect her privacy."

Sam felt the hope surge through her. "But how can we prove it? If she killed Ben, even if it was an accident, she'll never talk."

"Babe, I was a great prosecutor before I was a great defense attorney. You got the best of both talents on your side."

Sam smiled. "And a cocky attorney too."

"Only with you, baby. Only with you."

Sam blushed. She couldn't believe how quickly they'd fallen into the old corny banter of their early years. But her silly grin soon vanished and she wondered how her heart would recover from losing him a second time.

Caleb frowned at the silent receiver. "Sam?"

"Yeah, I'm here. Did your sister find out anything else?"

He noted the subtle withdrawal in her voice and scowled, but decided to ignore it for now. "Not as of midnight last night. Hold on a second. I'll check my emails."

"Okay." She listened as he clicked his keyboard and wished she could be there with him.

"Nope. Nothing else from Abby, but you got an email sent to me to deliver to you."

"I did?"

"Yep. I think I'm jealous. Maybe I'll just delete it."

"Who's it from?"

"My main competition. Cute guy named Tad. Seems to me he mentioned marriage last time you saw him."

"Tad! Read it to me."

"Okay, but if he proposes again, he and I are having a heart-to-heart." Caleb skimmed the email.

"'The spelling is a little hard to decipher. Phonetics, I think, but I can translate. 'Hi Sam. It's me Tad. I'm emailing you. Hope you get it soon. Can you and Wallie come see me and Eva? Dad says you're too busy and I should leave you alone but that you and Wallie can stay in the guest cabin for a few days if Mr. Caleb will assure him it's safe. What does assure mean? Can you tell Mr. Caleb to send Dad that assure? Don't worry; the cabin is safe. Eva and I play house in the cabin. Nobody yells if she pees. Love Tad.' I'm not sure I can compete with that. But at least I've got him beat on spelling."

"I do love that boy. I think I'll pack up and drive there tomorrow if you can get word to Anderson."

"I don't know, Sam. It might not be safe."

"Anderson?"

"Well, yeah, Anderson, driving to the house, going alone."

"You just said Anderson wasn't involved. Besides, sounds like Anderson wants assurances that his son is safe from me. If Anderson murdered Ben, he wouldn't need any assurances, would he? And I can tell you this—Anderson loves Tad and would never use him that way. I don't think I could be in a safer place. Anderson's house is a fortress and has a full staff. Tad will be glued to my side, and they even asked me to bring my own personal guard dog."

"You don't even have a phone. And it still bothers me that Anderson may have been with Weber the night he died. Just give me a couple of days to check out Sally's story again, and I'll go with you to the Andersons."

It was tempting. She missed him. But it was time to return to her regular life, depending on no one but herself. "No. You weren't invited. Plus, my trial is in a month, and I can't just sit here. I'm going crazy. I have got to get out of here."

"Yes, but Sam, someone did follow us to Chapel Hill."

"True. But it wasn't Anderson or we would have had a tail all the way to the library. You know as well as I do that it was probably a reporter. We haven't had any problems since. We weren't even followed after we left Briar Pharmaceuticals or when you got your car out of impound."

"True." Caleb paused. "Damn, you should have been an attorney. But I still don't like it. What if I need to talk to you about the case?"

Sam smiled. She knew she'd won. She reminded herself that she liked doing things alone. "Look, I'll borrow Maggie's cell phone. She has one she turns on the minute she sets foot in cell-phone land. I'll talk to you the entire trip until I'm behind Anderson's gated estate in Asheville. I'll stay through the weekend and meet you back either in Atlanta or Charleston on Monday, depending on what you find out from the Simpson woman."

Caleb reluctantly conceded and hung up the phone just as Sarah Mae buzzed in over the intercom. "You're going to be late for that hearing."

Caleb dashed out, grabbing his suit jacket and pulling it on over his wrinkled shirt.

CHAPTER TWENTY-SEVEN

"I can't believe I'm loaning you my phone. I've been telling you for years to get one," said Maggie.

"I know, but I never really needed one before."

"Yes, you did. It just messes with that whole run-and-hide routine you got going."

Sam scowled.

"Fine. But on one condition."

"Maggie, I've got to have the phone tomorrow. I'll give it back to you next week. I promise."

"One condition."

"Fine, blackmailer. What condition?"

"You get your own phone as soon as this mess is over."

"That's crap. Besides, I hear they don't allow cell phones in the big house."

"Don't even joke about that. You're not going to prison, even if I have to strap you on the back of one of my turtles and help you swim away to some new deserted island. Got that?"

Sam laughed. "Yeah, got that. But you do know I'd drown strapped to the back of one of those things. They hold their breath for days at a time."

Maggie joined in the laughter. "True, but believe me, Samantha darling, I make a much better girlfriend that those ugly prison bitches."

This time they both laughed.

"Hey, when I get back to Charleston, want me to pump Jim about you?" asked Sam.

"No way. If anyone's pumping Jim, it's me." Maggie's smile was wicked. "Hey, and don't answer any numbers you don't recognize on caller ID. My men are way too much for you to handle."

Sam climbed in the Jeep and went back home to pack. The ferry wouldn't arrive until ten a.m. the next day, and she had some invoices and paperwork to finish so she could mail them from the mainland.

She sat down at her desk and frowned. Wallie came over and nudged her hand until it plopped onto the top of his head, and she absently scratched between his ears. Something was different, but what? She looked at the white binders lined up along the back of the desk. Each had a color-coded label. That was it. Someone had moved them. They were straight, neat, and in alphabetical order from left to right. The straight and neat was normal, but for Sam, the alphabetical order was backwards. Sam enjoyed a dyslexic view of the world when it came to filing. Ben had been the only one that had ever noticed.

Would Jim have looked through her papers? Maggie had said he checked on her house every day. But why? Sam pulled out the notebooks one at a time to see if anything was missing. But other than the order, everything was the same.

Sam shook her head.

"I think I'm losing it, Wallie."

Wallie mumbled deep in his throat.

"You don't have to agree with me."

Sam finished her paperwork and stuck the envelopes in a bag to take with her. Next, she finished packing her clothes in her backpack along with her sleeping bag and some other essentials in case the guest cabin didn't have a bed. She hadn't unpacked her small camera bag since her last trip. Her heaviest bag was the one with Wallie's food. Sam looked at the backpack and two other bags by the door and decided the Andersons would take one look and worry she was moving back in.

It was after eight a.m. If she didn't hurry, she'd miss the ferry.

"Hold still, Wallie. I'm not playing. I just need you dry enough that you don't make my Jeep smell like wet dog for the next six hours."

Wallie was bouncing with energy. So much for wearing him out with a run before the long drive. He knew the suitcases meant she was leaving, and he was worried he wasn't invited.

"Calm down, nutcase. I'm not leaving you. You're about to meet your child bride Eva. Arranged marriages and all that."

Sam was sure she smelled like wet dog now and she didn't have time to take another shower. She changed clothes again and walked out to the Jeep with her arms full. Wallie dashed ahead of her.

"Back seat, wet mutt." He obliged with one leap, a silly grin, and a series of yips and grumbles. She wondered if she could teach him to say "Eva" before they reached Tad's house. Sometimes she swore he talked.

She returned to the house to get her last bag and lock the door. She was almost in the driver's seat when she remembered Maggie's cell phone was plugged in by her bed.

"Shit!"

Wallie barked once in agreement.

Dashing back in for the phone, Sam paused in front of the framed *Time* magazine cover. Something tugged at her memory. She stepped closer to study Tad. Wallie barked again with impatience.

"Right. Ferry." She grabbed the phone and its little charger. Then, on an impulse, she went to the shelf opposite her bed and pulled the binder holding the contact sheets and negatives from the *Time* photo shoot. She grabbed the loop off her light table, threw all of it in yet another tote bag, and dashed for the door.

"What took you so long? I was two seconds from jumping in my car and heading out to look for you."

"Geez, Caleb, maybe you should reconsider careers. Ever think of being a parole officer? Or maybe a prison warden," Sam began.

"I get the picture. But it's still almost one and the ferry was scheduled to leave that little island this morning. You promised to call."

"And I'm calling. It took a half hour to get off the ferry. Afterwards, I had to go by the post office, drop off my mail and pick up mail. Wallie had to pee, and I wanted a country ham biscuit for the trip. And of course, if I got a biscuit, Wallie wanted one too. And after that Wallie needed a second stop, and he takes his time finding just the right dump spot."

Caleb laughed. "So you've been busy. Or at least Wallie has been on the move, so to speak."

"Exactly," laughed Sam. "But we're finally on the interstate and my pain-in-the-butt lap dog is asleep in the back seat."

"Lap dog?" Caleb's heartbeat sped up again. "I thought you said Wallie was a guard dog?"

"Hey, no dog is too big to be a lap dog. Ask Wallie. He's a 95-pound rottweiller. Don't worry. He'll bare his teeth if any bad guys put a tail on me."

"That's not funny, Sam."

There was silence a moment.

"Caleb," said Sam, suddenly serious. "I'm not used to checking in with anyone. I know you're my attorney and you posted bail, but you've got to ease up on the leash a little bit."

"It's not because I'm your attorney, and you damn well know it."

Sam said nothing.

"Sam."

"Look, I think it's better if you just think of me as another client. Now that I've had some time. The mountains, well, that was just—I don't know. It shouldn't have happened. So let's just forget and move on. I need to talk to you about Jim."

"You're changing the subject."

"You're a smart one."

"Sam, we will talk." He didn't want the talk to be over a cell phone so he moved on. "Okay, I'll bite. What about Jim?"

"Did you tell him I'm gay?"

Caleb was glad she couldn't see him blush. "What would give you that crazy idea?"

"Maybe the fact that he thinks Maggie is my lesbian lover."

Caleb choked on his coffee. Sam was laughing so hard she woke up Wallie who started licking her ear.

"I never said that to Jim."

"So what did you say?"

"You know, I really need to get back to work. Hey, there's my other phone. Call me again in about an hour."

"Sure thing. Maybe you can give me some pointers on what kind of sweet nothings to whisper in Maggie's ear next time I see her." She laughed when she heard the click at the other end of the phone.

Sam leaned over and turned up the radio, and Wallie settled back down for a nap. The next time Sam called, Caleb only spoke a second. He was in a client meeting and told her to call when she got there.

Sam arrived at the Andersons about six-thirty p.m. She settled into the small cabin and tried dialing, but there was no cell service. She settled Wallie in and walked to the main house. Brick and stone-edged paths weaved through the

209

estate. Benches were placed under shady trees and the lawns were lush and green with perfect edges. The front of the house had a large verandah with perfectly spaced, overflowing flowerpots hanging between each archway. At the base of the wide steps stood two life-sized lions, one on each side, greeting guests with their stony stares. The knocker on the door was also a lion, and Sam wouldn't have been surprised if it came to life like the one in Mister Magoo's Christmas Carol.

Sam knocked on the door and waited.

Anderson opened the door. "Good evening, Miss Jennings."

"Hello, Mr. Anderson. I'm sorry to disturb you, but I had hoped to see Tad before I settled in for the evening. And, if it is not too much bother, I need to use your telephone. My cell doesn't seem to get service here."

Anderson opened the door wider, and Sam stepped in. "The phone is by the sofa. I will call Tad. I allowed him to wait up for you, but I had expected you earlier in the day."

"I apologize. The drive took longer than I expected." She lifted the phone and hesitated. "It's long distance, but I'll only be a minute. I just need to tell someone I arrived safely."

"Someone?"

"Caleb McCloud."

"Yes, certainly. Take your time. I'll be in my study." He paused and turned back. "You know, Miss Jennings, you're here solely on Mr. McCloud's word. I expect you to be careful with my son."

"I love Tad. I would never harm him. Or anyone else, for that matter."

"So I've been informed. Nevertheless, you will be watched."

"I'm here. I just unpacked and came back to call you. The cell phone doesn't work here."

"Great. So much for calling your lifeline. Sam, is everything okay there? I got that itch again." Caleb thought he was doing a great job of hiding the fact that he had been pacing back and forth in front of his office window for almost an hour. Every time he'd dialed her number, he'd gotten Maggie's voicemail. He was going to have to meet this woman one day.

Sam knew that his question carried double meanings.

"Everything is great here. No worries. It's just like when I was here before. Tad and I will have a wonderful weekend together and I'll meet you Monday. Or maybe even Sunday night."

Sunday? Caleb sat up straighter.

"Sam, something is wrong."

She sighed. He read her so well. "No, not the way you mean. It's just. Well, it's difficult being viewed as a murder suspect. My welcome has been a little cold. I guess I wasn't expecting it."

"I can be on a plane to Asheville within the hour. You and Wallie pick me up. We'll spend Saturday visiting Tad together and then drive to Ware Shoals."

"No, no. I'm just tired and being stupid. But I don't think I'll stay until Monday. I'll leave at lunch Sunday and meet you for dinner in Charleston at the same B&B. You know, it occurred to me that we never searched Ben's university office."

"Shit, I never even thought of that. Sam, I'd feel better with you by my side."

"No. I'll be fine. Besides, you're right. If Sally sees me, she probably won't talk." The picture of Ben's outline and the stained floor flashed in Sam's brain. "Caleb, be careful. If she did kill Ben, even if it was an accident, she could be dangerous."

"So you do care. Would you miss me if I floated off to heaven?" He said it light-heartedly, thinking one day she would admit it.

"I'm thinking that hot place below is more likely." She paused and her tone changed. Her voice became soft, almost a whisper. "Seems I've always missed you, Caleb McCloud. I love you."

Shit!

Sam slammed down the phone and stared at it in horror. She'd done it again? When was she ever going to learn how to play the game properly? The last time she had blurted out her true feelings, Caleb had left. Damn. Shit. Crap. She closed her eyes. Maybe, deep down, she wanted him to run so she could get back to her life. She just felt so alone here that the words popped out. She had told him just hours ago to forget the mountains.

"Sam!" The word was said with pure joy.

Sam turned and her heart lightened. "Tad!" She engulfed the small boy in her arms.

"You're here! I'm so happy. Where's Wallie? Didn't he come too?"

"Yep. We're both here. He's down at the cabin right now."

"I waited for you so we could eat together. Maybe Eva and Wallie could eat together too."

"Well, Wallie already ate. Maybe we could have just the two of us tonight, and the pups can meet each other tomorrow morning."

Tad lower lip stuck out and he started to protest but his father stepped up behind him and placed a hand on his shoulder.

"I think that's for the best," he said. "Tad, it's already after seven. You may eat dinner with Miss Jennings in the dining room; then Molly will put you to bed. I'm certain Miss Jennings is tired from her journey and would like to retire early."

Tad stiffened and ducked his head to stare at the floor. "Yes, sir."

Sam heard the command directed at her also, but it riled her. "Of course, your father is right, Tad. But since I have come all this way, maybe I could give Tad his bath and tuck him into bed with a story."

"Yes!" squealed Tad.

It was clear by Anderson's expression that he did mind. But she could have sworn his eyes softened slightly when he looked at Tad. The look was gone when he raised his head. "We follow strict routines here as you might recall, Miss Jennings. However, since you have just arrived, I see no harm in one short bedtime story after Molly has given Tad his bath."

Sam nodded at his clipped voice and coldness.

"Yay!" exclaimed Tad. Anderson avoided Tad's exuberant hug by stepping back and returning to his study, closing the door with an elegant click.

Tad's shoulders drooped for only a second before he spun around and grabbed Sam's hand.

"We're having grilled cheeses and salads. My favorite and yours. And you can meet Eva. She's hiding under the dining room table waiting for you. And for dropped food."

CHAPTER TWENTY-EIGHT

Sam spent Saturday morning feeling about twelve years old again. She and Tad took Eva and Wallie walking down to the river where the two mutts proceeded to jump in, roll in the dirt, and dart through the carefully laid out picnic. Eva grabbed a sandwich and escaped, running under Wallie before Tad could catch her. Wallie simply sat on her.

Tad had screamed with laughter when his puppy yipped and released the flattened sandwich. Declaring it full of dog germs, he divided it in half between the two dogs. With the dogs happy and sleeping in a pile under the shade tree, Sam and Tad had finished their lunches.

It amazed Sam that Tad was so energetic. Gone was the boy who was so thin and frail. The one who had looked as if his bones would break if he moved too quickly. Today, his cheeks were plump and rosy. His eyes twinkled with delight over a butterfly that landed on Sam's head. No longer did they sink back with pain. Sam reached over and brushed the dried mud from his arms. Normal little boy arms, dotted with mosquito bites instead of needle marks.

"Hey, we'd better go get washed up."

"I like being muddy."

"Well, some women do pay a lot of money to have mud caked all over them."

"Really? Why? That'd be fun." He frowned. "My step-mama wouldn't like it though. Something about being clean like God."

"Cleanliness is next to Godliness?"

"Yeah. That's it."

"Well, that's one more reason we'd better get cleaned up. Besides the gardener over there, the one hiding behind that skinny sunflower, looks like he's trying to decide if he should hose us off."

"That'd be fun!" Tad said. "But I'm not allowed to talk to the gardener. But you can! You can ask him."

Don't talk to the staff, thought Sam. Tad's stepmother had literally stepped into his mother's shoes, Prada shoes, at that. With a blind ambition only understood by other trophy wives, Sue Anderson lived for the society page.

At least fifteen years younger than her husband, she had bottle blonde hair that was never allowed to show a dark root. Her well-endowed figure rivaled Barbie's, but Sam's trained eye had her betting that it was a very expensive figure. Her outfits were Dior and Chanel. She was cool, remote and proper. Her hasty marriage had Sam wondering if the rumors about the ongoing affair had been true. But to give the woman credit, when Tad had become sick, she had been diligent, if not warm and fuzzy, in making sure he was well cared for and fighting for the experimental drug therapy.

Sam thought back. The initials PUD had sent fear coursing through every parent's veins. A tiny, three-year-old blonde girl named Emma was the first recorded casualty of PUD—Pediatric Ulcerative Disease. Emma had been a happy, healthy little girl who spent her days building sandcastles with her stay-at-home mom. But one day she stopped eating. Told her mom that little stomach people poked at the food with forks and it hurt. The tests were endless, but doctors could find no cause. For months, her desperate parents watched their daughter fade away, hollow blues eyes lost in a pale thin face.

Emma developed bleeding ulcers as the disease spread. Her white cell count rocketed up, and near the end of her tiny life, her ANA lab tests came back abnormally high. She was dead within nine months and the autopsy of her stomach seemed to confirm her fear of little people and pitch forks. And she was just the first.

PUD spread across the United States like an epidemic, striking only children under the age of six. The CDC worked furiously for a cause and a cure. There seemed no hope. Until Tad.

"Sam? Hey, Sam, look. I'm smearing mud just like those ladies. I made a cake too. Want some?"

Tad had spread mud all over his arms and legs and was now in the process of patting down the top of a lopsided mud cake."

Sam couldn't help laughing. "I've got a better idea. I saw a hose on the side of the house. Let's go find it before your stepmother returns."

"Yea! Eva and Wallie need a bath too."

That was an understatement, thought Sam, looking over at the dogs sleeping in a mud puddle.

They would have finished their impromptu garden shower before Mrs. Anderson returned if Eva hadn't tripped over her clumsy puppy feet and knocked Tad back into a brand new mud puddle. The boy and puppy were rolling in the mud when her car pulled up in the driveway.

Sue Anderson stepped out of her Mercedes and brushed her linen suit into place. Her round Chanel sunglasses hid her eyes, but Sam knew they were narrowed with anger.

"Theodore Joseph Anderson the Fourth, you and that mutt are filthy. Leave the dog outside and come in this minute. Don't touch anything."

"But Mama Sue."

"Mother Sue," she corrected. "And if you argue with me, you will spend the rest of the day in your room. As it is, Molly will help you bathe and you will not return downstairs until two o'clock."

Tad had started to argue and then thought the better of it.

"Yes, ma'am. I apologize for getting dirty."

"It will not happen again. Molly?" she called over her shoulder. Almost instantly a young woman appeared at the door. "Take Tad upstairs and see that he bathes and takes a nap."

"Yes, ma'am."

And they were gone.

During the entire exchange, Sue Anderson never took her eyes off Sam. "Miss Jennings, after you are clean and properly attired, I would like to see you in the parlor."

She hadn't waited for a response, but turned like royalty and walked into the house. Sam was left feeling like a mongrel that had sullied the queen's red carpet. Looking down at herself and the mud dripping off her legs onto the expanse of brick walkway, she decided that maybe she had.

"Come on, Wallie. I have been commanded to make myself presentable, and I think I'd better be quick about it."

"Mrs. Anderson."

"Please sit." She did not look up but continued to flip through the pages of the old *Time* magazine.

"I was reviewing the article you did on Tad, trying to convince myself that having you here is a good idea."

Sam started to speak but closed her lips when the chilly appraisal showed that the woman was not finished.

"Your photographs of Tad were moving. And I will concede that your article helped GloboHealth push the cure for PUD quickly through the FDA without the normal red tape. But, be aware, Miss Jennings, GloboHealth saved Tad and all those other children—not you. My husband believes that you are a saint. And now that Caleb McCloud, that political darling, has taken your case, he has decided you must be innocent.

"I am not so naive. Tad is the poster boy for GloboHealth and is thus a very valuable commodity to our company. I will not see you jeopardize his health with a garden hose."

"A commodity?" Sam recoiled at the word.

"Little boys can be bothersome, but Tad has proved his value. First, in his father's belief that every boy needs a mother, and then in the advancement of GloboHealth."

Sam eyes widened in shock and she glanced around. Sue Anderson laughed.

"I see that I have shocked you. Don't worry; we are quite alone. I would not endanger my position. I expect you out of my home by noon tomorrow. You will then make sure Tad forgets all about you."

"No matter what you say, Mrs. Anderson, I don't believe you can make Tad forget me. And I'm sure Mr. Anderson would be more than interested in your true feelings toward his son."

She smiled, and Sam felt as if she were sitting across from a classic Disney wicked stepmother.

"He will never believe you, my dear. I worked in his lab as a technician for four years before we married. Did you know that?"

She studied Sam for a moment before continuing. "Hmm, I see you did. Well, he was easy to seduce. His wife never had time for his needs after Tad was born. I filled the slot nicely. Her long illness and convenient death left Tad and his father alone. It was meant to be." She smiled. "And I keep Theodore very happy."

Sam heard the front door open and close.

"Sue, are you here?"

"In the parlor, darling. With Miss Jennings."

Mr. Anderson walked in, leaned over, and kissed Sue on the check. He was wearing a golf shirt and khaki pants. He was more relaxed but stiffened every so slightly when he noticed Sam sitting on the couch.

"Hello, Miss Jennings. I thought you'd be off entertaining Tad."

"She was, darling. Had him rolling around in the mud and bathing under the garden hose." She tsked.

"I see," he frowned. "Is Tad okay? He isn't feverish is he? It is a hot day, but this damp mountain air, and he has only recently recovered. I thought you were going to have him watched while I was gone, Sue."

She laughed. A lighthearted laugh, a one-eighty from the woman who had just labeled Tad a commodity. "He's fine, darling. Molly gave him a warm bath and tucked him in for a nap. You know I watch over him as if he were my own."

"Of course you do. But Miss Jennings, you must be careful with my son."

Sam nodded and stood to retreat from the rabbit hole. "I think I'll retire to my cabin until dinner."

"I think that's wise," said Anderson.

"It's all right, darling. She just forgot the rules for a moment. Didn't you, Samantha?"

Sam nodded. She turned to leave and decided she would say goodbye to Tad after dinner and drive to Charleston tonight. She'd wait and call Caleb tomorrow afternoon. She didn't want to interfere with his trip.

CHAPTER TWENTY-NINE

"Shit." Caleb hit the brakes hard and jerked the wheel. He felt the tires skid in the gravel before the car stopped dangerously close to the edge of a rocky cliff. There were two boards nailed to end posts and covered with chipped yellow paint marking the end of the road. He opened the driver's door, knocking a few more yellow chips to the ground, and stepped out to peer down the embankment.

"Holy shit," he exclaimed again. He couldn't see the bottom. Only a caldron of mist swirling up from what sounded like a river below. Caleb walked around and sat on the hood and decided he'd wait for the sun to do its job before getting back in his SUV. Already beams of light were melting the fog, breaking it into ribbons of ghostly beauty. And Caleb decided he'd appreciate that beauty as soon as he could cram his heart back in his chest.

He had obviously made the wrong turn, but that was understandable when you were driving through pea soup. When he got back to Atlanta, he was going to the dealer to get a refund on his fog lights. The only thing they did was light up the fog.

Caleb lay back against the hood and closed his eyes. Lord, he was tired. He couldn't sleep last night so he'd decided to get an early start to Ware Shoals. Of course, now he was here hours before anyone was awake. It was all Sam's fault.

How could she say she loved him and then hang up? And it had been so random. Right in the middle of a rant. And when had he started ranting?

Caleb laughed at himself. Now he was ranting in his mind. He hadn't realized how lonely he had been without Sam. His casework, both as a prosecutor and a defender, had been fast-paced and exciting. Because of his charisma with the press, after the first six months in the Atlanta prosecutor's office, he had been awarded the high profile cases. He seemed to have an innate gift in the courtroom. He was in the very midst of high society with a different girl on his arm at every fundraiser. His photograph appeared on the front page as well as the society page. Political editors called him a golden boy with a courtroom Midas touch, and the political cartoonists drew him with a cape. When interviewed, he was witty and intelligent with just enough self-deprecation to make him loved by Democrats and reluctantly admired by Republicans. He was exactly where he'd dreamed he'd be. He should be content. But he wasn't.

Caleb inhaled the rich, thick mountain air and sighed. He could hear the crash of water and feel the warm sun on his face. He sat up and opened his eyes.

Just below him, in the distance, was a waterfall pouring over the side of a dam. Out of the midst, a rainbow rose up to touch the sky. He smiled. He had found his pot of gold. He just had to save her first.

The color drained from Sally's face when she came to the screen door. Her home was tiny and old. It sat back from the main road, but the dust from passing cars billowed up and descended upon the front porch. Caleb stood, waiting for her to speak, careful to distribute his weight evenly in case the rotten floorboards gave way under him.

Her mother called from the back of the house. "Sally, who's at the door? You know I can't be late for Sunday school this morning. I'm teaching Edna's class while she's out with her bursitis."

Mrs. Simpson came to the door behind Sally and peered around, wiping her hands on a clean white dishcloth. "Oh, my. Hello, son," she said admiring the looks of the man before her. He was dressed in a nice pinstriped suit and just behind him she caught sight of his new SUV. "Sally, do you know this young man?"

"Hi," jumped in Caleb. "You must be Sally's mom. You have her looks. I'm Caleb McCloud, and Sally and I knew each other in Charleston. I'm a lawyer and she's been helping me with a case I've got going on there."

"A lawyer. Well, that's wonderful, but, oh, what kind of help is my Sally giving you? She's not in any kind of trouble is she?"

"No, I don't think so. Are you, Sally?"

Sally flushed and stepped out on the porch, pushing Caleb toward two rocking chairs.

"Of course not, Mama. I was just helping him with medical stuff from terms I learned in school is all. You go on and help Miss Edna with her class, and I'll come along later for church. I'm sure Mr. McCloud just has a few more questions about medical jargon. Right, Mr. McCloud?" Her eyes pleaded.

"Yes, ma'am. I was driving through on my way to a meeting and thought I'd stop by. Sorry I didn't call ahead."

Mrs. Simpson frowned slightly before glancing at her watch. "Well, I guess it'd be all right if you stayed on the porch and talked a bit. Sally, you get him some coffee and a little of that cake I made last night, and I'll just be on my way."

Caleb glanced around and saw no car. "Do you need a ride? I don't see your car."

Mrs. Simpson visibly relaxed. "That's sweet of you, son. But I enjoy the walking, and it's just up the road a spell. I walk it every day. I don't know if Sally told you, but I'm Pastor Wiggins' secretary."

"No. I didn't know. Well, if you're sure because it's no trouble at all."

"If I showed up in that fancy car for traveling only a few blocks, people would think I'd taken on airs. But thank you for your kindness. Sally, now you don't be late for service."

"Yes, ma'am." She turned to Caleb, her expression hesitant and fearful. "If you'll wait right here, I'll bring you some coffee and cake. She lowered her voice, "And give Mama time to get out of earshot, please."

Caleb nodded and settled down in a gray rocking chair. The arms were worn smooth in the center from years of use. He glanced toward the screen door listening for the sound of coffee cups and silverware. He hoped she didn't return with a gun.

She set the coffee and cake on a small table beside him and sat on the edge of the remaining rocker, turning to face him. He eyed the cup and looked back at her.

"You're not having any."

"I had my coffee earlier."

Caleb hesitated and then decided to risk poison because the nagging headache behind his eyes reminded him how much he needed the caffeine. He gulped down most of the cup before returning it to the table. He stared at her. She had dark circles beneath her eyes and her hair looked dull and unkempt. She twisted her hands in her lap, and her eyes looked like those of a doe ready to take flight.

"What do you want, Mr. McCloud?"

He paused until her fidgeting increased. He stared at her coldly before speaking. "You should have told me in Charleston that you're a murderer."

She squeaked. That was the best way to describe the sound that came out of her mouth—somewhere between a whimper of fear and a quelled scream. She grasped the ends of the rocker and leaned so far back in the chair, Caleb thought it might tip over.

"I'm not. I'm not." She squeezed her eyes shut, shaking her head from side to side.

"The facts say otherwise."

"You need to leave."

"I don't think so. I think you need to talk." Caleb paused to sip his coffee again. He was having a difficult time believing his bluff had worked. His mind scrambled at how to proceed.

"No. No. I just want to be left alone. Can't you just leave me alone?"

"I don't see that happening. If you'd like, I'll go with you to church, and we can sit down and discuss this with your mother afterwards. Maybe the preacher would like to hear your confession."

Sally's head drooped, and a tear tracked down the side of her cheek. Though he knew she was responsible for Sam's pain, he wanted to reach across the space and soothe her as you would a child with a skinned knee. She looked so small, so lost. It was clear her life had been a hard one. But that didn't excuse her. So he hardened his heart before she lifted her chin to face him.

"Please. She would lose her job if the pastor found out. Abortion is a sin."

"Abortion?" asked Caleb.

"And I didn't mean to have an abortion. I mean I was going to, but I didn't and then that woman came. But I swear, I didn't know."

Caleb sat silently and waited. Sally sobs were almost silent. He reached in his pocket and handed her a handkerchief but said nothing.

Suddenly, she reached forward and grabbed his hand. "Can you be a murderer if you didn't do it on purpose? I didn't do it on purpose. You're a lawyer. A good one. I read about you. Can you help me?"

So it had been an accident, thought Caleb. Well, that didn't surprise him. "Maybe you should start at the beginning. I already represent Miss Jennings, and I'm honor bound to help her first. But I'll be fair to you."

"You won't tell my mama?"

"No, I won't tell your mother or the pastor as long as you tell me everything."

She searched his eyes. Then nodded.

"It all started last fall. I was dating a guy named Jack. He was a third year medical student working on the same floor as me. I was having trouble drawing blood from an older patient. You know, bad veins. I went in search of my instructor, and Jack asked if he could help. He was short, but cute and funny. We started dating. I thought he loved me."

"Wait. You were dating this Jack guy? Not Ben?"

She took a deep breath. "Yeah, well I was—I had been, but he had stopped calling a few weeks before the new semester started. And then I had a class under Ben, but I kept having to leave because I was sick. Ben noticed. I was so stupid. I thought I had the flu. Here I was a nursing student, and I missed the obvious symptoms. Well, I was getting sick in the afternoons, not the mornings, so I guess it wasn't classic, but I should've known."

"So Ben questioned you about it?"

"Uh-huh. Ben asked me to stay after class one day, and I did. I thought he was gonna yell at me for leaving during his lectures. I just knew he was gonna flunk me, but he asked if I was okay. I told him yeah, but I thought I had some kind of flu bug 'cause my stomach was always upset. He looked at me kinda funnylike and said, 'A flu that lasts for several weeks with nausea that comes and goes and leaves you starving and sleepy?'"

She was staring at her hands now, and the tears had become steady rivers down her cheeks. "And I knew. I probably already knew, but I didn't want to know."

"Because Jack had stopped calling?"

She looked up and wiped her face and nodded. "Yeah, that and my mama. Mama got pregnant with me and had to get married. I never knew my dad 'cause he left right after I was born. Called my mama a whore and said he'd given the bastard his name and he didn't owe her any more than that. My mama scraped together money for me to go to school so I wouldn't have her life."

"What happened when you told Jack?"

"I didn't. I loved him, but I couldn't live my mama's life, having him hate me for trapping him. He called me a few more times, but I didn't call him back. I was scared I'd tell him."

"So you opted to have an abortion?"

"Well, yeah. I mean no. I went to an abortion clinic. Filled out all the paperwork. Even handed over five hundred dollars in cash after selling all my schoolbooks.

"I sat in that lobby and waited my turn as those other girls went behind the white door. Some just sat and chatted with their friends or boyfriends like it was nothing. Others were scared like me. When they called my name. . . ."

She looked up at Caleb.

"I couldn't get out of my chair. So this woman in a white coat stepped out and called my name again. I started crying. 'I can't,' I told her. 'I can't.' And I ran."

Caleb was silent a minute. He pulled a crisp white handkerchief from his pocket and handed it to her.

"So when did you go back?"

"I didn't. I never went back. But a woman came to me."

"A woman?"

"I don't know her name. Well, I think she told me, but I don't remember. It was three weeks later. This really fancy woman showed up at my door. I didn't know who she was, but when I let her in, she started talking about that clinic day and I kinda freaked. I remember she patted my hand and said she represented The Right to Life Something or other. She said she didn't work for the clinic but was a volunteer who helped unwed mothers who decided to have their babies. I was so scared and I couldn't afford a doctor. She'd come to my house, and one day, she told me that she was a friend of Ben's, but that he didn't want me to know because I might not let him help. She made me agree to keep it a secret."

"So Ben was just helping you because he was your teacher and worried but couldn't do more because you were his student."

Sally blushed. "Ben and I were kinda seeing each other, but I knew it could get him in trouble. He'd help me study on Mondays, and later we started having pizza on Friday nights and breakfast every Saturday morning. We got pretty close and he talked about the baby a lot."

"So he was going to marry you."

"I . . ." she began and stopped when his phone rang.

"Sorry, gotta get this," he said, recognizing the Anderson number. "Hello. Sam? Hello. You're breaking up."

"If you walk down to the end of the driveway, you'll be able to hear," said Sally.

"Okay, I'll just be a moment."

"I'll just dress for church and come back out."

Caleb nodded to Sally and yelled in the phone, "Sam, just hold on a second. Don't hang up."

He jogged to the end of the driveway. "Can you hear me now?"

"Yes," whispered Sam.

"Speak up. I can barely hear you."

"Listen, Caleb," she continued to whisper. "I think maybe we were right the first time. I was going to pack up and leave last night, but I needed to search Anderson's study."

"What the hell are you talking about?"

"Caleb, the *Time* photo of Tad. It was cropped. I looked at the original contact sheet last night. I think I found something, but I'm not sure. If I don't find it soon, I'm going to look again after lunch when Anderson leaves for golf."

"Sam, don't be an idiot."

"I don't have time to explain. But Caleb, Tad gave me something at breakfast this morning. He had it all wrapped up and told me to open it after church because it was a surprise. But I opened it when I got back to the cabin. I couldn't leave then. I have to make sure he's safe. I wanted to tell you but I've got to hurry."

"Sam, you're not making any sense. Slow down and tell me what is going on." He cringed when he heard a loud booming voice in the background.

"Miss Jennings, what are you doing in my study?'

"Oh, Mr. Anderson, I'm sorry. I was just using the phone."

"Well, use the one in the family room. I have work to do before Sue and Tad get back from morning services."

"Sam? Sam!"

"Oh, I had just finished. Sorry."

Caleb heard the click, but just before he could hit end and redial, he heard a second click and the phone went dead. Hitting end, he hit redial. The phone rang five times and a message machine picked up. Frustrated, he hung up and hit send again. This time he left a message to have Sam call him back.

A noisy truck engine sounded from somewhere behind the house. He heard chickens squawking from a pen he'd passed just up the road. The church bell rang to announce the start of service.

Caleb checked his watch and trudged back up the dirt driveway. He had just under three hours to make it to Anderson's house and Sally Simpson was going with him whether she liked it or not. There wasn't time to stop by the church so she'd just have to leave her mother a note. He felt a pang of guilt about manhandling Sally, but he had no choice. By the end of the day, he would have all the answers.

As soon as Sam's name was cleared, he'd do his best to help Sally.

Sally wasn't on the porch when he climbed the steps so he knocked on the screen and shouted. "Sally, I'm back. There's been a slight change of plans."

No answer. Caleb pushed the door open, leaned in and called out again.

"Sally?"

No answer. He walked in through the tiny living room to a kitchen with white metal cabinets and faded flowers on the wall. A table with two wooden chairs sat under a small window. Checkered yellow curtains blew inward and a note secured under a saltshaker flapped in the wind.

"I'm sorry. Tell Mama, I'm sorry. I can't stay here."

Caleb balled up the single sheet of paper and banged his fist on the table. The back door stood open and he could see a second driveway and a narrow dirt road leading down the mountain. He checked his watch and knew he couldn't go after her now. He smoothed out the piece of paper and withdrew his pen and wrote:

Mrs. Simpson, your daughter is in serious trouble. I'm sorry, but she was confessing to the murder of Ben Fuller when she took off. I don't think she meant to kill anyone—she said as much, but if she keeps running it will only be harder on her later. Please, if she calls you, would you tell her to call me? I'll try and help her.

He signed his name and placed the note, along with his business card, back under the saltshaker.

CHAPTER THIRTY

It was early afternoon, and Sam sat in the family room pretending to read when Mr. Anderson paused in front of her.

"Miss Jennings, I thought you were leaving today." He wore a pink golf shirt with neatly pressed navy pants. He glanced at his watch but seemed reluctant to leave now. "I believe Sue had a fund raiser this afternoon."

"Oh, yes, I know. I talked with Mrs. Anderson this morning, and she suggested I stay until after Tad's nap and take a few photographs for you. Tad wanted one with his puppy, but Mrs. Anderson preferred one of him in your desk chair. You know, just like the *Time* cover photo, only with a healthy boy this time. She said something about an ad campaign."

"She never mentioned it to me." Anderson frowned. "But it does sound like Sue. She is forever promoting the company."

He seemed lost in thought a moment. "Miss Jennings, I agreed with my wife the first time you photographed Tad. But flaunting our family publicly is not the Anderson way. My son is meant to run the company, not become its poster boy."

"I apologize, Mr. Anderson. I didn't know you disapproved. Maybe I could just stay to say good-bye to Tad. I could take a few snapshots of him and Eva. Just for your personal use, of course. Though I would like one for myself. I have missed Tad."

His expression softened. "Don't mistake my distaste for public displays as an attack against you, Miss Jennings. I believe I owe you a great deal for that article in *Time*. GloboHealth had been working diligently for a cure for PUD even before Tad became ill. But the FDA wanted years to test it. When Tad became ill, I was going to give it to him and damn the FDA. But Sue, thank the heavens for her level head, suggested the publicity might be a safer route. She pointed out that it would help other children who were suffering. Tad is an Anderson. And she was right. They allowed me to supply the drug under the supervision of the doctors at Saint Jude. And because of that, Tad is now a healthy, happy boy and not a single other child has died of PUD." Anderson's voice boomed with passion, and it was clear he had forgotten who his audience was.

"I know, Mr. Anderson. I also know that you would have given him the drug regardless of what the FDA said."

He looked taken aback, focusing on Sam's eyes for a moment. He nodded.

"You're probably right, Miss Jennings. But then that would have destroyed GloboHealth." He thought for a moment. "What you are unaware of at this time, but I am sure Sue is considering, is that we are on the verge of a vaccine for PUD. Within the next year, no child should ever suffer its symptoms again. I am sure that's why Sue wants the photograph. Take it. I'll decide what to do with it later."

He glanced at his watch. "Good luck with your trial, Miss Jennings. I believe I trust Mr. McCloud's instincts when it comes to justice and innocence." He turned and left. Sam sighed in relief, but fear coursed down her neck as she watched his car back out of the driveway.

Sam stood questioning her own instincts. He was a cold man, but a murderer? Maybe. Maybe if his son was in danger. But Ben would never harm a child. She had to search Anderson's study and quickly.

Sam waited until she could no longer hear Anderson's car. Glancing over her shoulder, she ducked into the study, pulling the door shut with a quiet click. She set the lens cap that Tad had given her last night down on the desk. Where had he found it? She would have to wait until he awoke and they were alone to ask. If need be, she'd take him with her. What was a kidnapping charge on top of a murder charge?

Sam turned and began searching the shelves. She had seen it on the contact sheet. A binder with the bold black words running vertically down the spine. Chemistry Eleven. She looked up at one more shelf, just above eye level, and felt along the edge. She reached into a gap between two thick textbooks and felt the vinyl side. It was there, pushed back just far enough to be hidden. Her hand trembled slightly when she pulled it down.

Sitting behind the desk, she flipped open the binder. Ben's handwriting. Pages of notes that meant nothing to Sam. At the back, were printed lab reports with a Briar Pharmaceuticals logo in bold black stamped in the corner. Numbers were circled in red, but they made no sense to Sam. A handwritten note in wiggling scribble appeared at the bottom of the last page:

> *Ben, you were right. It's synthetic, and it's in three of the five samples I ran. It was not in the second set of vials you sent. It is the Chernobyl of the pharmaceutical world. I don't envy your talk with Anderson.*

The itch was stronger and Caleb pushed the accelerator against the floorboard, gaining speed up the mountain. His cell phone rang.

"Sam!" he yelled when he flipped it open.

"Mr. McCloud. It's Sally."

"Sally."

"My mama called me. She thinks I murdered Ben. You told her I murdered Ben!"

Caleb yanked the car off the road at a scenic overpass before he lost reception.

"Sally, where are you?"

"My mama's hysterical. Why would you say such a thing to her?"

"Sally, you admitted murder. I heard you. Then, you ran."

"Not Ben. I didn't murder Ben. I found him there that morning. Blood everywhere. I told you. He was going to marry me and help me raise the baby even though he didn't love me and I loved Jack. He was the only person who cared about me other than my mama. I would never hurt him. Why would you say such a thing?"

"But you said. . . . Sally, if you didn't murder Ben, who did you murder?" His call waiting was ringing but he ignored it.

"The baby. I murdered the baby. But I didn't know I was. That woman. She said she was helping me and the baby. I thought it was vitamins. The IVs. She said they were vitamins and iron. Said I was too small and anemic."

"Sally, what woman?"

"I told you. She came to my house after the abortion clinic. Said she was there to help me through my pregnancy. The Right-to-Lifers, they do things like that. At least, that's what she said. The night before Ben died, she gave me a big IV. I had cramps all night. I wasn't going to Ben's that morning because I was sick. But she came to my door that morning. She had a gun. Told me I was to go to Ben's and take him some breakfast she had bought.

"I told her I was sick and needed to go to the hospital. She said no. The cramps were normal when you had an abortion.

"I told her I didn't have an abortion. She laughed at me. She drove me a block from Ben's and told me what to do and say. She said if I didn't she would hurt me. She didn't tell me Ben was dead. I was going to tell him about her. He would help me. I was scared."

"What did she look like, Sally?"

"Blonde and real classy. Like a model. I think she's really rich. She wore fancy clothes and high-heeled shoes. Not those white rubber soled things most nurses wear. She came back to my apartment that day I saw you. I thought she couldn't find me if I went home."

Caleb's heart raced. "Where are you now, Sally?"

"I'm in a Best Western in Greenville."

"Stay there until I call you back. You'll be safe there."

Caleb shut the phone and hit the speed dial.

"Abby!"

"Caleb, thank God, I've been calling you. The woman—the woman at the clinic and at Sally's! My guy got her tag number. The car belongs to Theodore Anderson. You've got to get Sam out of there. "

"I'm almost there. Call backup." He threw the phone in the passenger seat and held the wheel with both hands as he sped around the hairpin curves.

"So it was here all along."

Sam jumped. She hadn't heard the study door open.

"Ben was so clever. I would have never looked in my own home. Oh, and I see you found the lens cap too. My, my you've been busy. I know I shouldn't have kept a trophy, but I couldn't help it."

"You?" Sam gasped, her eyes locked on the gun. "You killed Ben? But I thought . . . . "

"You thought it was my husband." She laughed.

"But why?"

"You're reading the why right now."

Sam looked down at the lab pages in Ben's book. And looked back up at Sue in confusion.

"Oh, this is priceless. And they call me the dumb blonde. You have no idea what those lab results mean, do you?"

Sam shook her head.

"Ben worked for the company."

Sam nodded.

"Oh, you found out that much, interesting. I must admit I miscalculated by hiring him. He was too smart, but not smart enough to mind his own business. Well, in fairness to Ben, it began as a simple mix-up. I had him working on a new drug. Apparently, he picked up a couple of old vials of our kids' vaccine by mistake and ran an analysis. He found the synthetic virus in the vaccine. The stupid boy smuggled out some of the new vaccine vials and got his friend to run more tests.

"Synthetic virus?"

"A manmade virus. You know it better by its disease—PUD."

"PUD was in the vaccine? I don't understand. I thought you developed a vaccine to cure PUD. Was it a live virus?"

"No, darling, you're just not listening. GloboHealth has the government contract to provide childhood vaccines. Had it for as long as I had worked there. Not very profitable especially when people started suing, blaming their defective children on the vaccinations."

"Defective?"

"Autistic. The children became autistic and greedy parents used that to try and milk money out of GloboHealth. At first, I was angry, but then it gave me an idea. What if the vaccine really did cause kids to become sick?"

"You wanted to make kids sick?" Sam exclaimed. Her heart beat wildly as she tried to think of a way to distract the woman who stood calmly talking about infecting children as she waved a gun with each gesture. Keeping her eyes on Sue, Sam inched her fingers along the desk until she touched the edge of a letter opener.

"Honey, I thought I just explained that I'm not the dumb blonde. Now put that letter opener down and back up against that wall. That's better." Sue stepped further into the room so she was directly in front of Sam. The window behind Sue outlined her body with sunlight making her white silk shirt shimmer like angel wings.

Sam struggled for questions to keep Sue talking so she could think.

"Honey, you're an open book. You don't need to stall. I'm not going to shoot you yet. I need to tell you the whole story first. It's been so hard not to tell someone. Ben didn't really know. He suspected Theodore. Stiff, softheaded Theodore. It was so funny. Come to think of it, it's probably why he left the paper evidence here. Bet he was going to get the cops to search the house."

"This is what you were looking for in Ben's apartment?"

"In his apartment and in your house. I wasn't going to harm you. I needed you to go to jail for his murder. Oh, and there was Sally Simpson. She was just a bonus and made the story better. Lucky for me, Ben took me in as a confidant. He thought Theodore was using his son for fame and fortune, and I was of course helping Ben find the truth to protect Tad from such an evil cold man. Ben and I were old friends. We worked together at Briar Pharmaceuticals, did you know that?" She watched Sam's reaction. "No, I guess you didn't."

"We had a fling when he finished graduate school. A shame. I really liked him. He liked innocent, good girls so that's what I was for him. He told me all about you. He was heartsick. I decided he'd be my charity case. It was fun while it lasted. But really, I got sick of hearing how great you were."

She smiled. "So I moved on. I took a job with GloboHealth and met Anderson. A girl's gotta climb that corporate ladder. Good girl on the surface and bad girl in bed. Women can manipulate men so easily." She tsked before continuing.

"I really hated having to get rid of Ben. Such a shame. He really could have been a great addition to the company. And Theodore was beginning to bore me. A bit stuffy for my taste—always fighting my ideas for the company."

Sam stood shocked. Ben and Sue Anderson.

A light laugh filled the air. Not an evil laugh like one would expect. The sound reminded Sam of the giddy laughter of girls gossiping at a slumber party. The sound frightened her more than the gun. Sam ordered herself to think.

"But you killed Ben, and Mr. Anderson wasn't involved. I don't understand. Why would he kill Dr. Weber?"

"Dr. Weber?" Sue was surprised at the change of subject. "Now why would you think Theodore killed Weber?"

"He was seen. Mr. Anderson was seen coming out of Dr. Weber's office the night of the explosion. And Dr. Weber's reports are here." Sam pointed at the desk.

When Sue glanced at the desk, Sam started to lunge forward, but Sue turned back too quickly. The gun was pointed straight at Sam's stomach again.

"Oh, that's a whole different stroke of brilliance. I had Anderson drop by Weber's lab the night I blew him up. Poor silly old man, he thought Anderson was there to confront him about the lab results. Went pale as a sheet when we walked in. When Anderson simply stated that Ben had sent him to pick up some paperwork, the old guy just stammered and stuttered that he'd already given everything he had to Ben. Caught the old guy by surprise. While he was sputtering, it took me seconds to turn on the gas on a burner. I left the two talking and went to wait in the car. Theodore was just minutes behind me, grumbling about men too old and too forgetful to still be working.

"But I digress. I was going to tell you about how I single-handedly turned a failing old pharmaceutical company into the billion dollar success it is today."

Sam caught a movement outside the window just to the right of Sue. It was Wallie. She had left him outside with Eva, and he was panting from his play and looking for his shady porch. He was rambling and had not looked up. Sam shifted slightly, pretending to lean against the bookcase, testing its sturdiness.

"Don't get too comfortable," said Sue. "You will be leaving soon."

Everything happened at once. Tad came running into the study throwing the door open and seeing only Sam and running toward her. Sue swung the gun at Tad. Sam screamed and threw her body in front of Tad just as Sue fired. At her scream, Wallie crashed through the window.

Caleb was just reaching the gate when he heard the gun shot. He slammed the accelerator down to the floor, crashed through the gates up the driveway and leapt out of the still moving car.

"Sam?" he screamed. Broken glass covered the far end of the porch. A dog growled. Another whimpered. A small voice sobbed and screams split the air.

Caleb jumped through the shattered window. Sam was on the floor. Blood covered her chest and Tad was patting her face, tears streaming. A large rottweiller was wrestling with Sue Anderson. Her bloody arm was in his mouth and the screaming blonde woman was hitting him repeatedly with her other hand. Yet another woman in a white uniform was screaming just outside the open study door.

With one solid punch, Caleb knocked out Sue Anderson. He leaped over her body, grabbed the housekeeper by the shoulders and yelled, "Call 911. Tell them to send a helicopter ambulance. Hurry."

Caleb bent toward Sam, but found his way blocked by Wallie who lunged forward with teeth bared then fell back by Sam's side as Caleb jumped back.

"Tad, Tad? I need you to get Wallie to let me help Sam. Can you do that?"

He nodded. And pulled at the rottweiller's collar. For a split second, Caleb was afraid the dog was going to turn on Tad, but Tad's soft voice soothed the dog.

"Wallie, Wallie, lie down. Good boy."

Tad wrapped his hand around two of Caleb's fingers and pulled him toward Sam.

"Wallie, Mr. McCloud is good. He's good. He's gonna help Sam." He settled Caleb's hand on Sam's chest with his. Wallie seemed to understand and placed his head down beside Sam, but he continued growling low in his throat as Caleb checked her pulse. It was faint. Her eyes fluttered open.

"Tad?" whispered Sam. Wallie came to attention and began licking her face.

"He's fine. He's right here."

"Sam, you've got blood on you," said Tad in a soft voice.

Sam smiled with relief as she tried to focus on the small voice.

"Sam, tell Wallie to go outside with Tad."

"Wallie's here?"

"Just do it, Sam."

"I'm very tired."

"Do it, Sam." His voice was harsh but edged with fear. She did it but it seemed to sap her energy.

Alone with Sam, he stripped his shirt over his head and pressed against her wound, but it did not seem to help.

"Sue Anderson killed Ben." Her voice was barely above a whisper.

"I know, darling, don't talk. Help is on the way."

"Ben's book. The desk. Ben's book." Her eyes glazed. "Caleb." Her eyes closed. He pressed harder on her chest. Her pulse became slower and then stopped.

CHAPTER THIRTY-ONE

"Just breathe, Samantha, just breathe."

The nurse stood in the doorway, watching the beautiful man with the day old beard. Her heart went out to him. He held Samantha Jennings' hands in his, but clearly, she held his heart in hers.

"Mr. McCloud?" She tapped his shoulder and he turned red unfocused eyes toward her. She smiled tentatively and the tap became a pat. "You're not supposed to stay in the ICU room, but I don't think it can hurt anything. I brought you a pillow and blanket."

"Thank you." He refused to release Sam's cold hands to take the blanket. She set them by the foot of the chair and walked out the door, turning to watch him through the glass wall. The steady beat of the ventilator could be heard through the open door. Whoosh. Thump. Whoosh. Thump. The machine breathing in and out in rhythm with the steady beep of the heart monitor.

"Please, love, live. I love you. You are my life. Wake up, Sam. Breathe."

The nurse hesitated. She shook her head and returned to the nurses' station. The ICU rooms with their glass walls formed a circle, surrounding the station. Another nurse looked up and followed her gaze.

"He hasn't left that room since she got out of surgery yesterday. Doctor Landon suggested her family be called, that a decision had to be made. That man screamed he was her family and that Samantha Jennings made her own decisions."

"It's so difficult for the families."

"He's not really her family."

"Yeah, I know, but he says he's all she's got. Besides I'm with him. My bet's on Samantha. Any woman who can get a man to admit that a woman makes her own decisions even from a coma is strong enough to survive a bullet to the heart."

"Maybe you're right. I wouldn't have been in this job for the last fifteen years if people didn't beat the odds."

"I plan to be here when she wakes up."

"Me too."

"Just breathe."

"Mom?" Sam saw her in the distance. She looked the same. She was smiling and her arms were open. Maybe the hair was longer.

"Just breathe. Live. Love."

Sam tried to swallow. Her throat hurt. Where was she? She felt her mother's arms. Loving. Warm. Sam had forgotten her scent. She missed it. Sam tried to inhale, but she couldn't seem to pull the air into her lungs. The scent was becoming fainter. She struggled.

Sam moaned and tried to speak. Her eyes flew open. She was choking. She grabbed at her throat but someone pulled her hands away. She was thrashing. Eyes wild.

"Nurse! Nurse! She's awake. The tube! Hurry!"

A nurse ran into the room followed by a young physician.

"Don't let her touch the tube," ordered the doctor. "Miss Jennings, you're okay. Listen, you're okay. Look at me."

Wild blue eyes connected with patient brown ones. "You're okay. It's a breathing tube. Now, just take a breath through the tube. I know it's uncomfortable, but you're okay. Listen to me. He placed a hand on each side of her face to keep her still. Pull air through the tube. That's right. Once more. And again." Her eyes pleaded and the man nodded.

"Okay, I'm going to take it out. Now inhale deeply, and I'm going to remove the tube when you exhale."

Sam fought the panic and struggled to follow the instructions. She felt the tube pulled out of her throat and her hands were freed. She grabbed her throat. Dry heaved and coughed. A woman held a straw to her lips. She swallowed deeply and closed her eyes in relief.

The physician checked Sam's pulse, listened to her heart, and monitored her breathing for a few minutes. He straightened, smiled, and said, "Welcome back, Miss Jennings."

"My mom," Sam rasped.

"Excuse me?"

"My mom."

"I'm sorry. I was told you had no living family." He glared at Caleb. "If you give me her number, I'll call her immediately."

"She told me to breathe."

"What? No, no, Miss Jennings. Mr. Cloud was the only one in the room. As I understand it, he has been by your side all night, ordering you to breathe." The doctor glanced at the nurse who made the statement, and she had the grace to blush nervously.

"Caleb?"

"I'm here."

She turned her head and saw him. He was standing beside the bed just behind the nurse. He looked exhausted and anxious.

"I heard Mom. I saw her."

"Did you?" he asked softly.

The nurse shook her head. "No, Miss Jennings. We didn't know about your mother. I apologize for that. Mr. McCloud has been the only one here besides Dr. Walker and the nurses. It must have been one of the nurses you heard."

"No, I saw her."

The nurse looked confused, but the physician with the soft brown eyes suddenly smiled down at Sam.

"Where is your mother, Miss Jennings?"

"Heaven."

He nodded, knowingly. "Well, you'll see her again one day, but it will be many years from now; otherwise, you'll bruise my vanity, and heart surgeons are known for their vanity." He patted her hand. "We'll give you a little time with Mr. McCloud. He's been waiting for you."

She turned to Caleb. Tears were streaming down his face.

"Caleb?"

He gathered her in his arms, careful of the tubes and monitors. "I love you, Sam. I think I've always loved you. When I saw you lying there, blood everywhere. Your heart stopped, Sam. Just stopped. I don't know what I would have done if the life flight hadn't landed at that very second. As it was, they kept telling me it was too late." His voice quivered.

"Sam, marry me. Marry me, Sam. I love you."

"Oh, Caleb." She kissed him with such tenderness that he felt it to his soul. Slowly, she raised her eyes to his. Tears tracked silently down her cheeks. "I'm sorry. I can't. It would never work. It's too late for us. I just can't live that life. You were meant to be President. And this whole thing: Ben's death, the publicity. I can't live that way." Her eyes closed, wet lashes clinging to her high cheekbones, and she was asleep.

"Sam?" Alarmed, he checked her pulse. Felt her breath on his hand. Listened to the mild beeping of her heart monitor. He sighed in relief and smiled as he watched her breathe in and out. Within seconds, he was snoring softly.

CHAPTER THIRTY-TWO

Maggie raised her hand to order another martini and pointed at Sam's glass too. Sam put her hand over the top of hers.

"No more, Maggie. I've only been out of the hospital four weeks."

"Doctor didn't say you couldn't drink. Besides it's a much better way to ditch the past than running. Plus, if you play your cards right, you can replace Caleb before we even leave the bar. There's a cute guy at the end of the bar working up his nerve to come over here right now."

Sam glanced down the bar and shook her head. "I don't want a guy, Maggie."

"You will. A little time. Your heart will recover. And I'm not talking about from that bullet. Who would have thought he would just walk out on you like that? He stayed by your bed like a man possessed. Wouldn't even let me in. Who would have thought that the minute you're out of the ICU, he'd take off. You know, I bet Jim knows some hit men."

"Hey, leave me out of this. Caleb's my friend. If he left, he had a reason."

Maggie kicked him. "Men. You all stick together."

"And women don't?" he accused.

"Hasn't even called you. Damn him. Just dropped you like a hot potato and ran as soon as the doctor said you'd be fine. Well, drink up, Samantha. He's not worth the heartbreak. You wasted too many years over that man."

"Maggie, he didn't run out on me."

"The hell he didn't. You spent another week in that hospital and not a word from the man. I should know. I was glued to that phone. Just like before. Slept with you, had a little fun, and took off. Now, me, that's my kind of relationship . . . ."

"Now, wait a minute," began Jim.

Maggie ignored him and continued her rant. "But you, anyone who knows you knows you're a relationship girl. You're a Tammy."

"A what?" Sam laughed.

"A Tammy. You know," Maggie began to sing, "*I hear the whippoorwill whistlin' above, Tammy, Tammy, Tammy's in love.* Don't you watch those old movies?"

Sam rolled her eyes and laughed. Jim snorted beer out his nose.

"Maggie, he asked me to marry him."

"No one treats my best friend like that and lives to tell it. I'll . . . . What? He what?"

"He asked me to marry him."

Jim grinned. "That's my man. Knew he wasn't stupid."

"And you didn't tell me? Shit, Sam. Here you just let me seethe and you keep a secret like that to yourself. That's wonderful. I knew he was a great guy. You could make a girl believe in happily ever after. But where the hell did he go? Why did he leave when you got out of ICU without a word to anyone? Why have you spent the past month in sullen silence? Why isn't he here with you now? Work's no excuse. Call him and tell him to drive his sorry ass down here right now."

"I told him no."

Maggie and Jim stared at her, speechless.
"You told him no?" asked Maggie.
Sam nodded. Maggie stared.
"Holy shit," said Jim.

CHAPTER THIRTY-THREE

Sam sat at her desk and reread the letter. Theodore Anderson and his son had moved to London to start a new life. GloboHealth was bankrupt. Its assets were being doled out to families of PUD victims. Anderson was found blameless, but it didn't matter. He was ruined. Fortunately, his first wife also came from wealth and had left a substantial trust fund for her son. Because Sue Anderson had made Tad one of her victims, the public and the press had seen Theodore as a victim and had left him alone after his wife was arrested.

The day Sam was shot, an officer had driven Anderson from the golf course to the hospital where his wife was undergoing stitches under the watchful eye of a federal officer. He had listened to the story with disbelief and anger. Then, Tad walked into the ER covered with Sam's blood, and he had simply collapsed.

Sam looked down at the colorful drawing of Big Ben that Tad had sent her along with a note, 'Dad showed me how to do the PO Box so I could send this. I like it even better than email 'cause I can color. Dad says this is not your Ben but I thought you would like it. I miss you. Love Tad.'

Sam stood and taped the drawing on the front of the refrigerator. It had been almost six months since she had been shot. She knew the dull pain in her heart had nothing to do with a bullet wound.

She looked out the back door at the ocean. The peace was not there any longer. She knew she should move. She just didn't know where to go.

She patted Wallie's head and pushed the door open to let him run. The cold winter wind sent a chill down Sam, and she closed it as she watched her pup dash out to the ocean. Sam rubbed her hands up and down her arms. Turning back toward the sofa, she froze.

Caleb was standing just inside the front door watching her.

"Caleb." His name was little more than a sob, and she was in his arms.

"Oh, Caleb," she muttered into his wool sweater. "I thought I'd never see you again. I thought it would be okay. Not seeing you. Not hearing from you. I did it before. But every day is longer and emptier. I was never lonely before and now, I . . . ."

"Shhh." He was kissing her. An endless, soul-stripping kiss. His arms surrounded her, gentle and strong. He pulled away just far enough to kiss away the tears streaming silently down her cheeks.

"Sam, Sam. You are in my every dream. My every waking second." He swept her up in his arms and walked her to the couch with his mouth fused to hers. He set her down gently and went down on one knee.

"Marry me, Sam. I can't live without you."

Sam tensed and pushed away.

"I can't. Nothing has changed. I can't live your life of politics. I have thought of little else since you left. But I can't do it, Caleb. I panic at the thought. I need solitude. Privacy. You are meant to be a senator, a president."

"Sam, do you love me?"

"Of course I do, but nothing has changed."

"Are you really happy in your solitude?"

Sam blanched. Tears filled her eyes. Confusion. Fear. She couldn't answer.

Caleb dropped her hands, stood, and walked back out the front door. Panic shot through Sam, and she jumped up to follow. But the front door banged open again. Her heart skipped a beat as she watched him walk back inside with two large suitcases.

"So where do I put these? You know, I really like this house Sam, but it's a bit small. I'm gonna have to add a study."

"What?"

"I'm moving in. I sold my house, and I'm homeless at the moment. I thought I'd crash here."

She simply stared.

"Yeah, yeah. I know you said no, but I plan to change your mind. Marriage would be a lot better for my judicial image. But I'm willing to simply live together as long as there's a lot of sin involved. You're a stubborn woman, but I'm telling you, Sam, the minute you get pregnant, you're gonna have to make an honest man out of me or my mama will bring out the shotgun."

"Judicial image? What are you talking about? Can you do that and still run for senator? No one is going to let you run for president if you move in with me."

Caleb smiled. "I'm not running for president. I got a better offer. You're looking at the Honorable Caleb McCloud, the newest and youngest United States District Court Judge. Or at least I will be next November when I'm sworn in to replace Judge Oliver who is retiring."

"But, your dreams?"

Caleb smiled. "You are my dreams, Sam. I just had to grow up to find my past."

He kissed her before she could speak again, smiling at her dazed look. "Sam, darling, I realized that what I really want is to change the world. I don't need the fame and the glory. Or even that Oval Office—though that would have been pretty cool. Everyone knows a judge is much more powerful than the President. And there aren't term limits."

He saw the doubt in her eyes and something more. Hope.

"It's what I want, Sam. What I need. One thing though, how do you feel about a second home in Richmond? That's where I'll be based."

Sam threw her arms around him, "Yes, yes, yes!"

"Yes?"

"Yes to Richmond. Yes to marriage. Yes to us."

He kissed her again. Pulled a ring out of his pocket and slid it on her finger.

"Which way is our room?" She pointed with her right hand while staring at her left.

Caleb scooped her up again, leaving the bags for later.

"Oh, by the way, no leaving when I become the youngest United States Supreme Court Justice. Guy's gotta make a living, and I plan to be an alpha dog."

A wet Wallie growled an objection through the screen door on the back porch, and Caleb's laughter blended with Sam's as he kicked the bedroom door shut.

ABOUT THE AUTHOR

Kim Sanders lives in South Carolina with her husband. She spends her free time walking the beaches of the low country, enjoying the solitude.